UNNATURAL

DREAM WALKER BOOK 1

By H M DuVal

2

Praise for Unnatural

Wow! Just wow!

This book grabbed me from go. The world HM Duval creates is rich and feels real. I want to go back! I really can't wait for the second installment to come out!

Couldn't put it down!

DuVal's book pulls you into her dystopian world and you don't want to leave! Now I want to know what happens next. Thank you, Michelle, for an engaging read, even though I lost sleep for the past two nights because I couldn't put it down.

Looking forward to the next book in this series!

I just finished reading Unnatural and it was wonderful! The author's gift of description makes the scenery come alive around me, and the dialog is so natural! I am looking forward to the next book!

A Real Gem!

Duval unfolds an intricate and rewarding adventure in the finest tradition of Tolkien. Her elegiac voice should silence the objections of even the most persnickety fantasy genre devotees. Can't wait for the next book in the series.

H M DuVal

THE DREAM WALKER SERIES

UNNATURAL

UNTOUCHABLE

UNSTOPPABLE

6

UNNATURAL

DREAM WALKER BOOK 1

H M DuVal

UNNATURAL

Second Edition. Cover design by H M DuVal using Canva. Photo from Pixabay, credit Engin Akyurt.

Follow me on social media!
Instagram author.h.m.duval
Facebook H M DuVal - Author
www.duvalmichelle.wixsite.com/hmduval

ISBN: 979-8-9870854-1-7

Printed with IngramSpark (www.ingramspark.com)

DEDICATION

This book would not have been possible without my incredible support team.

To my husband, who always believes in and encourages the best, most vibrant version of myself. Thank you for holding sacred the space I need to be myself.

To my Beta Babes, whose enthusiasm and feedback helped me breathe life into this project at long last. Your investment into Pen's story was fuel to my fire and kept me going. Christina, Kelly, Caroline, and Erica — I couldn't ask for a better squad to stand at my back. Thank you.

Table of Contents

Praise for Unnatural   3

Dedication   9

Chapter One   17

Chapter Two   31

Chapter Three   39

Chapter Four   57

Chapter Five   65

Chapter Six   73

Chapter Seven   93

Chapter Eight   105

Chapter Nine   119

Chapter Ten   133

Chapter Eleven   147

Chapter Twelve   155

Chapter Thirteen   169

Chapter Fourteen   185

Chapter Fifteen   205

Chapter Sixteen   221

Chapter Seventeen   233

Chapter Eighteen   247

Chapter Nineteen 261

Chapter Twenty 275

Chapter Twenty One 283

Chapter Twenty Two 299

Chapter Twenty Three 311

Chapter Twenty Four 322

Exclusive Excerpt from UNTOUCHABLE 336

Author's Note 346

H M DuVal

14

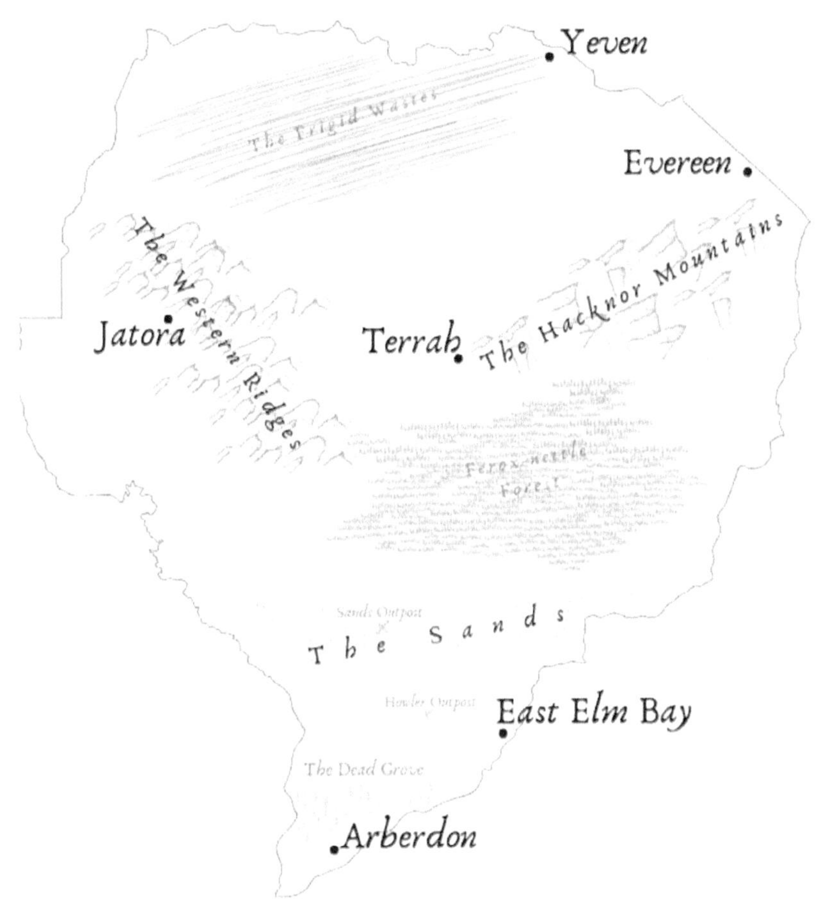
Yeven
Evereen
The Frigid Wastes
The Hacknor Mountains
The Western Ridges
Jatora
Terrah
Ferox-nettle Forest
Sands Outpost
The Sands
Howler Outpost
East Elm Bay
The Dead Grove
Arberdon

CHAPTER ONE

I sat on the front porch of my parents' house, taking in the sunset that roared through the sky. Small trails of sweat coursed past my temples and licked down my neck.

It was my favorite time of day, and for a few moments everything was perfect: I was an average person in an average town on an average day. I could forget, just for a little while. I took a deep breath and tried to hold the feeling inside me.

The air smelled of honeysuckle, dirt, and pollen, the dryness of it tickling the back of my throat. I listened to the sounds of the little town of Arberdon closing up for the night. I watched as my neighbors hustled home before curfew.

And then the moment passed and I was back to tracing a long, delicate brush through the barrel of my shotgun. Cross-legged on the wooden floor of the porch, I let my mind wander as my hands got back to work.

My hands were small but hard, having grown up farming the stubborn land we lived on. Trying to encourage even the most pitiful crops took full-time, brutal effort. And there were never enough hands to do the work, not even before the Executor enlistment requirement.

Not that it matters, I thought as I spat off the edge of the porch. The Executors set the requirements, and we fulfilled them. In exchange our small town got the aid we desperately needed, not to mention easier communication with other city havens.

With a sigh I leaned back on my hands, watching the last beams of light claw at the sky, as if the sun were trying to tear out of its fate at nightfall. Scratching my fingertips across the weathered wood of the porch, I watched the growing twilight and silently pitied the sun.

Somber shadows draped over Arberdon, a gray landscape of cluttered homes tumbling on top of one another in a desperate attempt to use every square inch inside the city walls. Inside safety. I'd heard of the other towns and cities like mine, other sanctuaries walled off from the deadly wilderness, but had only ever known Arberdon. My past, my present, my future. My entire life safely wrapped in the walls that protected our home.

My grandfather would sit with me on the porch when I was a child and fill my head with stories of our family guarding our property: generations running off throngs of wild creatures before the wall was built, tales of predecessors defending against bandits and working the land so vivid I felt like I knew them. Their lives were woven into the ancient beams of wood that held our home together, their struggle to survive paving the way for me to do the same.

He said to me, *"Penelope, this house is a legacy. This land is soaked with our blood. It's ours to protect, ours to preserve."*

I loved hearing his stories, but my father didn't approve. Many nights I could hear the two of them arguing after I'd gone to my room. Father wanted to forget about the *before* and move on, putting the violence to rest at last. Grandfather wanted to be prepared for when it started again. Because it always started again.

With dusk imminent and the final tendrils of light giving in and slipping below the horizon, it was time for me to finish my task. I turned my attention back to my gun and scrubbed the inside of the barrels with a vengeance.

Growing up, Grandfather's tales were fun, an entertainment, a way to pass the time. Arberdon seemed safe enough to me and my parents' land required attention and hard work.

My perspective changed when the town council opened a contract with the Executors. My entire world changed. I didn't have time for stories anymore.

Done cleaning, I put my tools into their respective pockets on my leather lap apron. I locked each component into its place, finding satisfaction in the melody of my gun coming back to life; sounds I trusted. My puzzle completed, I peered down the barrel to check my sights before refilling my ammo bag.

I hadn't known anything about weapons until the Executors mandated the enlistment of at least one member of each household. When governments collapsed along with everything else after The Great War, mankind was united under the direction of the Executors, a military group specialized in neutralizing the enemy. For as long as humanity had been trying to survive in the aftermath of The Great War, the Executors were preparing for The Second Great War. A final chance to settle the score with mankind's greatest threat, whom they called Unnaturals, or *Unnats*. Stars Above only knew why the creatures, with their freakish speed, strength, and savagery, were so set on killing off the last of us. It was said that their teeth were always stained with the blood of their latest victims and their blue-tinted skin crawled with filth. Abominations.

Though, to be fair, I'd never seen any creature resembling that description, or a battle for survival against the *Unnats*. Neither had my father. Neither had my grandfather. And there weren't any people around older than that to ask. Because of that, and the lack of records from the before, what knowledge we had about the species evolved into something more like lore.

The Executors took over regardless, using their resources and knowledge to turn us into a real army, complete with physical tests and rigorous training. More important were the addition of a hospital, school, and better infrastructure that we got in exchange. As a result, I knew how to clean a gun, not get knocked over when firing my gun, and how to do simple hand-to-hand combat moves. I was by far not the best soldier in our little army. Somehow, despite my below-average performance in training, I managed to catch the attention of the commander of the Executor branch assigned to Arberdon.

I grabbed a lantern in my spare hand and used my legs to press to my feet. With the sun gone for the night, it was time to start my shift. I trotted down the stairs, feeling the ring that hung from a chain around my neck bounce between my breasts. The sound of my boot heels striking the cobblestone street followed me as I strode toward the Southern Gate, my shotgun tucked under one arm. The town seemed to be sleeping already, but I knew better. Everyone was inside their locked doors and shuttered windows, including my family, waiting for the night to end. Only guards were allowed out after curfew.

The training from the Executors had left me quite strong for someone my size, and relatively more confident in my abilities. Once Ben had established his interest in me, though, he started pulling me from hand-to-hand combat training. He didn't want anyone else hurting me.

I stretched my neck and rolled my shoulders, trying to clear my mind so I could focus as I neared my post. It was my first shift since I'd been out on medical leave. I felt my face relax into a smile as I saluted the guard I was relieving.

"Randall! I didn't know you were pulling a double today."

"Evening, Penny." The guard saluted back. "How are you feeling?"

"Fine. What about you, though? You look like hell."

A tired laugh rumbled out of his big chest as he rubbed a hand over his ruddy face.

He didn't look that bad. In fact, my childhood friend Randall had grown into quite the man. He had broad shoulders, a strong body, and a kind face that lit up whenever he smiled. His wife was a very lucky woman, and I was pleased to say she knew it. Still, he had heavy bags under his eyes and his usual spark was gone.

"Yeah, I did a double," he sighed, taking his hand from his face and pushing it through his auburn hair instead. "Daylight shifts aren't very trying, though. Haven't ever seen an *Unnat*, let alone a spine-bear or flying possum, during the day. The worst threat is the sun exhaustion!" He laughed, the sound forced and hollow.

"How's Randa?" I asked, curling my fingers around his meaty arm.

He pressed his lips together, closing his eyes tightly, and I knew I'd guessed right about what was bothering him.

"I'll do as many doubles as I have to so I can afford that doctor from East Elm Bay. My baby girl was born sick, and we can't figure out what's wrong."

"Oh, Randall!" I tightened my grip on his arm. "Still? I thought she was getting better."

"She was," he rasped, holding my hand against him. He was shaking. "She was, and then she wasn't. I don't understand it. The doctors here, they've tried everything. They just increased her medicine again last week, but it isn't helping. It's like she's fading—" his voice cut off abruptly.

I frowned, feeling my heart twist and squeeze in my chest. "Why don't you go home and see how she's doing?"

He nodded, wrapping an arm around my shoulder as he started away. "You need to come visit," he chided with a weary smile. We both ignored the words he didn't say. *Come visit before it's too late, before she's gone.*

I cleared my throat, blinking my eyes until I could see him clearly. "I will, soon. I promise."

"Have a good shift, Penny. I'm glad you're feeling better."

I watched him retreat, my heart heavy in my chest. He and his wife had been trying for a family for years. They'd lost four babies before making it full term, despite the Executor doctors doing everything they could; it would be devastating for them to lose this little girl as well. I didn't need my qwell that badly. I'd have to find a way to give them some of my pay without it seeming like a handout. We Arberdonians were proud people, sometimes to a fault, and Randall was no exception for all that he wasn't native.

Unable to distinguish his frame from the deepening dark anymore, I turned away and scanned the field between the wall and the forest, letting out a long sigh with my worries. It was time to focus on my shift: just me, the night, and my shotgun.

Long shadows blanketed the land and stars were beginning to wink throughout the hazy sky. It wouldn't be long until the town was smothered in pitch black. There were always lamps and a huge fire pit burning in the center of town, but none of that light could reach all the way out to the Southern Gate where I stood.

The lantern, my only source of light for my shift, held enough fuel for five hours. That left roughly three hours of my shift without light. I preferred to stay in the dark so my eyes could adjust better, so I placed it on the ground beside my feet and settled into the strength of my legs. I would remain standing until my shift ended at dawn.

Hopefully when it gets later it will get cooler, too. I thought as sweat dripped down my back and flooded the bends in my elbows. Living my entire life in Arberdon meant I was accustomed to the summer heat. Being human meant I still didn't like it.

I unhinged my shotgun, letting the barrel hang over my forearm as I dug two shells out of my leather apron. I placed them in their respective barrels, snapped my gun closed, and checked my sights again. Satisfied, I held my shotgun in both hands where I could raise it quickly if needed.

Another sigh heaved out of my chest as I scanned the forest in the distance, wiping the sweat that coated my face with the back of my hand. It didn't help much.

The guard shifts, in my opinion, were a waste of time and resources, not to mention laborers who could otherwise be working in the fields, helping churn what crops we could from the ground. Stars Above knew, there wasn't much good protecting a town from an absentee enemy if that town starved to death in the process. But I wasn't asked for my opinion, only my enlistment. And so I did as I was told and stood in the dark, night after night, staring out at the deadly forest that surrounded us.

I balanced the butt of my gun on the ground and angled the barrel away from me, exhaling slowly. The air was stifling and I felt fidgety tonight. Full of adrenaline and expectation. I shook my free hand loose, trying to shake off my unsettled nerves. Breathing in took real effort and my chest felt heavy with the mugginess around me. It wouldn't be long before a thunderstorm came, and I could already feel the pounding in my temples that usually accompanied them.

I picked at the sweaty clothes that were glued to my skin. Ben's ring felt hot and uncomfortable between my breasts. I pulled the canteen out of my leg holster and allowed myself a small drink.

I rubbed my face and licked the salt off my lips. Taking a breath that stretched my lungs, I pulled a smile onto my face for practice. Though I didn't consider myself to have a particularly melancholy nature, lately just getting out of bed could be a challenge. If I were to let myself think about it, the idea of facing an endless expanse of identical days threatened to drive me out of my mind. My family didn't understand what staying up all night with a shotgun as your only companion did to a person, and I wouldn't want them to know. I was happy to enlist in order to save them from it. And sleeping all day in order to work all night certainly didn't allow for a thriving social life, or what social life there was to participate in for a small city like Arberdon.

Added to that, what sleep I had been getting lately hadn't been restful, strange dreams plaguing me that dissipated as soon as I gasped awake. I often felt more tired, off-kilter, when I rolled out of bed in the evening than I had when I'd laid down at the end of my shift. Like I'd been running, desperately searching for something, all day long.

If I were brave enough to be honest with myself, I would admit that I had every reason for my private depression. Or, rather, one large reason.

"Come on, Pen, *focus.*" I snapped at myself, determined to get my wandering mind back on track. Even if I thought my job was pointless, I believed in doing it well.

I started my usual calming technique, imagining a pitcher of water pouring slowly on the crown of my head that washed away my tension.

First I relaxed my scalp, then my brow. I softened my temples and unlocked my jaw. I let my tongue fall away from the roof of my mouth and my lips gently parted.

A cool whisper of air, hinted with the scent of a forest after rain, surrounded me. At first I welcomed the relief, breathing deeply and feeling the tightness in my chest lift. The storm must be closer than I'd thought if I could smell it on the wind and feel it stroke my skin.

I frowned at that thought and opened my eyes to scan my surroundings. The dry stalks of the fields remained still and scorched, a wildfire waiting to happen. The trees looked stiff and brittle.

There was no wind.

Had I imagined it? I furrowed my brow and sniffed again. The phantom smell of forest still hung damp in the air, made more of memory than substance. Around me the air remained stagnant even as my lungs pulled another breath of relief into my chest. I raised my gun to my shoulder and peered down the barrel. My hands were shaking, instinct clamoring noisily, insisting I wasn't alone.

Could it be an *Unnat*? Had I *smelled* one of those creatures?

I tried to remember if we'd been trained to scent *Unnats*, or even if it had been mentioned by the Executors. What I did remember from training was depressingly limited:

"My name is Commander Herald Brant. I'm here to teach you everything you need to know about Unnaturals. One: They're deadly. Two: They're strong. Three: They're fast. And most importantly, they die just like any other animal when you plug 'em full of lead. So shoot on sight, and we'll sort the rest out later."

A blur of something moving in the dark caught my attention and I remembered where I was.

Your mind is wandering.

I frowned and scoured the darkness. I had to pay attention and stop letting my mind wander! My heart drummed wildly in my chest and my mouth was dry. I held onto my lower lip with my teeth until it hurt, the pain sharpening my focus. Still the air smelled damp and green.

Everything's fine.

The longer I stood in the darkness, the more detail I was able to parse from my surroundings. Everything looked as it should. The fences around the fields took shape, and then stalks of grain and corn. The barren stretch of land between Arberdon and the forest was as still as death. Then came the trees that marked the edge of danger, either melting into one tangled mass or sorting into distinct branches depending on where I looked.

"Just your imagination, Pen." I muttered, relaxing my stance. "Your eyes are playing tricks on you." I shook my head, trying to clear it, and refocused my eyes on the forest.

And then I saw it, a figure standing perfectly still. Two golden orbs shining out at me, thirty feet away, tops. Two eyes watching me very closely.

I clamped my lips together to silence my gasp. Fear sat thick in my belly; it tasted like bile in my mouth. Hardly breathing, I shifted my thumb to the hammer of my gun and hesitated. Whether I was looking at a diseased Ursine this close to the gate or, Stars help me, an *Unnat*, I needed to take it down with my first shot. I tried not to think about what would happen if I needed my second.

Exhaling slowly to steady my arms, I pulled my right hammer into place and squeezed my first trigger, shattering the quiet night with a percussive *bang*. The sound reverberated, enveloping me, my target blurring and disappearing into the tall stalks of the corn field. I couldn't see it anywhere.

I hissed between my teeth, my heart thundering in my chest. No Ursine could move that fast.

I readied my second hammer, watching for the creature to reappear, a trembling finger hovering over the second trigger as I scanned the line of the field.

An *Unnat* broke cover and seemed to materialize in front of me. I closed my fingers around the trigger and felt the slam of the gun burrow into my shoulder a second time, but it was already too late. The *Unnat* snatched the barrel and wrenched my gun away, sending my shot off into the field as it grabbed the front of my shirt and lifted me off of the ground. The seams from my shirt cut painfully into the backs of my arms and neck as the thing pulled me toward its snarling face.

What are you doing?

Incredulous alarm barreled through my brain. I clawed at the *Unnat's* arm, gasping for air and kicking my feet uselessly. It smelled like dirt, and rain, and green things. I felt like I was breathing moss. Its eyes narrowed, breath falling over me in hot waves. A low growl rattled out of its chest as it pulled me closer to its face, sniffing the air around my head.

I couldn't make a sound, couldn't get my breath to stick to my lungs. I was glued to the intensity of its eyes, Stars Above, those *eyes!* A vibrant, burning gold that glowed like fire. I felt like they would burn straight through me, like they *saw* me. And that undeniable acknowledgment somehow brought the gaping, lonely expanse of my existence into clarity.

This is it, I thought as an eerie calmness settled over me, my frantic limbs settling. *This is how I die.* A bitter laugh tried to bubble out of my throat. *Well, at least I'm not alone.*

The *Unnat* snarled before setting me roughly back on the ground. My knees buckled under my weight.

Don't pass out, I begged myself.

The *Unnat's* sinuous arm snapped out and jerked me back onto my feet, flinching quickly away again as I balanced on rubbery legs. It stared intently at the town, those burning amber eyes piercing the darkness, before leveling me with its unnerving gaze.

"They're coming."

Every thought rushing through my mind came to a slamming halt. My throat tightened, wrapping around an impossibility. An obstruction I couldn't force away. A choking, damning, suffocating fact.

That was a voice. Those were words. *My* words, that I *understood.* Which meant it—no, not *it* but something far worse. He. With words and clothes and shoes it could be nothing other than *he. He* was saying something, his lips moving, but all I could hear was the frantic staccato of my heart, the gasping of my own breath. My mind grappled for traction, thoughts churning clumsily like slipped gears. I tried to take a step back, move toward safety, but my feet were as immovable as if they'd been staked to the ground. No matter how my mind screamed frantically to *do something* my body refused to move.

"The other guards. They're coming." The *Unnat* said again, his sharp eyes turning to me expectantly.

"You can speak?" I sputtered.

The *Unnat* rolled his eyes and grabbed the fabric of my shirt at my wrist, jerking me closer to the field, my legs flying to keep up with his long strides. In a daze I studied his hand, so close to my own skin. A smattering of scars decorated his blue knuckles, leading up to a forearm of tightly coiled muscle. And the strangest thought took shape in my flustered mind, sinking into me the same way his heat melted into my chilled skin. That I somehow knew those hands, that the thought of them made me tremble–

"Hey! Back off!" I twisted my arm in his grasp, trying to bluff my way out of being terrified. Just like that, reality came crashing back to me and I understood just how much danger I was in.

Stars Above, he was tall! And strong! My jaw quivered as I shifted my weight for better stability. There was no way I'd survive whatever happened next. Clenching my teeth, I pulled my sleeve free and raised my fists into a futile guard.

Don't pass out.

He looked down his large, straight nose at me, at the tiny fists I held up between us. The familiar feeling of being wholly inadequate snaked through my veins. I was not up to this task. The *Unnat's* lips pulled up, baring his teeth in a lopsided sneer.

Footsteps. From the corner of my eye I could just make out the bobbing of other lanterns, like flecks of gold dancing in the darkness, as the other guards closed in on my position. *Thank the Stars, help was coming!*

The *Unnat* considered me again, his eyes narrowing as he tilted his head, like he was listening carefully to a sound I couldn't hear. His mouth twisted with loathing. I tensed and threw an arm out as he stepped closer, barely aware of how he handed my gun back to me. The commotion headed our way grew louder.

"Ms. Kendall? Are you alright?"

"I heard shots!"

"Hurry, everyone! Penelope?" Ben's voice in the distance.

The *Unnat* and I stared at each other, holding gazes steadily. There was something...almost tangible about the way he looked at me. Like I had seen it before, in another place and time. His head tilted the other way, curious.

My arms wouldn't lift my gun. I had no reason not to. It was there in my hands, but my muscles refused to lift their burden. He showed his teeth again, a mocking slash across his face, as his gaze...his eyes...were so...

"Penelope?" Ben called my name from...somewhere. He sounded worried, genuine fear lacing his voice, which distantly registered as incredibly odd.

I felt like I was falling, spinning slowly, drifting through dust. My eyes were clouded, my ears were muffled, I couldn't breathe. But I didn't mind. It felt like falling asleep, in a way, and promised to be restful.

CHAPTER TWO

"Penelope?" Ben shouted in my ear. I started and spun around, blinking my eyes out of their trance. Ben's face was twisted with concern as he gripped my elbows.

"Are you alright?" He asked, sliding his hands down my arms so he could grab the gun from my tingling fingers. His pale eyes searched me.

"I—uh, what?" I looked around at the other guards. "I—I don't understand," I stammered, rubbing my temples. I couldn't get my eyes to focus and my head pounded like it had been in a vice. I swallowed compulsively.

"You discharged your weapon. Are you alright?" Ben's rough baritone broke into my confusion.

"I mean," I looked out to the field, blinking my eyes slowly. "I, um. There was...Well, I thought..."

I felt like I was going to be sick again. Breathing slowly and closing my eyes only made my spinning head worse, so I quickly opened them and stared at a spot on the ground that wasn't moving.

"Penelope," Ben tried to get me to look at him. His heavy hand grabbed my left shoulder.

"No!" The snarl ripped out of me and I knocked his hand away before I knew what I was doing.

"Penelope," his tone shifted. My pulse kicked up again in response.

"I thought I saw something," I cut him off, firming my jaw and lifting my chin. Now was not the time. "My imagination, I guess. But, Stars, I'm not sure," I finished softly, rubbing my face and fighting the urge to scream or cry or laugh or hurl.

Ben nodded once and regained his composure.

"We should send a team to check it out anyway. You three, head out into the field. Penelope, where did you see something?"

Ben turned back to me with a controlled expression. My heart squeezed.

"Um," I shook my head, trying to clear my mind of all the thoughts I wanted to avoid. *Not now not now not now!* I pointed in the distance. "I thought I saw something over there toward the trees. But I think my eyes were just playing tricks on me."

"We have to be thorough," One of the three guards, George something, said as they trotted into the darkness, their lanterns bobbing along beside them.

Ben stayed where he was, standing silently beside me as we watched them leave. His shoulders were tense, hands flexing at his hips. Words writhed on the back of my tongue, a squirming mass that dripped out as a whimper. I tried to swallow but my throat wouldn't open and I ended up with a mouth full of too much spit instead. I cleared my throat and spat in the dirt, trying to force my mouth to work right.

With precise movements, Ben took his communicator from his belt and walked back inside the city walls, where the device would actually work.

"Commander Joshen here." He called in to headquarters. "We're investigating the situation at South Gate. I have everything under control for now. I'll call back with a report in ten minutes. Over."

"Confirmed, Commander Joshen. Headquarters awaits your report. Headquarters out."

I watched him silently as he put the comm back on his belt. He took a deep breath, letting it out slowly. My heart tripped over inside my chest.

"Ben?" I said softly, not sure what I was asking for. My hands curled into fists that I kept at my sides.

He turned and took a step toward me, scanning my face like he wanted to say something. The weight of keeping my head up became too much and my gaze settled on the dry ground. If only I could liquify and sink into the crack that ran under my boot.

"Penelope," he breathed, easing into the space between us and cradling the back of my head with long fingers. He pressed his thumb under my jaw, tilting my head up. The pressure ached under my tongue but I resisted lifting my eyes to his. I wrapped my arms around my middle and stared at his chest instead. He pressed a kiss to my temple, nuzzling at me, his teeth scraping on my neck. I felt feverish and woozy, my heart and guts seizing together.

"I'm sorry," I whispered, pushing him gently away from me. "I just—I'm not—"

I turned away from him and let out a shaky breath of relief as he let his arms drop to his sides. It felt like I'd been having a hiccupping fit, that disgusting feeling in my diaphragm I wish I could dig out with a spoon. I pressed my fingertips to my mouth, breathing carefully so I wouldn't be sick. Adrenaline kept pumping into the gaping hole in my chest, threatening to drown me. I needed to focus on something else, something tangible. Stay grounded in the present.

Had I seen something? Had I *not* seen something? Was I going crazy?

"I told you I was sorry." He said quietly behind me.

He was talking about last week.

"I know." I answered just as quietly, feeling my throat constrict again with a mix of fear and shame. Try as I might, I couldn't choke it down.

Our silence loomed between us.

"I'm fine." I forced a smile, still clutching at my elbows.

Everything inside me felt strained, slightly off. I still had that lingering loopy sensation, like when you wake up in the middle of an intense dream. Or when you are still dreaming, but your mind is waking up. *Lucidity*, that was what it felt like.

Yup, I thought to myself, *this isn't real. It's a dream.*

Which made perfect sense, really. I'd been having bizarre dreams that I couldn't quite remember for what felt like ages. Clearly I'd just reached lucidity a bit early, my mind starting to wake up while I was still inside of a dream thick with adrenaline. If there actually were *Unnats*, and I'd actually shot at an *Unnat*, I'd be dead. And since I wasn't dead, the entire encounter couldn't have happened. Which meant I was, in fact, *not* on shift and was having a very elaborate dream.

I laughed in relief, shaking off my tension and looking around at the vivid scenery.

Ben nodded once when I glanced at him. His way of accepting what I had said, though I knew he didn't believe me. Apparently Dream-Ben had the same visual cues as Real-Ben. Which also made perfect sense, since Dream-Ben was built on my perception of Real-Ben. Knowing that I was dreaming eased the tight fist around my chest and I let out a shaking breath.

"I tried to comm you," he started, changing the subject.

"Did you?" I took the device out of my leather apron and made sure it was still turned on. It was. Of course it was. Dream-Me wouldn't have forgotten something like that because I would never forget something like that in real life. It was uncanny how the textures and weights of familiar objects felt real, even though I was dreaming. Or maybe they just seemed to be familiar because this was a dream and my perceptions bent to the whim of my mind's physics?

Ben was staring at me expectantly.

"What?"

Ben heaved a sigh, pinning me with a disappointed glare. "Why didn't you answer when I called?"

"I was standing outside of the gate, so it didn't work." I remembered.

"Right," he barked a laugh, his lips twisting. "So *why* are we standing outside the gate?"

"Because—" I started as I shoved the comm back in my pocket. *Because the Unnat was dragging me toward the field.*

But the Unnat wasn't real. It was a part of the elaborate dream I was still caught up in. It couldn't have been real. If it was real, I'd be dead. And if I were dead, I couldn't be dreaming. Still, some instinct warned me not to mention the *Unnat* to Ben.

"Because the thing I thought I saw pulled me out here." I laughed and shook my head. "Stars Above, that sounds stupid."

"Penelope," Ben said softly, his voice sliding like ice down my spine.

I laughed again, a harsh, cracking sound that burned the back of my throat. Why would my mind give me more of *this* to experience? Didn't I get enough as it was?

"How pathetic," I muttered to myself with disgust. How completely pathetic that my entire scope of experience could be boiled down to this stupid dream: stuck in the dark, alone with Ben. Didn't take an expert head doctor to analyze that symbolism.

"What did you say?"

"Seriously?" The word clawed out of my throat, the backs of my eyes beginning to prickle. "I can't do this anymore." I pressed my palm against my mouth, refusing to let any other words out. A dry heave racked me. Could someone throw up in a dream?

Ben's lips pulled down sharply. "What is wrong with you?"

I tried to swallow, my throat feeling thick and clammy. Something told me I was about to find out the answer to my own question.

"What *is* wrong with me?" I muttered when I could open my mouth without getting sick. My arm tingled underneath my sleeve, lingering heat from a hand that had never been there. I tried to chafe the feeling away.

I swung my gaze in the direction the other guards had gone, not quite seeing the landscape before me. If people you saw in a dream stepped out of your field of vision, were they still in the dream or did they stop existing until your brain conjured them again?

"Maybe I was wrong to schedule you so soon," he murmured as he studied me, crossing his arms over the crisp lines of his chest.

"So soon after this?" I gestured to my bruised left shoulder without thinking. But it didn't matter because this was a dream.

"Don't," he warned. I turned to look at him, shrinking out of habit.

"Ben, I—"

"I *said* I was *sorry!*" He devoured the space between us again, taking my face roughly in his hands. The size of his palms as they muffled all other sound, the way his fingertips bit into my head, was all perfectly familiar and overwhelming.

"I know." I whispered as another dry heave seized me. Unease sizzled in my gut, curling me inward.

It occurred to me that I never said it was okay, not any of the times we did this.

"Do you need to hear it again? Do you need to *feel* how sorry I am?" He leaned over me, his eyes fierce with anger, and crushed his mouth on mine.

Wake up, wake up, wake up!

I couldn't breathe, couldn't move. One of his hands held my jaw, the other snaked around my back and squeezed my bruised shoulder hard, trapping me. The pain had me gasping, opening underneath him. His tongue, wet and demanding. Forcing its way past my lips, groping inside me. Teeth on my skin. Blood in my mouth. The panic attack closing around me like a fist.

Stop this! You've got to stop this!

I wrestled my hands free and pushed as hard as I could, only just managing to get him off of me in time to violently hurl all over the ground between us.

I was sweating and cold at the same time, leaning on Ben's hips to save me from falling over into my sick. He held my shoulders and traced his fingers gently across my exposed neck. Sweetly. It wasn't right, the way his hands could lie like that.

"You should go home," he said.

I stood where I was, spitting bits of what used to be food off my lips. I felt weak.

What should I do? What—

"Your watch is over, Penelope. Go home. I'll come by later." Ben told me. It was a promise, but not one I wanted.

I could hear the other guards returning from their trek to the field. Ben waved to them to stay back, helping me to step away from my mess.

"Take my lantern, Penelope."

I numbly did as I was told, but my feet refused to move.

"Penelope, seriously, go home. We'll talk later." Ben turned me to the gate and gave me a push.

I stumbled into the city, dismay spreading through me as I made my way through the empty streets. The chain around my neck felt heavy.

I managed to make my way home, managed to get up the stairs into my attic bedroom, and managed to take off my sweaty, messy clothes and that Stars-forsaken chain before collapsing in a heap on my bed and crying until I passed out.

38

CHAPTER THREE

I walked quietly through the forest, though I didn't feel afraid. The forest was no more dangerous than any other powerful facet of nature; it was ignorance that harmed the unsuspecting, not evil. The haven of trees was my sanctuary and my home. I knew the way the ground swelled and dipped like I knew the shape of my own body. I took a deep breath, pulling in air heavy with the scent of life and growth. I felt my chest ease, the vise that usually clamped tight around me lessening with each step that I took toward my destination.

If only I could shake off my shackles so easily, *some lucid part of my mind yearned.* ***If only I could be free like this.***

"You can be," encouraged the trees that lined the North Road. "We can start over. Come to me and I can get you somewhere safe."

Safe*. My lucid mind mocked the idea as much as it craved it. I hadn't felt safe since—*

"Penelope," Ben's harsh voice cut through the trees, cut straight through my chest and down to my soul. I stopped, shaking, uncertain about which way to go.

"Penelope, where are you?"

My mind retreated, pulling back to that place of peace and the scent of green things.

Arberdon's crops never smelled that full of vitality. Too many generations stuck inside the walls, hiding from the wild. We had exhausted the ground within and would no doubt suffer the consequences soon enough.

"Penelope!"

I wrenched myself away from the voice, curling into a ball. I wasn't ready to be found.

* * *

I woke to the sounds of Arberdon coming to life, feeling gross and groggy. My mind came back to me slowly as the tendrils of some strange dream evaporated like fog in the light of day. Something about running, or maybe traveling? Rolling myself out of bed, I fumbled over to where I kept a pitcher of water on my dresser. I rinsed my mouth out a few times and used the rest to wash my face and pour over my head, letting the water spill on the floor around me.

It had been another week since I'd last worked a shift. Under the guise of still being sick, no one questioned my being a hermit. My family left me to my sick bed while they were up during the day, knowing I was accustomed to a nocturnal schedule. At night I would slip into my mother's old robe and shuffle downstairs to forage. It was threadbare silk, a luxurious fabric that was available before the Great War, before all the silkworms became extinct. My mother's robe was printed with bright swirling colors and large sleeves that always reminded me of wings. There was a stain on one arm and the hem that fell just past my knees was frayed, but it still felt like her. I loved it and felt comforted whenever I wore it. I stared at the robe through my cracked mirror now as it hung on my bedpost, wishing I felt comfort instead of dread as I considered it.

The first night Ben came to check on me, we sat across from each other at the kitchen table and he watched me eat whatever prize I'd found in the root cellar. I kept my mouth full so I didn't have to talk. What could I even say to him? My eyes traced the worn patch on the table in front of me, counting whorls in the ancient wood. I knew my silence bothered him, but he was only able to stay a few minutes before continuing his rounds. I couldn't help the sigh of relief when he left.

The second time Ben came, his impatience filled the air like flies intent on a corpse, his stare hot on my face. Clammy sweat broke out on my skin. Then the questions started:

Had anyone noticed my absence?

Was my family poking around in our personal lives?

Was Randall pestering me about him?

I assured him that no one had asked any unwanted questions. I'd been completely alone, and I still wasn't feeling well so appreciated being given the opportunity to rest.

He shoved away from the table not long after that, muttering to himself as he quietly closed the kitchen door behind him with the kind of control that left me shivering.

The third night he pulled his chair around the corner of the table and sat as close to me as he could. His restless fingers drummed intermittently on the table top or on his knees while his eyes drifted down from my face with uncomfortable frequency. I avoided focusing on him, the weight of his anger almost more than I could bear.

I had gotten up for water and to give myself some space when he grabbed me from behind, slamming my hips against the kitchen counter with his body. His left hand clamped over my mouth to muffle my scream, the fingers of his right hand twisting into my short, springy hair and pulling hard.

The edge of the counter pushed sharply into my belly while Ben pressed against me from behind, removing any doubt of his intent. He loosened the grip in my hair just enough that it wouldn't hurt so long as I didn't move.

"Where is your necklace, dear?" He ran his teeth across the muscles in my neck. "When did you stop wearing it?"

He didn't wait for an answer but slid his left hand down around my throat and squeezed. I gripped the kitchen sink until my fingertips hurt, breathing shallowly under the choking pressure of his hand. Struggling would only make it worse. Moving his lips down to the shell of my ear, he fervently hissed, "You will remember to wear my ring at all times! It is the symbol of our love; I can't take a break from loving you, so you can't take a break from bearing it!"

With a final squeeze to my throat, he sank his mouth into my shoulder, his teeth gnawing on me. Ben liked it when I fought back; that would only encourage him. I dug into the sink, praying this would be the worst of it, and endured.

He stormed off abruptly after that, needing to finish his rounds. Appetite lost, I retreated from the kitchen and barricaded myself in my room. Ben's chain glared at me from the top of my dresser. I glared back until I fell asleep.

The next night I didn't take a light with me when I ventured downstairs and sat quietly at the table, dreading the soft rap at the kitchen door that I knew was coming. I wore his ring, the weight of it pressing against my sternum. Making it hard to breathe.

When his knock came, I hesitated, hoping he would think I was upstairs sleeping as long as I didn't move. After a heavy moment of chewing my bottom lip, I heard the tell-tale sounds of him starting to pick the lock.

I scurried to the door, swearing I'd just gotten up from the cellar. He'd eyed me speculatively, noted my necklace with a smile, and in the end just breezed past me and pulled a chair out for me at the table.

Instead of taking his usual seat, he stood over me and let his hands fall heavy on my shoulders. I chewed on a bean while his hands kneaded my neck. The same hands that were at my throat the night before. The same hands that bruised the shoulder he was now trying to massage. The same hands whose fingers lovingly traced the patch of raised, irritated skin from his bite. The hands that I knew would kill me if I weren't careful.

I could never relax under those hands.

When he brought his lips gently to the skin behind my ear I all but bolted from my chair, situating the table between us.

"Penelope," his low voice coiled around me from across the room. "You need to kiss and make up."

I swallowed compulsively, knowing what those words meant. Ben stood where he was and studied me coolly, a patient hunter. I made some excuse about my monthlies and backed out of the kitchen, hit the stairs to the attic at a run, and bolted my door. With my ear pressed to my door and my heart in my throat, I waited for his next move.

After what felt like an eternity, I heard the kitchen door close quietly and Ben's footsteps outside. Moving to my window, I peered out at the moonlit night to watch his progress. Hands deep in his pockets and shoulders back, Ben prowled easily away from my house. When his silhouette was engulfed in darkness I could finally pull a ragged breath into my lungs. I didn't sleep for a long time.

Even standing in the morning light, I felt the night constricting me. Ben would return. Ben always returned. And Ben always got what he wanted.

Feeling another panic attack closing in, I poured what was left of the pitcher over my head and took a deep breath. As I slowly exhaled, I became hyper-aware of the water running over my body.

Fingers of water wove through my hair, caressed my neck, tickled down my back and my breasts, traced across the backs of my legs. As droplets fell to the floor with quiet *plops*, I settled into my calm space with a shiver and again denied the feeling of decay that threatened to claw its way out of my chest.

Right here, right now, I am alright, I reminded myself. *Right now I am safe.*

There you are!

I opened my eyes and frowned as I assessed my left shoulder. The bruising was mostly gone and wasn't as painful to move as it had been. It had a lighter hue now, too, which was good. A couple days more and it would be back to normal. Until then, I'd have to keep wearing shirts with sleeves in spite of the heat.

The bite on the right side of my neck where it met my shoulder was still red and angry. A darker bruise would take its place soon, the lines from Ben's teeth already changing color.

I turned from my dresser, equal parts thankful and resentful for the change in routine that had me getting up during the day. Maybe I wouldn't have to see Ben later, even if it meant going into town for an evaluation with the Executor medic. Digging out some clean clothes from the pile in my chair, I got dressed for the day and tied my leather apron around my waist where it belonged. Using some dirty clothes scattered around my floor, I mopped up the puddle of water in front of my dresser. I was about to leave my room when Ben's ring caught the light that filtered through the walls of my room. I crushed the delicate chain in my fingers and contemplated leaving it right where it was.

"Right," I muttered to myself. "Because getting caught without it would work out so well for me."

Regardless, I hated the way it felt between my breasts, gently pulsing against me with my heartbeat. I slipped the necklace into one of my apron pockets instead. If I saw him, then I would quickly put it on.

I took a shaky breath and squared my shoulders, telling myself that everything would be fine. And I believed myself. I felt safe in the daylight.

As I came down from the attic and reached the landing of the second floor hall, my sister came tearing out of her room and directly into me.

"Oof, Penny! You're up!"

"Good morning to you, too, Missy."

"I'm sorry, Penny. Good morning," She said, wrapping her arms around my neck and pressing her head into my shoulder. The pressure hurt, but the feel of her so close to me was worth it.

Missy, officially Melissandra, was ten years my junior, making her a bouncy, bubbly teenager teetering on the edge of being an adult. She was sweet and could only see the best in people. She was also the apple of my father's eye, the spitting image of our mother, made all the more precious since she died giving Missy life.

"What are you doing up so early?" Missy's voice broke through my thoughts, her broad lips and wide eyes smiling at me.

"I've got an eval with the medic in town."

"Is something wrong?" Her dark eyes sharpened, searching my face. I plastered a smile onto my cheeks and shook my head.

"Routine stuff, nothing for you to worry about."

For a moment, I thought she saw right through me. Her lips tightened, her eyes narrowed, her jaw flexed. But then her face blossomed with one of her signature smiles and she hooked her arm through mine. "If you say so. They won't make you work tonight if you've got to be up this early, will they?"

"No," I shook my head as we started down the stairs together. "I won't go back on shift until I get clearance from the medic."

Which I desperately, fervently needed. When I was on shift, Ben couldn't see me as often. He'd switched his shifts to match mine when I started working nights, but he couldn't interfere with my job. No matter how much he glowed in the eyes of the almighty Executor higher ups, they wouldn't allow that. I spent as much of the rest of the day sleeping as I could, tucked up safe in my attic behind my bustling family.

"Maybe I'll see you later?" Missy turned to me hopefully. "We could have dinner together tonight?"

"I'd like that." I agreed as we both stepped down to the main floor. "What are we having?"

"Lots of tomatoes,"

"As usual," I sighed. They were by far not my favorite, but were prolific enough to be a constant staple. But I knew better than to complain. We were fortunate to have food for every meal, a reality not everyone in Arberdon shared.

"Some corn is ready, and Gramps was talking about using some of last year's corn meal to make bread. Provided he can convince Hannah to part with some eggs."

"Old lady Hannah?" I smirked as we pushed our way into the kitchen. "If her birds are laying she won't share."

"She'll share with your Grandfather, she will." The oldest member of our family chuckled from the kitchen sink as Missy let out a scandalized squeal.

"You're up early," Father observed in the wake of Missy's noisy entrance.

"Yeah, medic eval today." I said, passing by the table to give him a peck on the cheek before scooting around the room to greet Grandfather. Father looked back at his tools, which were spread across the kitchen table in an orderly mess.

"There are my girls!" Grandfather said as he wiped his hands on a threadbare towel and gathered Missy and I both into a hug. "It's been too long since I hugged the both of you at once."

"Morning, Grandfather," I said, sliding out of the embrace and trying not to wince at the sudden ache in my chest. I clutched at the numbness I needed to hold myself together, too much of any feeling threatening my precarious calm.

I drifted to the drying rack and got a glass, filling it with water from the kitchen faucet as the pipes banged and rattled in protest. "What chores are you working on today?"

"We'll check the Eastern fields," he said, picking up a bag of supplies and heading toward the back door. "Something has been prowling the fence back there, checking weaknesses. It's got the equids riled up, and we can't have that. So we'll check the fence, mend what we can. I won't be upset if we catch sight of whatever critter has been snooping. I'm ready for those forest devils." He patted his bulging bag.

"Please be careful." I frowned, knowing he was carrying one of our guns. One of our *illegal* guns that we hadn't turned over to the Executors. "Don't let anyone—"

"Stop fretting, child. I know how to handle myself. Did it a long time before you came along. Come on, Missy, time's wasting!"

"Coming!" Missy took one of my hands in hers. "Later? Right?"

"Probably," I nodded, swallowing the emotions that were threatening to well up. She looked more like Mother every day.

"Good!" She gave my hand a quick squeeze and dashed out the door.

I set my hip against the counter and turned my attention to my glass of water, watching the sun filter through the cup and illuminate the floaters. For a time the only sound was Father tinkering with whatever tool he was mending. My head ached, my heart knocked dully in my chest. All I wanted to do was crawl back upstairs and hide in my bed, hide from the memories that assaulted me no matter where I looked, burrowing hateful fingers into my brain.

Trapped against the sink, his teeth in my flesh. Cowed at the kitchen table, his hands on my shoulders. His lips behind my ear. The predator in his eyes. *You need to kiss and make up.*

"You okay?" Father asked from his seat across the room. His dark eyes regarded me over the rim of his glasses.

"Yeah," I cleared my throat and took a deep breath, stuffing the errant feelings back down. "Just got an eval this morning."

"You already said that," he said quietly, turning his attention back to his task.

"Did I?" I forced a laugh. "Where are the farm hands?"

My parent's house had enough comfortable space for six inhabitants. My father, grandfather, younger sister, and I took up four of those rooms, and Father usually had at least two farm hands to occupy the other two rooms.

My father tended to collect people in need of help getting their feet under them in exchange for labor. The arrangement worked well; they got room and board, as well as an apprenticeship of sorts with Father. In exchange, we got help working the fields and making enough food to provide for everyone living in the house and, in bountiful years, enough to share with the rest of the town, too. When the hands were ready to branch out on their own, they did with enough confidence and skill to look out for themselves. And Father found a new apprentice.

"In the field already," he said, allowing the topic to change.

"What are their names again?"

"Dale and Rena."

"That's right!" Dale and Rena were orphans. Not quite old enough to join the Executors and too old to be wards of the town, Father took them in when he saw them begging in the market and was teaching them how to farm.

"Seeing as how they've been living here for two weeks," Father murmured, looking at me from under his brow while his hands kept working. "I know you'd remember their names. Unless there's something else on your mind?"

"Sorry," I muttered. "Must be fatigue. Has the water been pumped into the house yet today? The stuff in the pipe is looking murky."

"Nope," he shook his head, looking down at his tool again.

"I think I'll go do that."

"Good idea."

"Father?"

"Yes?" He set his tool aside and looked at me patiently.

His tone was steady, but held enough anticipation for me to know that he'd been waiting for this conversation. Hoping for it, even. My heart started pulsing loudly in my chest, feeling the edge of something important reaching out in front of me. And, even though I had no intention of confiding anything, his open gaze started pulling the words I kept buried deep toward my mouth.

Father, I'm trapped in a relationship with the most powerful man in Arberdon, and I don't know how to get out.

I'm not sure how it happened, how things got so wildly out of my control.

I haven't said anything because he would find ways to use you against me, use everyone I love.

But if I opened my mouth, if I spilled my poison, it would hurt my Father. Not just emotionally; Father would put himself between me and Commander Benjamin Joshen, and that was a dangerous place to be. A place I wouldn't put anyone I loved, not if I could help it.

It was too much. I shifted away from the precipice.

"I just...I love you, you know?" I pulled on one of my practiced smiles and went out the kitchen door as quickly as I could.

Outside in our courtyard I blinked hard in the morning light, the sun already climbing its way across the sky and bringing summer heat with it. The courtyard was boxed in by the back of our house, the front of our barn, and two stone walls. The walls were about eight feet tall and covered in decades of lichen and scorched weeds. Two small, rusted iron gates, one in the middle of each wall, allowed access without needing to walk through either building. The ground within the courtyard was tilled, planted, and tended into rows and rows of produce, and the center of the courtyard had a spigot pump connected to a deep underground stream that had saved our home from drought many times. A walkway made an 'X' through the courtyard: one long path stretched from the kitchen door to the barn, and one connected the two gates. I shielded my eyes as I gazed up at the web of heavy black cables that hummed, along with the ceaseless cicadas, above all the buildings of Arberdon.

Our town didn't have much in the way of electric power for personal use, though the Executors brought their own power and spread their cables all over our town. The phones the guards used inside the city required electricity, as did the computer housed inside their recruiter's office. The hospital had some equipment that ran on electricity, too.

Outside of Executor business, though, most people didn't have that kind of technology. Households collected rainwater in buckets or used a well. Our house had the spigot to the underground stream, and one of us had to go out and pump the water into the house manually each morning. The thunderstorm that came through last week hadn't completely broken the dry spell, but it did mean I wouldn't have to work as hard to coax water out of the ground.

My eyes adjusted to the glare and I set off for the pump. A network of hoses directed the water from the spigot to pipes inside the respective buildings. I made sure the hoses to the barn were closed off and started working on the spigot, forcing the handle to point at the sky before slamming it back down against the pipe. It was a lot of upper body effort, and the tight skin under the bite on my neck didn't appreciate it. The metal of the handle was already warm from the sun and my hands started sweating almost instantly.

Big inhale and pull up on the stubborn handle, big exhale and force the handle back down. *Clang.* Big inhale and pull up. Big exhale and force down. *Clang.* The buzzing of locusts, cicadas, and the power lines hummed around me lazily as the sun beat down on my head. *Clang.* The air was thick to breathe and my shoulders and neck started tingling with the familiar feeling of hard labor.

Clang.

I started to hear the sound of gurgling water in the pipe at my feet.

Clang.

It wouldn't be much longer now.

Clang.

Up the pipe came the gurgling.

Clang.

Down toward the house, the hoses slithering between the rows of plants as they began to fill with water.

Clang.

Soon my movements were accompanied by the sweet sound of rushing water. The handle became less stubborn as I continued.

Clang.

In a steady rhythm, it felt good to let go of my conscious mind and allow myself to be a machine. Here there were no decisions to be made, no feelings to unravel. The mindless work eased the aching in the middle of my chest.

Clang.

Clang.

Clang.

Clang.

Clang.

"I love watching you work."

I started and turned, not realizing I had an audience. Ben was leaning against the gate that led to town, his arms crossed over his muscled chest. Even at this distance, I could see the tension around his pale eyes, the tightness of his shoulders. I felt my own jaw clenching in response.

"How long have you been standing there?" I asked, deciding I had pumped enough water for the day. My heart continued galloping in my chest even though I'd stopped moving.

"Long enough to know you're upset." He said, pushing away from the gate and striding toward me. His movements were always silky, like a big Felinax hunting. "How are your hands?"

I looked at my palms, which were red from friction with the hot metal handle. I hadn't had to pump water in a while because I wasn't usually up early. They'd probably blister in a few spots.

"They're fine." I said, folding my fingers into my palms.

"Walk with me." He ordered, and took a step away from me toward the barn.

It sounded like a normal conversation, but I knew better. And I had no intention of being alone with Ben today.

"Uhm," I hesitated, mentally kicking myself for not wearing my stupid chain. "I need to leave. For my assessment." I said, digging the toe of my left boot into the dirt.

Ben turned to face me, his cool eyes narrowing dangerously. Then he pointed at my foot. "You're lying."

I abruptly planted both feet, heat rising to my face and under my arms. "Well, I wanted to get there early. The doctors are always so busy, and keeping them waiting would be rude and hold everyone else up in the schedule. So if I get there early, I can be ready for them when they're ready for me. Instead of the other way around," I trailed off, forcing my anxious tongue to settle.

Ben worked his jaw, studying my face. Trying to decide if I were telling the truth. Which I was, sort of. My face hurt with the effort to keep a neutral expression despite the grimace I felt in my soul.

Ben rocked back on his heels and slowly folded his arms over his chest. The movement was deliberate, swelling his stature. A form I found attractive once, years ago. Before things shifted between us.

"Then we can walk together." He spoke softly, but the fury in his expression was deafening.

"You don't have to do that. There's a lot of other, more important things that need your attention. I'm surprised you're up this early, actually."

"Hmm," he rubbed a hand over his face, replacing his anger with a mask of pleasantness. "No task is more important to me than you, Penelope." He cast me a beaming smile that almost fooled me.

"Thanks," I returned what I could of a smile, sensing an escape. "But you still don't have to—"

"Which is why I don't understand," Ben invaded my space, grabbing my wrists, twisting and dragging them painfully into his chest. "How you could have forgotten so easily. Dearest. I thought I'd made it perfectly clear that you shouldn't. Take off. My ring." He bit out the words, his lips curled back in a snarl.

Pain curdled in my throat as I tried and failed to stammer out an explanation. Sharp and hot, my tendons strained under the tension. I swallowed a whimper, refusing to give it to him.

"What was that?" He whispered, leaning down so his ear was nearer my mouth. He ran his lips over my jaw. "What are you saying?"

This isn't right. This isn't right!

"Working." I gritted out. Another breath hissed in through my teeth. "Pocket." My stomach churned as I spoke.

Ben glanced sidelong at me, and then turned his attention to my apron. He knew how I stored things, so he knew which pocket I normally left empty. He grabbed both of my thumbs in one hand and pulled them down sharply while he crushed my forearms to his chest.

"Shh, shh," he crooned with a heated gaze when I gasped in pain. Using his free hand, he wiggled two fingers into the small pocket where I'd stuck his chain, insistently pressing against my hip and thigh. He drew it out and held it in front of my face thoughtfully. "For safe keeping?" He mused.

My breath was choppy as I stood as still as I could, careful not to apply more pressure to my thumbs. He laid the chain over my head, smiling with satisfaction as it fell into place between my breasts.

"How thoughtful of you," he said, planting a quick, possessive kiss on my tense mouth. "Let's go," he said, releasing me and striding to the gate that led to town.

Chapter Four

I flexed my fingers compulsively to shake off the ache as I sat in the waiting room. Electrical wires snaked along the walls, drifting down corners to tunnel under the floor and feed current to the rooms below. The lights dotting the long chamber I sat in hummed overhead, much like the cicadas that blighted our crops each year. The pitch was all wrong, though, sounding like dissonance instead of home to my ears.

I glanced up at the young woman behind the desk, catching her studying me again. Whatever murmured conversation she and Ben had before he'd left must've been about me. She quickly moved her green eyes back to the paper in her hands, the susurrous sound as they slid against each other causing a shiver down my spine. Paper was not a common commodity, and only Executors made fresh batches for official purposes. Anything printed after The Great War came directly from those Executor presses, and anything from before had been destroyed, either in the War itself, or in the censor burns that came after.

Everything except for the library hidden in my parents basement, along with our unsanctioned guns.

I forced a smile onto my face when Ilsa, the pale woman behind the counter, looked up again. She tucked a stray lock of soft brown hair behind her ear, a bright flush coloring her cheeks.

"It shouldn't be too much longer now."

"That's fine," I nodded calmly, ignoring the unease that sat heavily in my gut about this entire situation. "Thank you, Ilsa."

She went back to her documents and I rolled my eyes to the ceiling, thinking about the rows and rows of contraband hidden in my parents house. The stories I'd devoured as a child, fiction and nonfiction alike. The pages that kept me sane after the loss of my Mother.

There were times that I marveled at my predecessor's foresight. At the generations who carefully kept seemingly useless volumes, pages and pages of what many thought of as only fire kindling. Protecting and preserving that history. Growing up I'd often wondered why we didn't share our library with others. It seemed a shame to keep it all to ourselves when it offered me so much knowledge and entertainment. Father and Grandfather explained that it made us too much of a target. We already had the largest free standing house on the largest plot of land. We had our own well, deep enough that we didn't worry much in droughts if we were careful. There were those who resented us for it, even before the Executors came. I didn't fully understand until I slipped up and mentioned the books to a friend when I was much younger. Having to turn over a small treasure of books, to convince the Executors that that was all we had, and watch them burn in the symbolic fire was one of the hardest and most painful experiences of my life. I still remembered the bite of my Father's fingers on my shoulder, holding me fast with Missy bundled in his other arm. How he'd stood beside me, silent, as tears ran down my young face and offered me that quiet strength.

I never mentioned the books again. I could only imagine what Ben would do if he found out—

No, I didn't want to think about that. I imagined a pitcher of water pouring slowly over my head and began my calming exercise, exhaling as I relaxed my scalp. My brow. My jaw. My lips. My throat.

*He **has** to stop. You have to stop him.*

With a firm grip on my emotions, I opened my eyes and found Ilsa looking at me. She startled and tucked that same stubborn lock of hair behind her ear.

"The—" she cleared her throat. "The doctor will see you now."

I pressed to my feet with a final steadying breath and walked to the door Ilsa had indicated. The humming lights hurt my eyes, shining harshly inside the concrete building. I pressed my fingertips against my eyes as I turned the handle, catching a whiff of fresh air from the open window behind the desk as I entered the doctor's office.

"Hmm," Dr. Kane murmured as I moved inside. She was a severe woman, everything about her efficient and functional. Her iron colored hair was pulled back tightly from her face. "Eyes still giving you trouble?"

"It's nothing." I assured her, quickly dropping my hand. "Just fatigue. And the lights. I'm not used to them."

"Hmm." She repeated. A lazy fan circled among the cables attached to the ceiling overhead, paddling the heated air around. "You know you can be honest with me here. You don't need to hide your hallucinations from me."

The unease in my gut tightened. Shivers raced down my neck despite the sweat that coated me.

"What?"

Dr. Kane nodded sagely. "Yes, I've already read through your pre-assessment paperwork. I know all about the hallucinations. Seeing things that aren't there, hearing things. Classic presentation of your affliction."

"I didn't fill out any paperwork," I protested, latching on to that fact. I assumed that I would fill out the routine questionnaire once I arrived. Surely there was a mistake, a mix up of forms.

"Commander Joshen did." She waved my protest aside. "Now, these hallucinations are a concern. How they have affected your sleep and relationships. Your safety is our main concern, of course, but we can't forget our concern for the other citizens of Arberdon."

"My relationships?" My voice sounded far away, small and not nearly substantial enough.

"Mm-hmm." Dr. Kane leaned forward, folding her hands against her desk. "How your mind makes you think your loved ones are doing things, saying things, that they aren't. Extreme fatigue can bring about these sorts of symptoms, a powerful stress response to intense pressure. It can fracture a perfectly functional mind." She cracked her fingers away from each other, a practiced expression on her face. "But proper rest, and monitoring of course, can heal those fractures before they become permanent. And before they cause harm to others."

"I'm not—" I shook my head, words failing me. My carefully constructed control threatened to unravel. "What?"

Dr. Kane nodded again, the hum in her throat taking on a sympathetic pitch.

"Harming others is a scary concept, I know. And I've known you for years, Penelope. I know how much of a nurturer you are at heart. How, well, how *unnatural* being an armed guard must feel for you, if you'll excuse the term."

"A *nurturer*?" I parroted in confusion. I'd always thought of myself as a protector.

"Which is why we want to help you find your way in a role that suits you better."

"We?"

"Mm-hmm. Commander Joshen and I have been working together to come up with a plan for you. To help you, before the symptoms become more pronounced."

Blood roaring in my ears. Hands shaking. The edges of the room wavered, darkening, as panic wound tightly around me. I watched Dr. Kane's mouth move, trying to interpret her words.

"What?" I forced out of stiff lips.

"Do you have any unexplained bruises, dear? Anything that your mind may have fabricated an explanation for? Self-harm is one of the first—"

Her voice faded to an incoherent jumble as I finally understood. This wasn't a doctor's appointment, or a routine psych eval. This was a trap. A neat way to explain away any evidence I had against my fiance, and bury me deeper under Commander Benjamin Joshen's control. He didn't even need to be present to control me.

I only had two ways to respond. Admit that I did have bruises, and attempt to fight the case Ben had already made against my character with the doctor. Or deny everything away, which would make it impossible to accuse Ben, but could maybe save me from whatever cage was rapidly closing around me.

"No!" I said abruptly. Dr. Kane paused, pressing her lips together against the interruption. I cleared my throat, folding my fingers tightly together. "No, I don't have any unexplained bruises. I haven't had any hallucinating episodes, either—"

"Are you sure?" Dr. Kane's gaze sharpened. She shuffled the papers on her desk, tapping the one on top with her finger as she found what she was looking for. "George James from last week's shift, the last one you worked, reported that you said, quote: 'I thought I saw something. My imagination I guess, but Stars, I'm not sure.' Do you deny his report, Penelope?"

I gripped my trembling fingers tighter to still them. "No."

"Speak up please. Do you confirm that those were your words?"

"Yes, ma'am, but that hardly—"

Dr. Kane pressed her hands to the top of her desk. "You discharged your weapon, Penelope. I don't think I need to tell you how serious a situation this is."

"I was doing my job!" I protested, fighting to lower my voice. "I thought I saw an Ursine. That close to the gate, it would have been diseased or mad—"

"But the other guards searched the area, correct? And did they find any sickly Ursines?"

I shook my head, the movement stiff and uncoordinated. "Surely the protocol supports using our weapons and training in the face of suspected threats to Arberdon. If I'd seen an Ursine but waited until it came closer—"

Dr. Kane stood up, coming around her desk to lean against it in front of me. I pressed myself as far back in my seat as I could, tilting my head back to see her eyes.

"Penelope," she sighed. "We're concerned. For you, and for the safety of everyone else. For that reason," she opened a palm like she would take my hand. I tightened my grip on myself and pretended not to notice the invitation. "I can't in good faith clear you for active guard duty."

My heart sank, dread weighing me down.

"Further, I think it best to remove you from guard rotation permanently. Commander Joshen and I agree that maintaining that post would not be possible after your marriage anyway. Perhaps it's time to focus on this new chapter instead. On building your own family. On being a married woman."

I stared at her mutely, unable to rationalize how severely my life had just changed.

"With adequate rest, careful monitoring, and maybe some help from our pharmacy, it should be no time before you're back to yourself and ready to start a family. Doesn't that sound nice?"

64

CHAPTER FIVE

It was just as hot out the front door of the hospital as it had been when I'd gone in for my appointment, but I finally felt like I could pull a breath into my lungs. Waves of heat danced off the cobblestone streets, making everything shimmer. I shielded my eyes from the sun, which was lazily climbing its way ever higher into the late summer sky, and tried to calm down.

Dr. Kane's words kept circling in my mind like a flock of carrion hawks honing in on a meal.

Hallucinations. Careful monitoring. Removed from duty. Start a family.

Before leaving, Ilsa had informed me that Ben had wanted me to wait for him outside, that he would be by shortly to walk me home, but I shoved away from the building. Damn the consequences, I needed to move.

I started down the steps, the heat of the sun against the crown of my head helping chase away my dark thoughts. It wasn't long before sweat was soaking through my clothes, the warm smell of it filling my nose. The whole town smelled of sweat, and scorched earth, and too many bodies. It was gross, but you got used to it.

Like how you got used to the way he treats you?

I shook the thought away, determined to be in the present only. I strolled past little houses that got gradually more congested as I came closer to the middle of town. Some of them were built before the Great War, just like my parent's, though they were in worse shape and didn't have much land for crops. However, the people of Arberdon were resourceful. Many residents grew vegetable patches inside stacks of old tires or boxes of dirt that sat along the side of the street. I waved at a man who sat in front of his house on an old bicycle. As he peddled, a belt that connected the gears of the bike and an agitator inside a barrel turned, washing his clothes. No matter where you looked, there was evidence of Arberdon's ingenuity, picking up the scraps and making something useful out of it.

Sounds swelled as I came to the section of Arberdon where buildings pressed into each other like a clutch of frightened jack-hoppers. Built with whatever was on hand following the Great War, usually the detritus from demolished buildings, the effect was a hodge-podge of recycled material that was as clever as it was depressing. Rugs or, if you were lucky, scrap metal hung in place of doors, tires stacked in tiers to make stairs, and PVC pipes held up slanted roofs. Any durable materials that could be found made their way into construction in the years following the end of the war. Wood was never used, like what my parent's home was made out of, despite us being surrounded by forests. No one was willing to harvest the raw material from outside the walls.

In one of the clustered buildings, on the second floor, was Randall and Levita's place. It was no wonder my feet carried me toward his home.

Randall's family had relocated to Arberdon when I was very young. As one of the only walled cities in the area, Arberdon was a settlement for refugees of the wilderness. They usually came in small bands and were scruffy-looking at best. Time outside the walls gave each of them that *haunted* look. I never really understood what drove people to travel like that, endangering themselves. But, then again, I'd only ever been inside my own walls. Randall assured me that their old life was sufficiently dangerous and unstable enough to risk the journey, and I never pressed him beyond that.

Randall was five years younger than me, but he looked five years older. His early life, and that *haunted* look, aged him more than my life had me. But I didn't care about any of that when we became friends, and I still didn't care. Being an outsider, no other kids had been eager to befriend him. Add his strange origins to his strange complexion (he was ruddy, we were brown), and he was about as desperate for companionship as I had been.

Reminiscing about Randall and I had a rare genuine smile tugging at my lips as I milled through the center of town, letting myself get lost in the general public. Bodies surged and wove past each other in an efficient dance, each person knowing exactly where they were going and when they had to be there. The great fire sat in its pit in the middle of Arberdon's main square, crackling and throwing sparks as it consumed its fuel, blazing in spite of the heat. The words on the metal plaque bolted to the pit's stone face glinted in the sun: *'Through the darkest night, we are the Bright Illumination. Executors for Life.'*

I frowned to myself, ignoring the anxiety those words inspired, and continued around the fire pit, edging past traffic moving in the opposite direction.

Two young Executor recruits, who couldn't have been much older than Missy, stood on post at the West side of the pit, ensuring the gas lines that fed the flames were never compromised. They nodded to me as I strode past, taking their jobs very seriously. I nodded back, smoothing out my scowl, and pressed on toward Randall and Levita's home. The fire growled as I swerved around the pit, belching up smoke and oppressive heat. Sweat slicked across my skin and down my spine, whisking my thoughts away from Executors and my own troubles and leaving muted awareness in its wake. My mind lingered over the pulse of my heart at my temples and under my tongue, savored the crunch of my boots over the dirt that coated the cobblestones, was mesmerized by the wavering lines of heat that danced into my vision, was soothed by the smell of the air, cool and damp, that caressed me. It felt familiar, almost like—

The night was hot, my clothes sticking to me uncomfortably with sweat.

Bodies around me slowed, moving in dream-like thickness as the sound of my heart pounding overwhelmed everything else. I sucked in a breath, ignoring the concerned faces of the recruits beside me, and tried to keep walking as though nothing was wrong, as though I weren't seeing two different realities playing out at once; one where I walked down the street with agonizing slowness, and one where I was an observer of my final shift last week.

I wouldn't light my lantern unless I needed it, much later in my shift. My eyes adjusted better without it.

I stumbled, the fall taking more time than it should. While my body was trapped moving at a glacial pace, my mind reeled. Panic threatened, vibrating through my veins. Was this actually happening, my mind fracturing just like Dr. Kane had predicted? Heavy pressure gripped my head, too many thoughts and images trying to fit in my mind at once.

I caught my fall on my palms and knees, the pain feeling muffled and distant. My skin was scuffed up and bloody from the cobblestones when I finally got my feet under me again. A monumental effort had me waving off the two recruits who had moved to assist me. I couldn't let them help me, or I'd be locked up in the hospital by the end of the afternoon.

"It's not real," I hissed under my breath. "None of it is real." I knew it wasn't real. That meant I wasn't crazy. Right?

Suddenly I saw it at the edge of the forest. Two eyes watching me very closely.

"I'm not crazy. I'm not crazy." I chanted under my breath. I just needed to sort my thoughts, just take a moment and collect myself. Then everything would be fine, surely.

Maybe Ben and Dr. Kane were right and I needed medication and supervision. Maybe I was a danger to everyone around me. What other explanation did I have for what was happening?

What *was* happening?

My eyes scanned Arberdon's center frantically. My body, heavy and sluggish, refused to respond to my urgent desire to move, to run. Neighbors and strangers alike shuffled past me slowly, oblivious to my panic. The day was covered in a bright haze that made it hard to see and I struggled to shield my eyes with my hand as I turned in a slow circle.

I took aim, breathing out to steady my arms, and squeezed my first trigger.

Nothing *looked* out of the ordinary, other than the impossibly slow population around me. I tracked a bug fly across the main square, noticing each undulating flap of its wings. No one else looked up at the tiny rainbows shed by its flight. No one noticed me having a breakdown in the middle of the street.

Bang!

I jumped even though I knew it was coming. Just like that night on shift, none of the hazy vision superimposed on the world around me was real. I was feeling confused and emotional, tired after too many nightmares and not enough sleep, and that made me see things that weren't there.

They were right. They had to be right, I was hallucinating things. A danger to society.

I readied my second hammer as I scanned the field, looking for movement.

As much as I tried to convince myself I was imagining things, to talk myself back to reality, I couldn't shake free of the mirage that gripped me.

I forced my neck to turn my head, searching for something, *anything*, that would explain what was happening. Paths stretched out before me: the long stretch to my parent's house cut in half by the track leading to the North and South Gates.

Suddenly it appeared beside me, seeming to materialize.

Old Hannah fanned herself in slow motion with her hand while she sat on a bench with her eyes closed, her clothes damp with sweat just like everyone else. A few of her precious birds scratched the dirt around her feet.

And yet, as I kept turning, I started to feel cool. A chill tickled my spine and goosebumps seized my skin.

I pulled my second trigger, but it was too late.

I faced the Western Gate and the Executor buildings.

He grabbed my gun, wrenching it away from me and sending my shot out to the field.

And then I noticed him.

The seams of my shirt dug into my back as he lifted me, dragging me toward his snarling face.

A man stood, mostly hidden, in the shadow just outside of the Western Gate. Where in the name of all the Stars was the Western Gate guard? The man in the shadow was far enough away that I couldn't make out any of his features, but I could tell he was a tall man, a *very* tall man, with broad shoulders, standing in the heavy shade of the city walls. We stared at each other, me and the very tall man.

His eyes, Stars Above, his eyes!

"Penelope!" Someone called my name, and I tripped as my awareness slammed back into my body. I was sweating because it was hot; it was incredibly hot, and it smelled like hot dirt and bodies. I turned back in the direction of the Western Gate, but there wasn't anything remarkable there.

"Penelope!" My name was called again, and this time I paid attention and turned to the voice. It was Randall, jogging toward me from the Southern Gate on his way home.

"What the hell are you doing up this early?" He laughed as he collided into me with an arm wrapped around my waist.

"Hey, Randall! Aren't you chipper today?" I laughed and shoved his shoulder playfully. "I was actually on my way to visit you and Levita. Do you guys have a minute?"

"Of course! Always, for you." He smiled. "Come on to the house," he said, and strode forward to lead the way.

I looked back at the Western Gate and an ominous feeling settled into my gut. There was something seriously wrong with me.

CHAPTER SIX

I trotted forward to catch up to Randall, trying to shake the crazy out of my head as I went. *Just act normal and you'll be fine*, I assured myself on a shaking exhale.

The doctor is wrong, there's nothing wrong with you.

An old, rusty pull-down ladder led to their front door on the second floor of their apartment building, and I followed Randall up. My friend had managed to make a real door for their home, and it locked from the inside and slid on tracks along the wall. He was pretty good at creating those kinds of time- and space-saving contraptions.

"I like the door!" I commented as we stood on the landing outside their home.

"Thanks! It took some figuring to get it to work, but Levita appreciates the added security."

He knocked on the door quietly and I could hear Levita rise to open the door inside.

"Well hello!" Levita gave me a hushed greeting, moving back and letting us both come inside. Levita was younger than me, so we never spent much time together growing up. That changed when she and Randall took a shine to each other as teens. While I never felt as close to her as I did to Randall, she had become a dear friend. "What a nice surprise," she smiled and hugged me. She seemed tired, and she felt thin.

"I hope I'm not intruding too much," I murmured as I returned her hug. "I really should have visited before now. I'm sorry I've been so...distracted."

"Don't be," Levita brushed my apology aside as she ushered me to a chair. "We all have our lives to live."

Their apartment had everything they needed in the smallest amount of space possible. Just inside the door to the right was a sink basin and one gas burner. There was no running water, but Randall had created a contraption that would siphon water from their rain barrel into the sink. From there, it would drain to another barrel and be used in their bathroom. To the left of the sink was a cold box, another one of Randall's genius creations. It maintained temperature so well that Randall could fill it with ice in the winter and keep things cold all the way into spring. It went a long way toward helping them keep provisions for the lean months before fresh crops started coming in.

The other side of the room held a number of chairs and cushions that Levita had made or restored, and served as their living room and eating area. A hallway separated the kitchen half and the living half of their place and led to the bedroom, which they shared with their daughter. A curtain separated their sleeping area from a wash basin and toilet.

"So," said Levita, breaking the silence and pulling me out of my visual tour of their space. "What brings you?"

"I just," I floundered for a moment, wondering how I'd even ended up in their apartment. I shook my head. My whole life was a disaster. "I wanted to check in, see how you and Randa were doing."

Randall smiled, proud father that he was, but a heaviness settled over Levita at the mention of her daughter.

"I know I've been an abysmal friend–"

"None of that, Penny. You've always been unrealistically hard on yourself."

I took Levita's hand in mine, offering a squeeze in gratitude for her words as much as in comfort. "How is she?"

Levita held my gaze, her lips pressing together lightly. The gentle curve of her mouth never reached the faint lines beside her eyes.

"I think she might be getting stronger," Randall volunteered.

"Yes, perhaps." Levita nodded. She pressed her fingers to mine one more time before withdrawing. "She's resting now, but you can see her in a bit if you stay a while."

"I'd like that. I feel like I've been so out of touch. And here I've come to visit, but I also have a self-serving motive."

"Oh?" smiled Levita, casting me a knowing look. She resettled herself more comfortably next to Randall, who wrapped a beefy arm around her shoulders. "Nonsense, Penny, we know you care. You've been sick these past few weeks, so we wouldn't have wanted you to visit until you were well anyway."

"Right," my lips twisted at the reminder.

I *was* still sick. Sick of the lies I told to the people I loved the most, sick of how cut off I was from everyone else. Sick of the way Ben thought he controlled me, the way he *did* control me. The room felt suddenly stifling, the walls too close and the air too thick. It was a trap, a slowly shrinking cage that I knew would eventually crush me.

I took a deep breath, letting it out slowly to settle the panic rising up my throat.

You've got to get out. You've got to stop him.

"Penny? Are you alright?" Randall asked, a frown wrinkling his brow. "You seemed to go pretty far away there for a minute."

"I'm fine. Totally fine." I cleared my throat and tried to shake away the thoughts that crowded my mind. To forget the last hour in the hospital that marked the end of my life as I understood it. "Just didn't sleep much last night."

"Hmm," Randall pressed his lips into a line while he tugged on his beard. He knew I was hiding something. He was my best friend so of course he could tell, but fortunately decided to let it go. "Tell me about this self-serving motive you mentioned."

I folded my fingers together, taking a moment to get my thoughts organized. "I haven't been able to help at home much since I started guard duty. And my father has Rena and Dale to help, and Missy and my grandfather, but I know he could use an extra pair of hands to lessen the load that I'm not pulling anymore, you know?"

That you may not get to pull again, if Ben and Dr. Kane have their way, the thought invaded my mind unbidden, and I couldn't shake it once it appeared. *Monitoring and medicine to keep me calm and docile, marriage to Ben and living in his house—*

"Go on," Levita prompted and I got the impression that they weren't going to say anything else until I finished, so I cleared my throat and continued.

"I was wondering if I could ask for your help, assuming you have the time."

"Anything we can do to help." Randall offered. "That's what family does." Levita nodded, though she looked decidedly less enthusiastic than her husband. I couldn't blame her.

"I don't want to stretch either of you too thin, so it wouldn't be every day or set hours. Just whenever you make time. And I would pay you well, that's non-negotiable."

Levita returned my smile tiredly, likely seeing straight through my motivation to hire her.

"We'll talk about it and figure out what would work for us," she said, laying a hand on Randall's arm.

"Of course," Randall agreed as he placed one of his hands on top of hers.

He looked down at her with such affection, such devotion that it hurt. The pain of longing echoed in the cavern of my chest.

A weak cry came from down the hall and Levita instantly rose.

"Give me a minute to change and nurse her, and then you can come back to say hello," Levita said. "She does better to eat without distractions."

"Okay," I said, standing when she did and suddenly finding my stomach in knots. I wasn't often in the company of newborns; not since Mother died and I took care of Missy. I rubbed a hand over my tight chest and looked around to distract myself from the memory.

Randall watched his wife walk down their hallway and then turned to me, his face a collection of hard lines.

"Come stand on the landing with me," he said. Without waiting for me to reply he opened their front door and stepped outside.

The knots in my stomach clenched tighter.

I rolled the front door closed behind me as quietly as I could. Randall leaned against the rusted metal banister and looked out toward the center of town where the Executor fire constantly burned.

"Swear it on our friendship." He said without looking at me.

Randall had invented swearing the big, important stuff 'on our friendship' when we were kids. It was his version of a solemn oath, and I knew that I should never and could never break it.

"Swear what?" My attempt at being casual sounded pitiful even to me.

He let out a frustrated growl as he turned to me.

"Damn it, Penny. I don't like this. I don't like what's happening here."

"What are you talking about?"

"Don't play dumb, it doesn't suit you." He huffed as he returned to leaning on the railing. I leaned next to him and waited, knowing I'd have to hear him out even if I wasn't ready to.

"Things have been...straining you more these past years. I didn't think anything of it when you started keeping to yourself more after you got engaged. I mean, that's what you do when you start a family of your own. And Levita and I were..."

He trailed off, struggling with his words.

"You needed to focus on each other. You've both been through so much," I couldn't go on, and I didn't need to. Randall placed a big hand over mine and gave a quick squeeze as he cleared his throat.

"True. But there's something troubling you, and I don't like it. And now, when I look at you, all I can see is this...shell. You say all the right things, do all the right things. But I can't find *you*." He raked his hands back through his shaggy hair and let out a shaking breath.

"Randall, I'm fi—"

"He's killing my friend, isn't he?"

Sweat turned cold on my skin. It didn't matter that he was absolutely right, that I felt the festering decay in my soul more with each passing day. I was *so tired* of trying to hold it together, trying to appease Ben and navigate what used to be a relationship but had morphed into a prison. I wanted out, but I had to be careful. One wrong step could end my future even if he didn't kill me. The appointment with Dr. Kane just that morning confirmed it. I wasn't about to let Randall get wrapped up in whatever fallout was headed my way. No one I cared about would be hurt, that was all that mattered.

"Look, Randall, I know I've been distant lately, but nothing has changed about how much you know you can trust me, right?"

"Trust you to do what, exactly?" He turned, his eyes searching mine. "What's going on here? What's he done?"

"Nothing!" I said too quickly, panic tightening my throat. I ran my hands down my face and let out a slow breath. It was too much, holding back the wave of panic that crested again. I tried anyway, lifting my gaze back to his and continuing as calmly as I could.

"Randall, I'll admit that things have been...straining for me, like you said. But it's nothing that I can't handle. And I *am* handling it. Which is why you need to leave it be. You can't go...poking around and asking questions."

"Poking around!" Randall threw his arms in the air, his rising anger bringing a brighter shade of red to his cheeks. I immediately hated saying the words Ben had used to question me just the other night.

"That's not how I—"

"What the hell has he done to you, Penny?"

"Randall, please, listen to me. You *can't* bring Ben into this. Please don't. Don't talk about him, don't let other people hear you talking about him, and for my sake *don't confront him*. I'll handle it. I promise." I grabbed his broad shoulders and tried to stare him down, though he was a good foot taller than my five foot four. "*Please*, Randall."

He held my gaze for a full minute, his jaw working as he studied me. I made a valiant attempt to keep my expression calm and confident, to prevent him from seeing the cracks in my armor.

Finally he dropped his eyes and shook his head.

"*Shit*," he hissed. "I failed you."

"What? No you didn't—"

"I did." He took a deep breath and rubbed the back of his hand over his eyes. "Penny, I'm your best friend, and I didn't even notice what he was doing. How did I not notice?" He asked miserably.

"This isn't about you." I snapped, forcing my eyes to focus. I would *not* cry in front of him. "This is my mess, my problem. I'll handle it."

"What does John say?"

"Father doesn't know. No one knows."

"What?"

"And it needs to stay that way. For now."

"Why?"

"Because—"

"Because you love him? Because he's going to change? Because he's misunderstood?"

"No!"

"Dammit, *what*, then?"

"Because he's too powerful!"

Randall slid back a step like I had hit him. And the moment I said it, I knew it was the real reason I'd stayed with Ben over the years as things turned sour between us. I closed my eyes, trying to sort the words that were flooding my mind, begging to tumble out of my mouth.

"He's our *boss*, Randall." I said, immediately shaking my head. "No, it's more than that. He's the Executor's darling boy, and that means he runs this town. He *owns* this town. Someone breaks the law? *He* arrests them. Someone has a dispute? You take it to the Executor Judge. And *he* is in charge of the judge, too. You need a loan? You need a doctor? Where do you go?"

"To the Executors," he murmured.

I nodded. "And *he* is in charge of the Executors here." Silence stretched out between us and, in spite of the fear I felt from sharing so much with Randall, I felt like I could breathe for the first time in months. I filled my lungs, feeling lighter and more exhausted at the same time. His silence encouraged me to keep going.

"What I need the most is to know that no one else is going to get involved. That no one else will feel the fallout."

He blew out between his teeth, his lips a tense line. I could see him arguing with himself.

"Randall," I said softly, putting a hand on his arm. "Randall, you have a family. You have—"

"Randa."

I nodded. "And you need a doctor from East Elm Bay. From *the Executors* in East Elm Bay. Let me handle Ben."

He considered me quietly for a time. Then, "Do you think he'd really..."

"Make getting a doctor for your daughter really inconvenient and difficult as a way to get back at me?" I smiled bitterly, remembering my appointment with Dr. Kane. How her opinion had already been made before ever seeing me, all based on a report that Ben had created. "He can be spiteful, petty."

"I do not like this, Penny. Not one bit." He crossed his arms roughly on his chest. "None of this feels right."

"I'll handle it."

"Is he hurting you?"

"Randall, stop!" The sick feeling crept back into my stomach, the ghost of Ben's hands on my body taunting me.

Randall studied me, watching my reaction, and his cheeks flushed red with his rage.

"That sick son of a—" he swallowed his words with a quick glance at his door.

"Randall, *please*." I gripped his arm. "Please. For me, for them," I gestured to his door, "don't ask questions. I will handle this."

Now I could hear Levita moving, too. Finally he took my hands in his and tipped his head so he could look me in the eyes.

"Penelope Kendall, I swear on our friendship that I will keep my mouth shut, but just for now. Just for a day or two. And if you need *anything*, you will come to me and my house and we will help you."

Relief flooded through me so fast it hurt.

"But you swear to me that he won't touch you again. Don't let him touch you, Penny."

I nodded automatically, the weight of his concern twisting inside my chest.

"Swear it, Penny."

I ran my tongue around my mouth so I could force the words out, finding a promise that didn't feel like a lie. "Randall Krull, I swear on our friendship that I will be fine and I will handle this. I will find a way out that doesn't involve anyone else. And I will tell you if I can't."

"Randall?" Levita's voice was muffled through the door. "You can come back now."

He nodded once, stone faced, and ushered me back inside.

* * *

It felt like days had passed with all that had happened since I woke up. Randa Grace was as beautiful as ever, with ten perfect fingers and ten perfect toes. Her eyes were a muddy green, like Randall's, but her face was all Levita, her skin a soft, warm shade blended between her parents.

She was lovely, but her breathing was labored, and her little brow was almost always crumpled with pitiful whimpers that tore at my heart. Her regular regimen of medicines from the doctors didn't seem to do anything to alleviate her struggles, though Randall was quick to point out how strong her grip was, how solid her appetite. His usually booming voice fell a bit flat and uncertain, like he was trying to convince himself. Levita was quiet, watching her daughter with wary eyes full of yearning and pain.

I didn't stay too long with them. The heavy worry for their daughter filled the apartment like a fog, and all the emotions I felt being there with them threatened to tear me out of my carefully constructed calm. I had to get out before I lost it.

Walking down the cobblestone street back to my parents' house, I couldn't help but glance over my shoulder at the Western Gate. The guard was at their post, Arberdon's citizens milled around doing their business, and all was as it should be. And yet I couldn't quite shake the feeling that I was being watched. I shook my head, told myself to get a grip, and kept walking.

The sun's position told me it was just past noon, with the high heat of the day pounding down on my head and neck. Heatwaves danced up from the street and played with my vision, but I knew my path by heart. I lowered my lids to block the sun's glare and strolled in thoughtful silence, the constant drone of cicadas drowning out the sound of the town around me.

Randall would keep his word for his daughter's sake, I knew. He and Levita had already exhausted the resources available at our hospital, and the doctors had given her medicines as soon as she was born to help her immune system, but it wasn't doing enough. They'd increased her dose as high as they could, but they referred her case to the doctors at the hospital in East Elm Bay, our nearest neighbor with more resources than we had. The Bay city was two days of rough, dangerous wilderness away, and the doctors wouldn't agree to come see Randa without substantial compensation for their trouble. Even assuming they did come, there was no guarantee that the doctors would survive the journey. Arberdon's doctors encouraged Randall and Levita to have courage; hope for the best, prepare for the worst.

I kicked at a loose pebble on the street, sending it skittering into the gutter.

"It's just not fair," I muttered, closing my eyes to block out the tears that were suddenly threatening to spill. I rubbed my face roughly and rolled my shoulders. *I will remain calm,* I told myself firmly.

"You don't seem any happier after going to see your friends."

My steps faltered with surprise, but I recovered before giving him an excuse to touch me.

"Their daughter is really sick. I'm worried about her, about them." I told Ben, wrapping my arms across my chest.

He nodded, tucking his hands into the front pockets of his trousers as he peered up at the sky.

"You didn't wait for me."

"I never heard you ask me to." I said carefully, keeping my eyes averted.

"Your Father went to town to barter for some tools he couldn't fix. Everyone else is in the field. Why don't we go talk where it's quiet?" He waved casually at a fellow Executor as we walked past, as if he weren't threatening me with the invitation.

Fear shivered over my skin, making me forget about the hot sun and the stink of the town and poor Randa.

"I need to be alone right now, to think,"

"What you *need* to do is stop avoiding me." Ben's low snarl cut me off as his hand clamped into the back of my neck. His teeth pressed against my temple, sharp, as he tasted the salt on my skin. To anyone watching, it looked sweet and intimate. But his fingers dug into my nerves, forcing me to go wherever he led. I sucked in a breath and swallowed my pain, refusing to give it to him.

"Let's get you out of his heat."

We walked in silence the rest of the way to the Eastern edge of town and my parents' property. Every step grew heavier, every beat of my heart harder. There was no escape.

He opened the courtyard gate and led me inside, closing the gate behind us and shoving me in front of him toward the barn. I stumbled a step or two forward, furiously fighting to stay calm.

"Ben—"

"Not yet." He said softly, spinning me around by my shoulders and roughing me into a march.

Maybe it'll be different this time. Maybe it won't end the same, I tried to convince myself. My throat felt tight and I tried to ignore the dread that was crawling out of my stomach the closer we got to being isolated together. I knew it wouldn't be different, just like every other time I had held onto that futile hope.

Ben was right behind me, his breath hot on my neck, his hands eager to push me forward anytime I hesitated.

The path seemed shorter today and, before I knew it, we were stepping into the confines of the old stone barn.

"That's better," Ben smiled, and the kindness of it almost touched his eyes. "Out of the heat, right?" He slid the barn door closed and leaned back against it, looking at me expectantly. I moved cautiously away from him, blinking in the sudden shade. Pressing my hands into the stone at my back, I willed the wall to hold me up.

"That's Arberdon," I agreed, my dry throat working to swallow. "The heat can get oppressive." Ben didn't ever tell me much about his hometown, Yeven, but I knew it was a good bit cooler than Arberdon on average.

He nodded, his mouth pursing thoughtfully.

Be careful.

"We should talk," he said at last.

Earlier, I'd said I would do just that. But as I stood here, with the stone at my back and the scabs and bruises decorating my skin throbbing, my resolve slunk away from me like a beat dog.

Fitting, I thought bitterly as I stared at the toes of my boots. Steel-toed, for safety. Except that the greatest threat to my safety wasn't a dropped ax, but the man standing against the barn door.

"You want to start?" I asked, hating myself.

Ben clenched his jaw. "You're avoiding me."

I bit my lips to keep from saying anything I would regret.

"You're *still* avoiding me." The growl in his voice told me there was no friendly smile on his face anymore. He gave an exasperated sigh as he pushed away from the door and took a step toward me.

"How do you think this feels, Penelope? You're holding yourself away from me like bait, and I'm always the bad guy for taking the bait, for falling into your traps."

"*What?*"

"Don't think I'm not aware of the game you play, the way you twist things in your mind." He regarded me coolly. "I don't like what you make me do. But I'm trying to help you. I'm still willing to take you, despite your affliction."

He spoke so calmly, so matter-of-factly. Was it possible that I'd actually caused all of this?

No! Don't doubt yourself.

"I'm not *making* you do anything, Ben." I said quietly, confidence cautiously blooming inside me. "I'm not in charge of the things you do. The things you know aren't right."

Slowly, painfully slowly, Ben closed the space between us. I didn't run; I had nowhere to run to. And he always did love a chase.

He stopped when he stood directly in front of me, his expression dangerously calm. My heart pounded, the pulse of it throbbing in my throat. My tongue felt fat and heavy, saliva pooling at the back of my mouth. I rubbed my palms against my thighs, willing myself to meet Ben's stare. I would *not* back down this time.

"Please leave me alone." I whispered.

"*What?*" He laughed unkindly. "I'll never leave you alone, dear. You're *mine*."

Say it again. Don't falter.

"Leave me alone." I said again, a little bolder. My jaw was trembling and my stomach was twisted into knots, but I felt a strength filling me, pumping out from my chest and pouring into my limbs. This time *would* be different. I would be different, and I would make it so.

"What I need to do is teach you a lesson," he growled, his hands coming up to grab my shoulders. I dodged quickly, knocking his hands away and managing to slip out of his grasp by surprising him. I'd been resigned and complacent for a long time.

"You need to leave me alone." I said in a clearer voice, gaining momentum. The fear in my belly was melting into adrenaline.

"You are an ungrateful *bitch*!" He snarled, blocking my dash toward the barn door. Rough hands shoved me backward and I stumbled. "After everything I've done for you? For your family? You think you've earned the right to talk to me like that?"

"Ben, I'm not—"

"Get back here!" Fingers biting into my arms, flinging me against the wall.

"Stop it!"

"It's time you thought about someone other than yourself. It's time you remembered your place and made amends." He roughed his belt off and snapped it between his hands. "You need to get your head on straight."

I shook my head, keeping his gaze. "I won't let you touch me like that again."

Something flickered behind his eyes, something dark and dangerous. His chest heaved and his jaw flexed. "Who is it?"

"What?" My heart tripped over inside my chest. "No—"

With a snarl he rushed me and I automatically threw my hands up, guarding my face. But he didn't try to hit me, grabbing my left wrist instead and wrenching it so hard between us I thought my shoulder would snap. My back hit his chest with a thud, the shock of pain making me see stars. He wrestled his other arm over my chest and set his teeth against my neck.

"*Stop*," I wheezed.

"Who is it? Who do you want?" His breath was hot, his mouth wet where he latched onto me. My lungs spasmed, barely able to pull air in past his hold.

I squeezed my eyes shut and fought back the panic. Maybe I could retreat into my mind again, pick up the pieces and reconstruct myself after. Maybe it would be easier to escape him later, when he wasn't in a rage.

No, please! Don't give up, Pen, please don't give up!

My arms were pinned uselessly, but my legs still worked and were stronger. I struck out behind me, hoping for a shin or a knee cap. He grunted when I made contact, but it wasn't a solid hit. Instead of distracting him all I did was piss him off. He kicked my feet far enough apart that I could hardly stand.

"You think someone else will love you better than I can?"

I rocked my head back, trying to break his nose, but he was too close to do any damage. He slammed us both into a workbench, folding me over onto my stomach.

"Because they won't! I'm the only one who gives a damn about you, the only one who would bother with you, you understand me?"

No no no!

I struggled, trying to straighten up or get my feet beneath me. The heat pounding through my veins fought to turn my panic into rage, but it was losing the battle.

"You think anyone else would take you now? I know how this backward town thinks. You're *mine*!"

"No, I'm not," I sobbed, rocking my shoulders as much as I could. "Please Ben, you have to know this isn't right!"

"Shut up!" He hissed, pressing an arm to the back of my neck, pinning me to the workbench. The weight of his elbow sent pain radiating up and down the back of my neck and dulled my hearing. My vision blurred. "You're so *selfish*! Only thinking of yourself. But what of *me*? What of *my* needs? How long are you going to keep playing this game?"

"Stop it, Ben!"

"Stop it, Ben!" He mocked me, slamming his hips into my backside with each repetition. *"Stop it, stop it!* Is that how it's going to be? I'll make you change your tune. I'll make you want me!" He fumbled with the front of my pants, trying to get under my leather apron.

"Ben! *No!"* I tried to push away from the table, but he slammed me back. The weight of his body against me made it hard to breathe, but my right arm was finally free. I clawed behind me, trying to grab at his eyes or an ear. His hands grew frantic at the front of my pants.

"I'll make you love me, you'll see!" He cried, tearing my apron from my hips.

A silhouette appeared in the door of the barn.

"What the hell is going on here?" Father bellowed.

Ben grabbed his pistol and whirled around.

All thought evaporated from my mind. Every fear clanging around my skull crystallized into one awful realization.

Ben was going to kill my father.

I launched my elbow behind my head and finally made a good connection. Ben stumbled back, his firing arm faltering to his side without discharging, his other hand clutching at his face. A searing pain sang down my arm, but I didn't hesitate. I grabbed a small anvil hammer from the workbench and swung it at the knee closest to me.

"Dammit, Penelope, I wasn't going to—"

It made a satisfying *crunch* as it met its mark and he shouted, dropping his pistol to the floor as he stumbled. I kicked the pistol away from him and brought my elbow back across his face, ignoring the explosion of pain in my own limb as I felt his jaw give way. He fell backward again and I advanced, bringing my hammer down.

Ben struggled to regain his footing, his right arm shielding his face, but his left leg wouldn't support him. His right eye was already swelling shut, but he instinctively dropped into a grappling stance. Even half blinded and with one useless knee, Ben was a better fighter than I was and dodged most of my advances. But I knew my surroundings better.

I charged with my hammer, swinging wildly. Chunks of stone from the barn wall broke free and clattered into the aisle as he scrambled out of the way.

He stepped on the blade of a hoe that was leaning against the wall, its long handle springing forward and clapping into the back of his head. The distraction was enough for me to break through his defenses, landing a sound blow to his chest. Bones buckled and Ben slumped to the floor with a *whoosh* of breath, clutching his ribs. I dropped the hammer, driving him to his back with a knee to his temple. I sank down on top of him, planting my fist into his face.

Pounding.

And pounding.

And pounding.

My father's hands eased onto my shoulders, his palms cupping my arms gently and heavily.

"That's enough." His voice was calm, but his tone was wrong, foreign. He sounded shaken. "I don't think he's getting up. Penny? Baby?"

My punches were barely more than pitiful slaps now, my throat raw and aching. I sucked a ragged breath into my screaming lungs and covered my damp face with my hands.

"Daddy!" I sobbed as he lifted me to my feet, burying my face against his chest. He smelled like sweat and tools and everything that I needed.

I was barely aware of him carrying me through the courtyard and into the house. Hardly noticed him easing up the narrow flight of stairs that led to the attic. By the time he laid me in my own bed, I was drifting into an exhausted void.

91

CHAPTER SEVEN

"You're here," the trees murmured as I drifted aimlessly past. My fingertips traced along branches that shuddered. "Are you alright?"

A sad smile pulled at my face and I didn't bother answering. I didn't want to think about what ha—

"Penelope," a second voice cut through the forest. It used to be my name, but had evolved into a curse.

I pressed my eyes closed, leaning against a tree by the side of the North Road. I clutched the soft fronds of leaves, trying to sink into the forest and be forgotten. The branches curled around me.

"Penelope!" Ben's voice slithered through the underbrush, wrapping around my ankles and freezing me in place.

"Please, no," I shivered. I just wanted to dream, to drift away. I wasn't ready to—

Ben's voice solidified into a hand, fingers constricting around my lower leg. "Got you," he snarled.

"Wake up!" The trees shouted.

* * *

My body ached. My elbow throbbed, my eyes burned. Shifting beneath the light blanket sent a surge of hot pain through the abrasions on my knuckles and roused me enough to take inventory.

Long, late sun shadows stretched through my bedroom. A large flybug that had gotten caught inside pelted itself endlessly against the broken glass of my window. I watched it idly; how much time would pass before it realized there was an opening it could escape through a few inches to the left of where it was currently committing suicide?

Perhaps it'll never get free again, I thought. *Maybe it'll be trapped until it dies.*

I bolted up, untangling myself from my bed.

"I'm here, angel." My father rose from the only chair in my room and came to sit on the side of my mattress. "I'm here and you're here and it's okay." He was using his soothing voice again as he pulled me down beside him. The familiar tone tied my gut in knots, reminding me of Mother's death, the announcement of the enlistment requirement, and all the things I wanted to forget.

"Oh, Stars, what have I done?" I slumped miserably and looked at my hands. Ben's blood still colored my fingers, stuck stubbornly to my dried skin, though I could tell Father had tried to wipe them clean. I could feel the tears in my eyes, hear the quiver in my voice. "Did I kill him?" I whispered.

"No, angel." He took my hands in his own and turned me to look at him. "No, but you beat him pretty solidly. He's back at the Executor's now, with the surgeon." He paused uncomfortably.

"Was he conscious?" I stared at the floor, unwilling to meet my father's eyes. Afraid to see censure or fear in his face.

He was silent long enough to force me to look up.

"I don't give a damn about him, angel." He said quietly, his voice shaking with emotion. His eyes were red, glassy. "I want to hear about you."

Brushing him off would be the convenient thing to do, somehow pretending my way back to the normal flow of life. Being silent hurt, but saying the words out loud, pulling back the facade and being honest with myself and my father...that kind of pain promised to be excruciating. Neither one of us would be the same after. So yes, making excuses while trying to patch the tattered remains of the image I projected would protect the status quo, would protect the lives of the ones I loved.

I opened my mouth. Took a breath.

But something happened when I snapped in that barn. Some desperate animal that I'd kept on a tight leash in my chest broke free, and that part of myself couldn't, *wouldn't*, tolerate my old existence anymore.

I couldn't bear to look at him, couldn't bear to stop and think about the narrative that was flooding out of my mouth. He cradled me in his arms, rubbing my shoulders like he had when I was a child, stroking a hand across the back of my head. I heard the ragged breaths he took, felt the trembles of his own stifled sobs as I laid my heart bare.

* * *

It was after midnight when I considered the aftermath of my unequivocally horrible day.

The moon was high in the clear night sky, splashing silvery light into my room. I was tucked onto the window ledge, my arms banded around my drawn up knees, gazing at the town below me. The glow from that infernal fire could still be seen from my cracked window on the Eastern outskirts of Arberdon, reminding me of the heavy weight of my awful, impulsive actions.

My pack lay against the wall near my door. Stuffed with everything I thought I might need for...an indefinite length of time. My shotgun was strapped to the top, extra ammo packed in the outside pocket.

I took a deep breath and forced it out slowly, pushing my shoulders back and trying to convince myself that this reality was better than what I'd been doing before. Or at least survivable.

After my tearful confession, my Father had stayed beside me, assuring me we'd find a way through this cluster together. His guilt-wracked apologies only made me feel more awful, and we held each other and cried until I passed out again.

But I knew how this turn of events would really play out. Because I knew Ben. And Ben always got what he wanted.

My fists clenched on my knees. He was already working on declaring me mentally unstable, and what happened earlier would only support his case. I could claim self-defense, but I knew how it looked. One way or another, there would be repercussions handed down to me from the Executors. And Father, feeling the need to protect me, would attempt to temper the blow. And the blowback from that would put Father, Grandfather, and Missy at risk.

"Unacceptable risk," I muttered to myself, memorizing the view from my window. I would never allow harm to come to my family if I could help it. And *nothing* was getting at Missy through me.

I had spent most of my adolescent years raising Missy while Father worked hard to provide for us and battled his depression at the same time. I wasn't sure how he would respond to his youngest daughter after Mother died in the birthing, but he only ever showed her love and tenderness. He kept his tears and grief to himself, as he did with most things.

We still hadn't discussed that time of loss much; we just sort of understood the pain we both felt. We both lost our best friend.

I blinked back moisture, pressing my furrowed brow against the cracked glass of my window. My mother was as bright as the sun. Her perspective on life helped balance my father's less optimistic views. They both worked hard to show me love and teach me how to live, but I was always closer to my mother. We would talk about everything and nothing in the kitchen while canning, or sing songs from her youth while mending fences. If Father was my rock who kept me grounded, always silently present and supportive, Mother was my wings, lilting with stories and adventures and teaching me to find the beauty around me. When I lost her, I lost everything good and lovely in my world. I had learned to soar on her love. When she died, getting off the ground seemed impossible. I was crushed.

In that pain, Father and I leaned on each other wordlessly to prevent our sadness from drowning Missy. And so she grew to be our ball of sunshine, keeping me and Father in high spirits when the world felt like it was closing in.

I'd be damned if I let any fallout of mine touch her light.

And so, my only option was clear.

My bag was full of clothes and blankets. I didn't really own anything else except the small collection of baubles I'd received from Ben, but I didn't want to touch them. Having never been outside of Arberdon, I had no idea what to expect outside the walls of the city. I had no idea what I would need or where to go. I didn't even have an accurate map.

"Keep it together, Pen." I muttered. I took another deep breath and steeled myself against the reality that it would be a very long time before I lived in this room and in this house again.

I looked around the attic, committing it to memory.

The bare wood of my room was hundreds of years old, the treasured beams shrunken and cracked. My small bed in a metal frame that wheezed with every movement; the old overstuffed chair that sat next to it with its pesky spring that pressed up in the seat, making it impossible to sit in straight; the cracked mirror that hung above the water pitcher perched on my dresser; the canopy, one of my mother's colorful scarves, hanging from the rafters. That old scrap the only bit of whimsy I let into my private space.

I stood, easing my cramped legs straight, and ran a palm over the smooth walls. They sloped with the roofline, making it compact as well as stifling. It was the quietest room in the house, however, so I'd moved out of the room I'd shared with Missy and into this space when I joined the Executors and was posted on night guard. I missed the time I'd spent with my sister, but this room felt more mine than any other place in the house. It was my sanctuary.

I roughed the back of my hand against my damp cheeks and glared out the window.

A dark shape moved within the shadows of the town, avoiding the light of the moon.

"What are *you* doing?" I hissed under my breath, recognizing Randall's gait as my eyes adjusted.

I watched my best friend creep closer until he finally disappeared into the courtyard behind my parent's house. Then I turned away from the window with a grim set to my lips, hefted my pack, and quietly slipped down the stairs.

"—to press charges. They're claiming assault." Randall's harsh whisper drifted through the door that separated the kitchen from the rest of the house. I closed my eyes against their persistent sting as my Father let loose an impressive string of curses.

"They'll come at dawn with an arrest warrant, and commitment papers for the psych ward if that isn't enough."

"I'll be damned if they take my baby." Father growled.

"No one's getting Penny." Grandfather said firmly. "Over my dead body."

That's the whole point, I thought, scrubbing my eyes. *It will be over your dead body. And Father's. And probably mine, too. And then what about Missy?*

I eased my pack down to the floor and strode into the kitchen.

"Hey, Randall." I sighed as his beefy arms gobbled me up into a hug. "You shouldn't be here."

"Like hell, Penny." He shook me firmly. "You're family. Family stands together."

"And *you* have Randa and Levita to think of." I countered, crossing my arms over my chest and facing Father. I swallowed thickly. *Keep it together*, I mentally chanted. "Where's Missy?"

"At home." It was Randall who answered. "She's tucked in with Levita, safe and sound. She can stay as long as she needs to." He added with a meaningful look at my Grandfather, who nodded grimly.

And now they're all at risk, I gritted my teeth.

"Thanks for the advance warning, son." My Father said, gripping Randall's shoulder and hauling him in for a hug. He squeezed the back of his neck, pressing their foreheads together, before stepping back. "But Penelope's right. You're putting yours at risk just coming here, though we're not ungrateful."

My best friend nodded, already backing toward the kitchen door. "I'm not going to let you be caught unaware, if possible. I'll do what I can, share what I know, and keep Missy safe. I swear. Penny, on our friendship, I swear."

I breathed carefully past the tight grip on my chest and dipped my chin at him. "Thank you, Randall. I'm s—"

"If that's an apology, shut your mouth!" He snapped with a forced grin, startling a watery laugh from me. I noticed his mouth quivering before he pulled me into his arms again.

The smell of him, warm and comforting and familiar, threatened to dissolve me on the spot. I held on, held my breath, my fingers digging into the fabric on his shoulders.

"We've got you," he whispered fervently. I nodded, sniffing hard.

Message delivered, he slipped out the back door and faded into the night.

"We'd best get ready." Grandfather said into the silence that followed. Father let out a long breath and the two of them turned toward the cellar door. To the illegal weapons stashed beneath the floorboards, along with the books.

"Wait!" I wrapped my arms around their necks. "I love you both so much," I said fiercely. "I love you."

"We know, girl." Grandfather's voice was more gruff than usual. He squeezed me back as tightly as I held him.

"We'll find a way out of this. We'll be fine, Penny-girl. We'll be fine."

I savored the feel of their arms around me, wanting to linger just a little longer. Tempted to give up on my impossible idea and stand beside them at dawn instead.

They will be fine on their own.

I stepped back and forced a smile on my face, clearing my throat. "I just wanted to make sure you knew that before, well. I just wanted you to know that."

Father squeezed my elbow, smarting the bruise from my fight with Ben. It was a good reminder that I wasn't helpless. I wasn't weak. I wouldn't break.

"Come on, John." My Grandfather said, holding my hand just a moment longer. They turned to the cellar door again, and I didn't stop them as I heard their footsteps fade beneath the house.

"Please forgive me." I whispered, reclaiming my pack from the other room and creeping out the back door. "Please understand."

I eased the latch closed on the door and slung my pack across my shoulders, taking off at a slight jog across the courtyard toward the fence.

On the other side of the fence, beyond a carefully maintained swath of barren ground, loomed the forest.

"Stars, what am I doing?" My steps faltered. No map, no experience, no real plan...oh this was a very bad idea!

You will be safe. You will survive. They will be fine.

I took a deep breath and tried to convince myself that leaving was the right decision. I veered to the right side of the stone barn, vaulting myself at the courtyard wall and hooking my arms over the barrier. The angle between the wall of the barn and the courtyard wall made it easier for me to scale the craggy surfaces. I scrambled, finally managing to fling a leg over the top of the wall and pull myself over.

It wouldn't be long before my Father and Grandfather realized I'd left. I had no time to pause, releasing my hold on the top of the wall and sliding down the other side. I landed hard, trudging to my feet and taking off at a dead run toward the trees.

The guards would check the perimeter periodically, so I hustled to cross the barren buffer before being seen. The woods were, ironically, going to be my sanctuary.

You will be safe. You will survive.

The mantra looped through my mind in cadence with my stride. And then I was ducking into the deeper darkness of the forest.

A chill danced down my spine as a blast of adrenaline and something else charged out of my heart. Excitement? Victory? A manic laugh bubbled up inside me and I gasped around it, a smile splitting across my face. I did it! I was out of Arberdon! I was in the forest!

Stars Above! I was IN the FOREST! The giggle threatened to turn into hysteria and I swallowed it down, goosebumps breaking out along my skin. Who knew what sorts of creatures were cloaked in darkness with me, watching me, stalking...

"Focus, Pen." I gasped, taking a deep breath and thinking of my calming exercise. I controlled my breath, bringing it back into rhythm with my running feet. The ache of oxygen burn started in my lungs and legs, but I knew I had to press on and get as much distance between myself and Arberdon as possible. Father and Grandfather wouldn't report me missing when they realized I'd run off, and the Executors weren't supposed to arrive until dawn, which gave me the rest of the night to escape.

Night, when the predators were active. I shook my fists loose, trying to shake off my fear with it.

Don't worry about that.

I brought my attention back to my breathing and staying calm. Inhale for two strides, long exhale for three. Loose fingers meant loose shoulders. Strong core, quick feet. The uneven terrain and choked foliage impaired me, the pack making it even harder to make progress while crashing through the greenery. I needed to stay quiet, and I needed to make good time, so I swung toward the North Road that led away from town. If I stayed close to the ditch I should be able to keep my speed up, while still having enough time to throw myself under cover if I heard pursuit.

I hoped, at least.

I broke from the trees at the side of the road, finally able to straighten, and settled into my endurance pace. The sound of my breathing enveloped me and I kept my gaze on the ground a few feet in front of me, adjusting my stride as needed. I licked my lips, spitting over my shoulder to clear my throat.

My body protested the work, clamoring about injuries and exhaustion, but slowly the physical demand that I stop eased away as I found my groove and rode it.

Hours passed, though I have no idea how many. I knew only the burn of my muscles, the ache of my shoulders, the chafing of my back under the pack as some obscure, distant marker of time. Stopping wasn't an option, so I pushed forward. My body's complaints were a dull hum in the back of my mind, muffled by my compulsion to keep moving. At some point, my mind wandering, I began to dream.

I'd been running so long, my breath screeching in and out of my lungs. My legs hurt, my arms hurt, my chest hurt, my feet hurt. I lost a shoe somewhere, but didn't dare stop or go back for it.

They *would find me.* ***They*** *would catch me. There would be punishment for what I did.*

What did I do? Oh, Momma!

A twig snapped in the forest beside me and I shrieked before I could help myself. I clamped a hand over my mouth and plunged further away from home.

*What would happen if **they** found me? No, when, because of course **they** were faster, and stronger. I was so tired already.*

Another sob threatened to choke me and I bit my tongue instead, teeth biting into my flesh. I had to get away, had to survive. I had to grow stronger.

And when I did, I would kill them all.

Chapter Eight

The sun had just crested the horizon to my right, its brilliance smothered by trees, but there were other signs that a new day had come. The black canvas of night eased to a soft gray. Birdsong tentatively warmed up and those awful gnat-stingers were coalescing into clouds around me. I swung my arms weakly at them as I allowed my heavy legs to trudge to a lurching stop. My throat wheezed and I licked my lips, my tongue sticky instead of slick. Trying to swallow just about choked me.

I braced for a moment on quivering thighs, taking in the forest around me. I had no idea where I was, though I knew I still followed the North Road. Eventually I'd find my way to East Elm Bay if I kept going in the same direction...though I wasn't sure I should. After exhausting a search of Arberdon, the Executors would no doubt check there. It *was* the closest city, after all.

But I'd figure that out later. More immediate was my need for water and a rest.

I gingerly slung my bag down from my shoulders, my hands shaking as I tried to grip the canteen. I ignored the determined gnat-stingers that stuck to the sweat of whatever skin they could find, wiggling uselessly as they drowned. I didn't care that they were nipping at me, swirling around me in an incessant haze. What I needed was purchase on my Stars-forsaken metal bottle. What I needed was its water, sweet elixir, nectar of heaven, in my mouth. Everything else was background noise.

I sipped carefully, water threatening to spill in my uncoordinated attempt at drinking. I swallowed with effort, took a deep breath, spitting out a few gnat-stingers who tried to join me, and tried again with marginally more success.

After replacing my canteen I dug out a hunk of corn bread from the top of my bag, breaking off small pieces as I stretched out my legs. I knew better than to collapse into the trembling heap that I wanted to. If I didn't keep my legs limber I'd never get up again. And I knew I wasn't stopping, just resting for a moment before I had to start running again.

I didn't even want to think about that.

So I nibbled at the bread while I paced in the ditch and stretched, letting my mind be empty of all but the physical discomfort that throbbed through my body.

After finishing my food, I arched my back and swung my arms before deciding that sitting down and stretching would be permissible. I used my pack to help lower my unwieldy limbs, my quads screaming the whole time, and reached for my toes.

"Being alive feels good," I muttered, easing my legs out straight. "This is a good feeling." My mantra kept my mind distracted as I regained feeling in the soles of my feet, as my heart rate eased back from a thundering pace.

I had no real concept for how long I had been running, not knowing when I started, and I didn't think knowing would make me feel any better. But the urgency to put more distance between me and Ben's Executors ate at me and I knew I had to get moving again. Biting back a groan, I rolled to my knees and reached for my pack.

It was only then I noticed the cautious silence around me.

"Don't move," The low whisper wrapped around me like a spell, freezing me in place. My throat locked around a scream that wanted to rip out of my chest, but instead I held my breath.

"Whatever you do," the eerie voice whispered again. "Don't. Move."

Adrenaline poured through my body, limbs humming with a need to explode into movement. By some miracle I held my stillness, despite every instinct clamoring for me to move.

In the corner of my eye I could just make out the crouched form of a man. His outline was hazy and indistinct, but I could tell he clutched a weapon of some kind. My ears ringing and my heart pounding in my throat, I forced my gaze to the shotgun strapped to my bag.

Rustling sounded from the brush across the road from me, jerking my attention away from the threat behind me. *Large* rustling, to be exact. The kind of rustling that you would expect to precede a large, dangerous, deadly creature.

I swallowed against the bile in my throat.

With a snarl, the anticipated large, dangerous, deadly creature stepped boldly onto the road. Knowing it was coming did nothing to stop terror from flooding through me. I couldn't help my whimper as I took in the hulking form of the Mountain Canid.

The size of a small plow-equid, its blunt nose and boxy head met a neck thick with muscle before sloping into a pair of powerful shoulders. Its barrel chest was as wide as the trees that lined the North Road, its legs tapering into large, clawed paws. Its whipcord tail stood up in the air like a challenge, the whole of it quivering back and forth with barely contained rage.

I'd never seen a Mountain Canid before, but there was no mistaking what stood before me now. Randall had told me all about what he'd seen when out on Roving Patrol with the Executors, and Canids were some of the worst. They were vicious and tenacious, and I was pretty sure that I didn't need to worry about which city I would hide in because I was about to be killed in the ditch just outside Arberdon.

My gut clenched and I wasn't sure which of the fight or flight survival instincts would overpower me first. Or if I would save the Canid the hassle and just drop dead beside my pack.

The Canid growled and paced forward a few more steps, claiming the road, flashing teeth as its hackles rose in a spikey ridge along its back. It snapped toward me quickly three times and I didn't even notice as I peed myself.

Suddenly, the figure from behind me launched from the foliage, vaulting with the assistance of a long staff, and landed on the road between me and the Canid. He swung his staff back and forth in an unpredictable pattern, shaking tatters of a red scarf that hung from one end, sending up puffs of dust as he tapped out a tattoo on the ground. The Canid stiffened and stopped advancing, analyzing the new threat.

The man's shoulders bunched under his brown shirt, strong legs pushing against the fabric of his pants as he slowly circled in front of me, keeping the Canid's attention.

My body vibrated with the urgent need to *do something*! But I knelt there, utterly useless, staring at them.

Having decided that I was the lesser threat, the Canid rotated with the man in the middle of the road. It did that three-snap lunge thing toward him, but he didn't even falter in the rhythm of his staff. His left arm held the wood of the staff steady, dancing the red tassels at the end effortlessly, while he arched his right arm out to the side, making himself appear larger. His dark hair fell in a messy braid from the crown of his head to the base of his shoulders, the sides shaved bare to reveal skin decorated with a multitude of scars.

Skin tinted *blue*.

"Oh," the word dropped out of my mouth as I absorbed his profile in horror.

The *Unnat*.

The *Unnat* from my dream.

The *Unnat* I'd tried to shoot.

The *Unnat* who grabbed me, lifted me with the power of one arm.

The *Unnat* who was, apparently, *real*.

"Oh," the back of my throat burned and I swallowed compulsively.

An *Unnat* and a Mountain Canid, two of the most deadly creatures I'd ever heard of, were about to do battle in the middle of the North Road while I crouched in the ditch like a sniveling idiot. When they were done with each other, what would they do to me?

I was *not* sticking around to find out.

With a shout, the *Unnat* threw his body forward, charging the Canid and shaking the staff in its face. The Canid recoiled and bunched its legs to retaliate.

And I heaved my pack and ran like hell.

I tore through the foliage, plunging blindly away from the road, and cursed my lack of foresight in lashing my shotgun to the top of my bag instead of keeping it in my hands. Though a shotgun probably wouldn't drop either one of those creatures, so maybe I was better off.

With my hands free, I batted branches and vines out of my face, the sound of the fight fading behind me. Or maybe just being drowned out by the scream of my breath, the pounding of my feet. The woods blurred around me, my eyes watering and lungs burning. Birds tore up from the ground as I approached, screeching at me and warning others away. Or maybe drawing more predators toward me.

I wove in and out of trees, dodged branches that grabbed at my clothes, scrambled over boulders, and crashed through thick brambles. My palms were torn open, my face was scratched and bleeding, but I couldn't feel anything except for the hot burn of my muscles and the taste of blood in my throat.

With a yelp I tumbled down a ridge, the ground rolling out from under me. The pack landed hard on my back, knocking the wind out of my lungs. I wheezed, blinking the stars out of my eyes, and struggled to my hands and knees.

Like a miracle straight from heaven, with rays of sunlight shining all around like it was caressed by the hand of fate, I looked up and saw my salvation.

A rover sat in front of me.

"Oh *please* work!" I wept and stumbled to the machine.

Complete with chain tracks and a plow spearhead, it was made to navigate the forest. The Executors had a fleet of them in Arberdon, but this one was clearly custom. I tried not to think about where the driver was.

Using the handlebars to sling my heavy body onto the leather seat, I checked for the keys. Still in the ignition.

"Thank you," I breathed. The engine roared to life when I turned it over, coughing out a few clouds of dark smoke before settling into a steady purr.

It was already facing away from the North Road, which suited me fine, so I revved the engine and tore off. Leaves and bracken took flight as the tracks dug into the earth, fishtailing slightly, before catching and launching away. I bounced over the uneven ground, the rover crawling over all manner of obstacles and plowing smaller trees out of the way entirely. The handlebars vibrated under my bloody palms, and before long both of my arms were buzzing. But I didn't care. I was tearing through the forest at a break-neck pace away from what was very likely going to kill me, so I'd take numb arms with a smile on my face.

Having no idea where I was or what direction I was going in, I kept the rover pointed straight as best I could to put the most distance between me and the North Road. I prayed I didn't drive directly back into Arberdon. Or off a cliff.

The rover splashed through a few different small streams, churning the water with mud but not once slowing down. It was pulling up a small rise when I noticed a drop in power.

It's nothing, I insisted to myself. *It's just the hill. Everything is fine.*

I crested another hill, speeding across a clearing toward looming trees, when the rover slowed with a pitiful cough and died. For a moment I thought it was idling, my arms and backside tingling hard with pins and needles.

I grabbed the key and turned.

Click click click.

Even though I knew it was stupid, I tried to turn the key harder.

Click click click.

"No no no no," I stood up in the seat and shook the handlebars.

I slung down from the seat and shoved my hands through my short hair, my legs protesting the sudden movement after sitting still so long. My gut twisted and I could barely hold myself upright.

The sun was nearing its apex, peeking above the trees that surrounded me, and the droning of cicadas filled my ears. I could hear them clearly because the rover was dead.

The *rover* was *dead!* I cursed hard and tugged my hair at the roots. I had no idea where I was, I had no idea where I was going, and the rover was dead. This was somehow so much worse than running along beside a known road that led to a known town. What was I *thinking* running into the forest to save myself? The forest would *kill* me, not save me!

I had to get back to the road, there was clearly no other option.

"Great, just *great*, Pen. Real good plan." I cursed myself some more as I tried to rough the rover around to point in the opposite direction. The heavy machine wasn't impressed with my efforts. But why bother turning it around when it wouldn't turn on? On a whim, I tried the key again.

Click click click.

"No gas." Said a rough, breathless voice behind me.

I reached behind my left shoulder, vaulting over the rover for cover as I whipped my shotgun up to position and sighted at the same time. My speed surprised myself as much as it surprised the *Unnat.*

"Stay back!" I shouted boldly, though it came out more hysterical.

"Be easy," he soothed, his eyes narrowed with irritation. He raised his hands beside his head. His muscles bunched and flexed under a brown shirt darkened with sweat.

He stood not fifteen feet away, just over the rise and onto the level clearing. As we stared at each other, his skin returned to its normal blue hue, the flush of exertion quickly fading away.

"Don't try me," I growled, readying both hammers because *of course* my gun was loaded. He could play cautious all he wanted, but I'd seen how fast he could move. If he decided I should die, I wouldn't have time to unload my two slugs, but I would sure as hell try. I clenched my jaw shut and tried to be brave.

He watched me as he reached the rest of the way up to the hair on his head, unraveling his tangled braid and redoing it with deft fingers. It was an odd thing to do with a shotgun pointed at his chest. Something about the movement pricked at my mind, the weave not as tight as it should be. He tied off his hair with a leather strap and let his hands hang casually at his sides.

"Don't get nasty."

"*Nasty?*" I screeched, finger safely on the guard above the trigger. "You're chasing me!"

"No."

"Oh, *please*! First was the night of my shift,"

"You *shot* at me—"

"*Then* I saw you in town,"

"—and I still don't know why!"

"And now you're *here!* What do you want?"

"What you took from me, for starters."

"I didn't—"

He gestured with his head toward the rover.

I swallowed, shame stealing my protests as my stomach dropped to the ground between my feet.

"This is *your* rover?" My voice was small and pathetic. Good thing he had excellent hearing.

He nodded once, slowly, his uncanny eyes burning into me.

I swallowed my embarrassment and backed away, keeping my gun trained on him. "Okay, you can have it."

He didn't move forward, just frowned between his eyes a little more. I slid backwards another step, putting more space between us.

"Stop," He barked, nodding toward the trees behind me. "Don't go that way."

My steps faltered, but I recovered. "And why should I listen to you?"

He sighed, like he was long-suffering the novice survivalist. Which he was.

"Because I know. Nothing survives in the Dead Grove."

An embarrassingly high pitched titter escaped me. "Dead Grove? *Seriously*?"

He did that single, solemn nod thing again, his eyes penetrating. I believed that gaze could incinerate on command. I shifted uncomfortably.

"Look for yourself." He said, his deep voice rolling over me like waves. "See the line."

I narrowed my eyes at him, refusing to turn around, though the need to look behind me burned like an itch. He laughed once, harshly, his features twisted into an angry snarl.

"Fine, do what you like. You'll be dead before dark." He reached down to the ground, retrieved his staff, and walked back down the hill without looking at me or his rover again.

I kept my gun up and aimed at the hillcrest. I couldn't help myself, though I knew a shotgun wouldn't do me any good against him. It made me feel better. I turned slightly so I could see both the edge of the rise and the forest behind me.

Skeletal branches reached for the sky, covered in long, sagging hair-like clumps of what I guessed were leaves. Bark the color of grease, covered in thick rivulets of oozing sap.

I glanced back at the rise, but the *Unnat* was out of sight. Taking a fortifying breath, I sidled closer to the treeline. Was it just me, or did the branches shiver at my approach? I reached down, bracing my shotgun steady on my hip, and groped around for a rock. My palm closed around a jagged lump, pulling it free from the dirt. With one final glance over my shoulder, I took aim and threw the rock into the forest.

Snap!

The dark branches were more like heavy vines, the closest ones shifting unerringly toward the rock I threw.

"Trapper Trees." I muttered.

Carnivorous plants that rode the line between flora and fauna. Their sap acted like a lure, attracting smaller animals and insects toward the sweet smelling liquid, which they then attacked with their branches. Their prey would be overwhelmed by the rope-like appendages, then pushed down into the dirt and slowly absorbed through the roots as they rotted.

They weren't incredibly fast, but the grove in front of me was thick with them; I hadn't realized any grew close to Arberdon. Then again, I was at least half a day's rover ride away from Arberdon, and Stars only knew how far from the North Road. If I had made it to the edge of the clearing, would the rover have been enough to carry me through?

I closed my eyes and cursed myself some more. What choice did I have, really? What exactly was I planning to do out in the wilderness? My heart stuttered, but I took a deep breath and remembered how to calm myself.

"Hello?" I called weakly, unable to fully process what I was doing. The words stuck to my throat, like they didn't want to leave my mouth. I ran my tongue over my teeth and tried to project my voice farther. "Are you still there?"

I opened my eyes, and there he was as though he'd never left. He leaned on his long staff, the tasseled end reaching back behind him. Sunlight glinted off of a sharp blade hidden among the pretty red fabric.

Had the tassels always been red? I wondered.

"Don't you want your rover?" I fished lamely, not sure how to broach my latest absolutely horrible idea.

He considered the machine before sliding those burning eyes back to my face. He shrugged one shoulder.

Silence stretched between us, taut and painful like a burn on your skin. I shifted. He didn't.

Fingers trembling, I returned my shotgun to its holster behind me. Then took a few tentative steps closer to the rover. And still those burning, unfathomable eyes watched me.

"Do...do you know how to get back to the North Road?" In all my life I never thought I'd be asking for directions from a wild creature in the forest.

"I do." He finally confirmed.

The relief I felt at his words fizzled away in the expectant silence that followed. *Why wasn't he telling me?* Couldn't he at least point and let me be on my way?

"Will you tell me?" I pushed the question out between my teeth.

The *Unnat* considered me, his gaze communicating things I didn't understand. Uncertainty squirmed in my chest.

"Probably."

I fisted my hands against my hips, fear burning away to irritation. Heat rose to flush my cheeks.

"Well? What do you want?" I snapped.

"An apology would be nice."

"An *apology*? For what?"

His stare took my measure before he finally shook his head and dropped his gaze. I couldn't help feeling that whatever he saw, I didn't measure up.

"Nothing," he muttered. "Let's go."

"What?" I sputtered. "Go where?" Was he going to walk me to the North Road? Could I trust him that long?

"You need to come with me," he rubbed a large hand across the back of his neck, rubbing the tight muscles there. "Because you're going to die."

"Excuse me?" I shrieked and, like it would do me any good, took cover behind the rover again. My gun was back in my hands, though I didn't remember getting it.

"Without help. You'll die *without help* out here. Because you don't know what you're doing."

I couldn't argue with that, so I said nothing.

"I'll help you get where you're going, and you help me when we get there. Then you'll be in another city and I'll go on my own." Harsh lines bracketed his mouth.

"How do you know where I'm going?"

"You're running from something." It was not a question.

"Maybe."

"Something bad enough to drive you out *here*." He continued over me, gesturing around him with one hand. "With the beasts." His eyes bored into mine. He didn't need to gesture to himself to get his point across. "You need to be anywhere but there." He pointed through the trees toward what I assumed was Arberdon.

An unexpected pang of longing tore through me. *Home*, with Missy, Randall, Grandfather, Father...and Ben. My heart twisted with a strange combination of longing and loathing. Everything I knew, the sum of my entire existence, was somewhere in that general direction, and I might never see any of it again.

I sucked in a breath and bit the inside of my cheek. Now was not the time for a breakdown.

"So," the *Unnat* was continuing anyway, "I'll escort you to Terrah, you complete one task for me in exchange, and then we're done."

"That's it?"

The single nod made another appearance.

Terrah was at least a week and a half away on foot. It was a much bigger city, with a much bigger Executor presence, but still...the idea had merit. It would be easier to disappear in a larger city. And the Executors likely wouldn't search for me there, seeing as it was impossible to survive that far between walled cities.

Impossible on my own, rather.

"Why can't you do it?" As soon as the question leaped out of my mouth I wished I could suck it back in again. He looked very pointedly at me, taking in all of my appearance, and an unfamiliar shiver flushed up my neck in response. Breath seized in my lungs, shock at my body's reaction. *Like my body wanted*–no, that was preposterous.

Then he gave the same perusal to himself. He met my eyes again, arching a dark eyebrow.

"Right, just pretend I didn't ask that." I heaved another breath into my lungs. Really, what did I have to lose?

You can do this, Pen. I tried to boost my confidence. *This is a slightly less horrible idea than what you were doing before.*

"Just one small task?"

The *Unnat* smiled, full lips peeling back from his serrated teeth in a lopsided grin full of condescension. Oh yeah, he knew he had me.

Chapter Nine

The sun was finally slinking down from its height and taking the smothering heat with it as I trudged through the forest, pushing a rover. To be fair, the *Unnat* was also pushing the rover, but I was carrying my pack and had been up running all night. I was exhausted and grumpy, and felt entitled to it.

Sweat coated my body, crystalizing across my back and shoulders where my pack rubbed incessantly, and slicking *every single* crease of skin I had. I smelled like sweat and piss, and I didn't want to think too hard about how I got that way. I felt disgusting. I *was* disgusting and tried to distract myself from how miserable I was by going over the insanity that was my life.

The *Unnat* said he'd explain everything to me after we made it back to his camp, wherever that was, and I was completely aware of how gullible that made me. But what choice did I have? Die in the forest from any number of things trying to kill me, not to mention my monumental ignorance, or maybe possibly *not die* by following this guide. At least if he were going to kill me I knew it would be fast. And if he really did have a task that needed doing in Terrah he couldn't kill me before we got there, right? If I needed to, I could just stroll into the city and disappear without doing his task. It wasn't like he could come after me, unlike—

Flashes of Ben's rages tore through my mind, a chaotic blur of all the worst I'd ever received. I stumbled over the rocks we were crossing, smarting an ankle and skidding to my knees.

I sucked in a breath, not caring about my stupid ankle or shredded kneecaps while I calmed myself and slammed that mental door closed. Now was not the time. Never was the time, preferably.

Never again, I swore to myself.

Never *again.*

A chill danced across my skin, the sensation like a caress across my mind. When I felt the panic easing out of my chest, I opened my eyes and used the rover to pull myself to my feet.

"Almost there." The *Unnat* grunted over his shoulder, his face twisted into a snarl.

After galumphing for hours through the wilderness in somewhat companionable, though grudging, silence we didn't notice each other's bad attitudes anymore. At least, I stopped being concerned about his. I was beyond exhausted and struggling to keep my feet moving on the dregs of my adrenaline. There was only so much a body could worry about at once, apparently.

I said nothing to the *Unnat,* just got ready to put my back into the rover and continue pushing up the inhospitable incline. But before I could make contact, the machine lurched away from me. I stared, shocked dumb and sputtering, as the *Unnat* finished pushing the rover over the rocky hill we were climbing *by himself.*

Words failed me. I stared at the place where the rover had been a moment before, then looked up to the crest of the hill the *Unnat* had just disappeared over. And back. And forth. One more time, just to make sure I wasn't imagining.

I closed my eyes against the feeling of incredulous despair that wanted to unfurl out of my chest. Tingling heat bloomed behind my eyelids.

Crying was *not* an option. I snapped my eyes open and looked up at the white heat on the edges of the sun's aura, trying to burn the tears away. I would not start sniveling in front of the *Unnat*. Angry was better, *much* better, than pathetic and lost and scared and...I clenched my fists at my sides, grinding my molars as I picked my way up the hill after him.

When I finally scrambled onto the outcropping, the incredible view was almost enough to derail my ire. Only about twenty feet above was a final ledge, the sharp horizon of land giving way to maples and oaks that stroked the sky. Overhead was an intense blue, interrupted by snaps of green and yellow dancing on the ends of branches. Massive rocks, bleached from exposure, surged from the soil all around as though they were living, growing things alongside the mature trees. The cicadas still screamed through the heat, the air just as thick and hard to breathe as it was in Arberdon.

I quelled another surge of homesickness and forced my attention back to the present. The outcropping we stood on, just large enough for the two of us and the custom rover, had three sides that dropped off abruptly to form an isolated peninsula. The fourth side was a huge rock formation behind the *Unnat*.

My guide was busy pulling a camo-tarp over the rover. Before I could even suck in a breath to demand some kind of an explanation for *telling me he needed my help* to push his Stars-forsaken machine all the way back to camp, he spoke.

"Done it without you before." He said it with no inflection. He didn't even look up.

"Excuse me?"

He sighed again. He'd been doing that a lot. "I have moved this thing before. Without you."

Having finished his task, he turned to face me, crossing strong blue tinted arms across the chest of his dark shirt, and quirked that same unimpressed black eyebrow in my direction.

My righteous anger diffused, leaving me feeling hollowed out and rather slow to have forgotten how much stronger he was.

Strong enough to snap you in half, and you were ready to march right up to him and shake a finger in his face. Good call, Pen. I felt heat flood my cheeks and prickle down my spine. My arms wrapped protectively around me.

"Maybe your friends helped?" I swallowed, only just realizing that there was no guarantee he was alone. *Naïve, Pen, real naïve.*

He barked out a harsh laugh. "Apparently I don't have friends."

"So then *why* did you tell me you needed my help to push that thing?" I was not whining, no matter what it sounded like.

"Didn't say that."

I frowned, feeling a flicker of my anger return. "Yes, you di—"

"I asked you to push. Didn't say I needed help."

My mouth shut with a *click*.

"Since your next question is 'why,' I wanted to keep your hands busy."

I blinked at him.

"I'd rather not test my reaction time to a shotgun point-blank to the back of my head. You know, in case you decided to go your own way after all."

Having dismissed me at that point, he turned, retrieved his spear, and walked into a crevice nestled into the rock behind him.

I frowned after him and felt all the energy drain out of my body, like a marionette with all its strings cut. Something in my chest crumpled just like the useless doll I envisioned. Clearly I wasn't the only one feeling dubious about our partnership. Assuming his exit was my invitation, I dragged my feet after him.

Slipping into the rock was like stepping into another world. My eyes were momentarily blinded, my body instantly cooler. I inhaled a deep breath of damp, earthy air and took in my surroundings.

The crevice cut into the side of the rise like a hall, opening abruptly into a large circular space. Across the chamber, another opening led into deeper darkness. The ground was smooth and bare, save for a pallet of furs to the left, where the *Unnat* was busy digging through his things. Colorful layers of rock made the walls, and the roof was a collection of jagged spires reaching down. The immense space swallowed me, and I hunched a little closer to the crack that led back to daylight. Somewhere further away water dripped faintly.

"You can follow through there to wash, but don't drink." The *Unnat* said, jerking my attention back to him.

The now shirtless *Unnat*.

"Oh!" I felt heat creep up my cheeks again, and then swallowed my nausea.

Three deep gashes ran down his torso from his right pec to the base of his left rib cage.

He glanced up at me from cleaning the wound with the edge of his shirt, that eyebrow quirking again.

"Are you—that is—uh—that looks bad." I closed my eyes and tried to get control of myself. Who was the stammering idiot in charge of my mouth?

The *Unnat* ignored my fluster and went back to his first aid. His shoulder lifted again, opening the cuts and spilling a trickle of intensely red blood.

"Dance with a Canid, you're likely to get scratched."

"Dance?" I huffed a surprised laugh. "Well, I guess I should thank you for killing it. If the outcome had been reversed, I doubt the Canid would have brought me home after." And why did that sound so inappropriate when I said it out loud? A flush stole up my neck and I pressed my lips together before I said anything else ridiculous.

"Didn't kill the Canid."

"How is that even possible?"

He glanced back at me with barely contained disdain as he tossed his bloodied shirt aside and started rubbing salve roughly into the gashes. My stomach roiled again and I watched his face instead.

"Death shouldn't be dealt lightly." His scowl seemed more intense. Probably from whatever he was doing to his torso.

"But it was going to kill you!"

"Wouldn't have attacked if *you* hadn't gotten between her and her pups."

"How was I supposed to know that?" I bristled at his tone. "I was just following the road!"

"Actions have consequences, regardless of intent." He muttered, closing his eyes for a moment. He took a deep breath and let it out slowly. "You couldn't have known. Just glad I was close."

I nodded mutely, my guts trembling at the thought. What if he *hadn't* been right there? What would have happened with the Canid then? I gulped down my panic, feeling faint.

"Thanks." I breathed, gripping my elbows tightly. "For saving me."

He grunted and shrugged into a new shirt, this one dark blue. Where did he get his clothes from?

"You smell like piss." He said flatly, nodding toward the other tunnel without looking at me.

I sputtered, but couldn't argue. My cheeks burned hot, indignation and embarrassment and exhaustion rushing together in an emotional tide. My vision wavered. A litany of curses marched through my mind as I stiffly made my way to the crevice. I glared at the *Unnat* as I passed. His mouth screwed shut, he kept his eyes on the leftover bandages he was rewinding across his fist.

"You *hairless bristle-boar!*" I spat at him as I passed. The *Unnat* turned, his mouth opening as if to say something. "Stuff it. I'm going, alright?"

The second tunnel was narrower than the first, and I thought about leaving my pack in the outer cavern. But I didn't trust anything of mine with that *Unnat*. Heat slipped down my cheeks, leaving a wet trail through the grit coating my face.

The crevice finally opened up into a smaller cavern as I shuffled forward with my hand against the wall. Fear trickled down my spine, pushing all other thoughts aside. My eyes had adjusted to the lack of light as much as they were going to and I couldn't see a thing. More tears built, threatening to siphon what little energy I had left and leave me in a heap on the floor.

But no, I wouldn't give the *Unnat* the satisfaction of falling apart. I clenched my jaw and shut my eyes. At least then it felt like the darkness was my choice.

My hands pressed firmly onto the rock beside me, I inched along. Parts of the wall felt soft, smooth, and old. Other parts felt rough-hewn and sharp, like they had been intentionally carved to make the passage a bit easier.

I followed the sound of water around a corner and stumbled into a natural basin about waist high. The burbling sound echoed all around, indicating how large the space was that I was in. I'd have to be careful not to get separated from my pack or the wall that led back out; I'd very likely never find them again.

Leaning over the basin, I slid my palm against the damp rock until I found the source of the stream, the water licking over my hand before splashing into the basin below. The cool liquid instantly chilled me, helping me recenter myself. Plunging my hands into the basin, I scooped up the water and splashed it across my face. I gasped, repeating the motion again and again until the tears threatening my eyes retreated.

I shrugged out of my pack, setting it down on the ground against my leg, and attempted to get clean. I washed my body in shifts, picking fresh clothes from my pack by feel and luck. Once done, I blindly washed and rung out my old clothes, managing to bark my knuckles against the sides of the rocky basin in my haste.

But once those chores were over, every noxious swirling thought threatened to overtake me. I forced my fists to relax as I draped my final piece of wet fabric around the basin's rim and slid to the floor. I did *not* want to go back into the other cavern. My breathing hitched and my throat constricted with new tears.

Not now, not now, not now, I demanded of myself. There were too many thoughts churning in my brain, too many things that had happened. I wasn't ready to face anything yet; not my feelings and not my unlikely traveling companion. What I needed was the peace I got from numbness. A protective shell to separate me from everything except the next moment and what needed to be done. I breathed deeply in through my nose and held it, slowly exhaling as I started my calming exercise.

Somewhere around relaxing my hands I fell asleep.

* * *

"Penelope!"

The shout echoed like a shot through my mind, setting me quaking down to my soul.

My fingers clutched at the sides of my head, gripping at my scalp and pulling. I curled my knees into my chest and held my breath. If I didn't open my eyes, if I didn't draw attention to myself, maybe he wouldn't find me.

"Penelope, where are you?"

I shook my head, curling tighter around myself. No, I wouldn't make a noise. My lips pressed tighter together, struggling to hold back the heat that simmered in my chest.

"You can't hide from me, Penelope."

I would absolutely hide. I would hide and hide until there was no more danger. No more fear and pain. I bit my lips, refusing to make space for the burning pressure that was building behind my ribs.

"Come out, Penelope. Come out and face me."

My stomach rolled, hot nausea climbing up my throat. I didn't want to think about him, didn't want to remember. My hands trembled, whether from fear or the need to defend myself again I couldn't tell. I curled my fingers into my palms, tucked my limbs up tight to my belly. I barely dared to breathe.

"Don't make it harder on yourself. You know how this ends."

No I don't, *I thought, desperately clinging to the idea.* **I don't know, and neither do you!**

Abruptly the space around me stilled, the complete absence of sound jolting my body like an electrical wire. Dismay poured into my chest; somehow he'd heard my thoughts.

"Penelope? Lovely lady, where are you?"

My lips twisted into a snarl at the pet name he'd used at the beginning of our courtship. As though the reminder could be anything but repulsive to me. Fear started melting in the rage that pumped out of my heart. How dare *he try to lure me with sweet words. Words I'd longed to hear as a young girl, but now knew them for the poison they were. How* dare *he manipulate me, manipulate my medical records, manipulate my life!*

"I'm just trying to help. You know you need help. You are scared and alone. I know how you hate to be alone."

Lies. It was always lies, and the knowledge of that tainted everything I'd ever longed for and thought I'd experience with him. He'd hurt me, cut me down to where my dreams lived, dug them out and warped them and beat them until I couldn't remember what it was like before. I couldn't remember who I was without the shame and the fear that came from living under Ben's thumb.

"Show yourself!"

I had, and he'd taken what I'd foolishly given him and twisted it into something ugly and hateful. I would not be foolish like that again.

He wanted to see me? I was different now. I was stronger. Harder. I had to be. I would not *go back in that cage. Like gas feeding a fire, the heat and pressure inside me reached a boiling point, surging up my throat and filling my mouth.*

"Enough!"

My shout manifested into something wild, something large and powerful, amplifying in the dream and ricocheting inside the walls of my mind. The wind whorled with my echoing voice, sucking my breath away. I was jostled, tossed, tumbled like a brittle leaf in that wind, spirited away to someplace else. As I was carried by the wind, something warm, alive, and other *flickered through my chest and I tensed against the sensation. My limbs fought to lock, to find purchase on something,* anything *to stop my lurching flight. But resisting only made the wind howl harder. I was overpowered.*

As suddenly as the gale came, it left me behind. I lay still, the world shivering in the wake of that powerful wind. Slowly, even that vibration settled and I dared to open my eyes.

Wherever I was, I'd never been there before. Though, to be fair, I could hardly make out a thing in the gloom that cocooned me. With a bolstering breath, I pressed gingerly to my feet.

A strange aura seemed to emanate from my skin, pressing softly against the darkness that surrounded me. Raising my hand, I could see every detail clearly, as though I were lit from within. But everything outside of my body was as black as pitch. My foot connected with solid ground when I took a step forward, and the sound of my footsteps echoed around me, indicating the vastness of whatever place I'd found myself in. But the two were strangely disjointed, like they didn't belong together.

I turned in a circle, looking for an exit or a clue. Even though I was stuck where I was, without sight or any idea what was happening, I didn't feel afraid. The lack of fear was foreign, and welcome. Instead I felt curious, ready to get on with the 'next' that would take me somewhere...More. More interesting? More fulfilling? I wasn't sure what I was looking for.

"Hello?" I called out to the void. "Is anyone there?"

The sound of a match sparking to life, or maybe it was a gong sounding, or rocks crashing, shattered the silence.

A match striking was probably the appropriate sound, since a single white-yellow lick of fire suddenly flickered in front of my face. There was no match, though, just that little spot of light defying the dark.

"What are you*?" I murmured, leaning in. It pulsed with knowledge, with some kind of unfathomable awareness that coaxed me closer.*

The flame sighed a lilting tune and grew a little bigger.

I reached out, wanting to grab that vital flame and hold it in my hand.

The fire danced back out of my reach.

I snatched at the air again.

It dodged me again.

My brows pulled together as I made another desperate grab. I wanted, no, I needed *to catch that thing. Whatever it was, it was mine, I could feel that certainty down to my bones. I narrowed my eyes and made another grab.*

I dove, I ran, I lunged until I was sweating and swearing, and still that little light drifted just a little faster and farther than I could go.

Panting, I stopped and braced my hands on my thighs, sweat dappling my skin. The flame sighed sweetly as it slid in front of my face once again.

I glared.

It burned.

"What do you want from me?" I growled, breaking our stalemate to stand and wipe the back of my hand across my damp face.

Some instinct clamored for my attention, halting my casual movement. I looked at my hand, looked at the pulsing, brilliant light that filtered out of my skin, then considered the flame in front of me. I could feel it thrumming with energy, the same energy that charged my own skin, waiting to see if I could figure it out.

It wanted me to figure it out.

I wiped my hand against my pants, suddenly nervous. What if I was wrong? What if it rejected me?

I would never know unless I tried.

I raised my hands, palms up, like I had cupped water from the cavern, and waited.

The flame shivered and sighed, growing bigger. Then it drifted lightly into my waiting hands.

"Ohh," I breathed in wonder, bringing it closer to inspect. Small images flickered in the flames, pictures I could almost—

The fire flared, diving into my eyes and piercing through my chest like a spear. I opened my mouth, screaming, and flames burned down my throat. Heat roared in my ears, constricted my chest, and I fell endlessly, kicking and crying, and was consumed.

* * *

I woke with a jolt, gasping and patting my torso down, looking for fire.

A deep voice shouted, the sound booming against the walls around me, and I squawked in alarm. Sound surged, cresting and cracking against the cavern walls. The heavy steps of a massive predator charging toward me with wild, burning eyes that shone out of the dark.

My *Unnat* guide.

I scrambled to my feet, pressing myself against the stone basin and sliding around until I found the rock wall. My knuckles ached against the fabric of my pack, clutching it in front of me. I swallowed, frantically reminding myself that he wasn't my enemy. At least, not at the moment.

"You screamed." he accused. Only his eyes gleamed eerily in the darkness, pinning me in place. I leaned harder into the stone wall.

Just like that night on watch, eyes like an animal shining in the dark, I shivered.

"Bad dream." I wheezed, and it wasn't quite an apology.

He narrowed his eyes, no doubt studying my face. He must have been able to see a lot better than I could in the cavern.

"We're leaving now." He growled and turned from me, striding toward what I guessed was the tunnel in the rock. I frantically grabbed my still damp clothes, keeping one palm against the wall so I wouldn't lose my way.

"These clothes aren't dry yet."

"Pack them wet or leave them behind." His voice echoed back to me.

Unwilling to lose any of the supplies I had, I rolled the damp cloth together and stuffed it in my pack, cringing. No doubt they would make everything smell moldy by the time we stopped again. I draped my shotgun over my left arm, double checking that I'd already loaded it by feel. Satisfied, I snapped the barrel closed and put my hand to the rock, edging my way around the room until I found the opening to the tunnel.

When I emerged into the first cavern, the *Unnat* stood silhouetted against the mouth of the cave. His pack strapped to his broad back, his spear in his hand. He regarded me impatiently.

"Let's go," he intoned and turned toward the opening.

Chapter Ten

It was full night, and the sky above us glittered with layers and layers of brilliant, trembling white stars. I couldn't help myself, stopping and craning my neck to take it all in.

Night looked different here, so far away from everything familiar, without the hum of electrical cables arcing overhead, or the crackle of the great fire sending sparks into the sky. Night felt different too; softer and heavier at the same time, like I could reach up and brush my hand against it. Wisps of gray clouds, backlit by the celestial brilliance, drifted lazily overhead like gossamer ribbons. *Velvet and silk,* I thought, and a thrill ghosted under my skin.

"Come on, woman." The *Unnat* called from the edge of the precipice. Apparently he wasn't interested in taking in the sights.

"I have a name." I grumbled as I walked toward him.

"Uh-huh." He groused back, rolling his eyes. "Watch your step here." He started down the incline in front of me, angling slightly so he could keep an eye on me. Probably to make sure I wouldn't shoot him.

"You could *ask*." I replied sourly. "Why aren't we taking the rover?"

"Still no gas." He didn't need to add the *duh, idiot* for me to hear it. "And why should I? Watch this rock, it's loose."

My brow furrowed as I stepped lightly where he had indicated over the stones. He was right, of course. Almost a full day around each other, and neither one of us had bothered to introduce ourselves. Why hadn't I asked his name?

Because you don't care, I thought, and immediately burned from the admission.

I thought back to my life in Arberdon, secluded behind the walls. Organized and directed by the Executors. I wanted to believe that I thought for myself and didn't blindly buy into propaganda, but here I was, treating him like a means to an end. And why? What had this creature done to me to deserve my disdain?

He'd seen me on my night shift, but hadn't harmed me. In fact, he handed my gun back to me after I'd already tried to shoot him.

He'd saved me from the Canid, at extreme risk to himself.

He was guiding me to safety and freedom. Safety from my own people. Safety from the Executors of Arberdon. Safety from Ben.

Safety.

My chest seized at the thought. How long had it been since I felt truly safe in Arberdon? The past handful of years under the weight of Commander Benjamin Joshen left me feeling numb, hollowed out. Watching what I said, who I spoke with, what I did. Never knowing what would trickle back to the shining star of the Executors, or knowing what would set him off. Curling in on myself tighter and tighter for what? To feel safe? To protect myself? In reality I'd lost myself entirely.

Who was this person, arrogantly following an *Unnat* through the wilderness and relying on him as a guide, but not willing to recognize his personhood?

"Stars," I muttered. "You're right."

He grunted in response as we skidded a few feet to the bottom of the incline.

"Well. I'm Penelope," I reached my right hand out toward him.

"Don't touch me!" He snarled, practically falling in his effort to put space between us.

"Excuse me!" I snapped back at him, embarrassment blazing across my skin. "Here I was, just trying to," I floundered, my face screwing up. "Start over or something, I don't know! I guess I shouldn't have bothered!"

I threw my hands in the air, disgusted, and stomped past him muttering about rude, nasty, impossible beasts. Maybe there was a good reason our people were enemies.

And yet, I couldn't shake the feeling that there *wasn't* a good reason. Because this stranger, this *Unnat*, had risked his life to save mine. He warned me about loose rocks. And that had to count for something, didn't it?

I hated it when my conscience was right.

Whatever. I muscled the straps of my pack angrily. *He's also a jerk.*

"Wrong way," he called.

I hung my head, squeezing the straps that cut into my shoulders. I had no idea where we were going, so of course I couldn't stride off in indignation. I didn't bother looking up as I walked back to where he waited, keeping my eyes on the undergrowth and picking my way through the brush. I blew out a relieved breath when he didn't say anything about our argument, just turned and led the way.

We walked.

Sticks and small plants crunched under our boots, though his steps were significantly less encumbered than mine. Practice, I guess.

I assumed we were headed for Terrah, but without a map and with no idea where we actually were, I was at his mercy. Not a comfortable place to be, I decided. As soon as I was in Terrah I would find a map and learn some survival skills. I didn't want to be at anyone's mercy.

Never again.

The scenery continued on in a blur of indistinguishable foliage in every direction. Trees, brush, rocks. We didn't follow any path that I could discern, and I felt like one of the lumbering oxen from my parent's farm crashing through the brambles. Thorns snagged at my pant legs, leaves smacked my face. I learned to walk with my hand in front of my face and my mouth closed very quickly. Orb-weaver webs were tenacious.

A moon-bird called somewhere in the distance. Some creature alighted from the branches above us with a cackle. I gripped my gun a little tighter, stepping closer to my guide. He might be a rude prick, but he was keeping me alive.

For now, I reminded myself sternly. It was too easy to slip into trusting him, and that was frighteningly dangerous. There was no certainty after we got to Terrah and I did his task. I pressed my lips into a frown. What was the task he needed me to do?

"Abel." He said gruffly, shattering the silence between us.

"What?"

"My name. It's Abel." His hands gripped the leather straps of his pack so tightly they squealed under the pressure. "Since we're starting over."

"Oh. Hi." *'Hi'? Really, Pen?*

"And I'm serious. Don't ever touch me." His burning eyes slanted toward me, his lips pressed down furiously.

"Yeah, message received there, Abel." I gave him a salute. "No problem."

He muttered something in that growling voice, tearing his hands through the hair on the crown of his head before roughly ripping the leather thong away from his horribly sloppy braid and throwing the length of it up into a knot.

We walked the rest of the night in silence, save for a few directions from Abel. *Step here,* or *Watch the branch,* or, my personal favorite, *Can you move any faster?*

I was thankful for being able to rest during the day, but my muscles still protested being abused again. I tried to ignore the sharp, snapping pain that wrapped around my legs with every step, or the ache in my neck and shoulders from my pack. Or the tingling throb that radiated out of the soles of my feet with every step. My throat felt raw, and fatigue made every move heavy and uncoordinated.

I was doing a really poor job of ignoring my discomfort.

Abel set what I considered to be a relentless pace, though the way he kept sending impatient glances over his shoulder at me told me how he felt about it.

"*Try* not to disturb the whole forest?" He muttered.

I sighed and readjusted my pack, my earlier wonder at the scenery fading as my awareness blurred around me. Shocks of light fluttered at the edges of my vision, pulsing and dancing like little flames. When I glanced at them, they disappeared.

"Do you see fire?" I slurred at Abel's back, tripping over a root. Another sigh rolled through his shoulders as he glanced at me. He shook his head and continued leading us forward.

I kept my eyes trained on the ground in front of me, looking for the path of least resistance, Abel just ahead forging the way. The only option was to keep moving, and I became intimately acquainted with the meaning of 'trudge.'

We finally stopped at another bolt hole as the sound of song birds filled the air and the eastern horizon began to turn pale and rosy. I stumbled into the tunnel Abel indicated and dropped my pack to the floor, thoughts of food or stretching flitting briefly through my mind before falling immediately asleep.

* * *

I was in that strange dark place again. I looked around, still unable to see anything except myself. I lifted my hands and studied their inner glow.

"It's brighter this time," I murmured, my brow furrowing.

Even though I couldn't make out any details about the space I was in, I instinctively knew I wasn't alone.

"Hello?" I called into the inky darkness, my voice ricocheting around and returning to me unrecognizable.

Hello!

The voice was at once a whisper and a rush of wind, resonating with intensity that my ears couldn't pick up but I could feel vibrating in my bones. It seemed layered over and woven through the very fabric of space. I couldn't place an accent, or a gender, or an age. The voice just was.

My chest constricted and burned. My breath quaked into my lungs, shuddered past a tightness in my throat, bloomed into something dazzling that melted through every cell of my being. And the little flame from before darted out from between my ribs.

"You!" I accused, wondering if I should take a step back. "You hurt me."

A wave of amusement and something else rolled over me from the fire. Affection?

The flame, so bright it was hard to look at, flickered and sighed in front of me, undulating on air currents I couldn't feel. When I closed my eyes, I could almost make out pictures dancing in the afterimage.

"Why isn't there anything here?" I gestured around. "What is this place?"

The silence stretched between us until I started to shift awkwardly.

"Okay, so you can't talk." A sense of intelligence still radiated from the fire, so I didn't feel like too much of an imbecile talking through my thoughts. "What's going on here?"

I scratched my nose and pursed my lips. This had to be one of the strangest dream sequences I had ever had. I took my time turning around, trying to take in the dimensions of wherever this place was. But still all I could see was darkness. I stomped my feet, but couldn't tell if the ground was soft or hard, stone or dirt or wood. The only feedback I got was that weird, dislocated echo of my movements. I turned again to the flame and cleared my throat, trying to figure out what to do.

"I'm not sure what to ask." *I started, and the echo of my voice thundered around me once more, cascading and coalescing into one booming word.*

Ask.

Ask what? I wanted to say, but the words sprang out of my mouth before I knew I'd formed them:

"Why am I here?"

* * *

I awoke to Abel nudging me with the end of his spear. The tassel-free end, thankfully. I rolled over groggily, rubbing the heavy sleep out of my eyes. He waited nearby, standing tall with his arms crossed over his chest, like some silent, impatient sentinel. We left as soon as I'd seen to my necessities and strode out into another spectacular night.

The ground undulated softly under its blanket of greenery, trees pushing through tall, skinny, and straight. The plants were all tired and thirsty at this time of year, crackling and brittle around their edges, twigs snapping and falling to the ground as we passed.

Hours passed in our barely tolerant silence. Him most likely impatient to the point of tears by my lack of experience, stealth, and speed; me under the unmistakable impression that he was a grump and a boor of an individual. We had nothing to say to each other.

The ground we covered grew gradually more level, and the trees younger and thinner until, just up ahead, I could make out a massive clearing. We edged toward it, Abel seeming to be absorbed into the darkness. I tried to copy his posture, doing what could only be described as a scuttle compared to his graceful slink. He held a fist in the air, casting a snarl in my general direction over his shoulder. I froze, sinking a little lower into the brush.

Eyes wide, breathing as quietly as I could, I watched Abel transform.

He didn't *actually* change, of course. But seeing him drop his mantle of humanity was like getting a glimpse into another world.

It's not becoming less human, I thought as I studied him, *it's becoming something* more.

The past two nights we had traveled in the thick of the forest. And, I assumed, his usual territory. Just like I'd learned the creaks and shifts of my parent's old farmhouse, it was easier to detect a threat in a familiar environment. He would be more cautious moving forward, I gathered, or at least more focused.

He tilted his chin up slightly, closing his brilliant golden eyes, and drew a short breath in through his nose. His lips parted slightly as he drew in another breath, scenting and tasting the air. I felt my stomach coil slowly with an unexpected awareness of his mouth.

Wait, what? I inhaled sharply, expanding a chest that felt too tight for all the wrong reasons, and dug my fingernails into my palms. *Focus, Pen.*

Abel moved toward the edge of the clearing, gathering shadows around him as he melted through the foliage. He moved like magic, the plants practically folding themselves out of his way. Each step was precise and controlled, his tall frame defying the laws of nature. It shouldn't be possible for someone that big, that strong, to also be graceful and quiet. He possessed his movements, his body humming with contained power in the dappled moonlight.

Two nights past the full moon meant the light was waning, but still powerful. Dry clouds drifted like smoke across the stars, casting eerie shadows on the ground. Abel crouched in the bracken and scanned the distance with those powerful eyes. I could imagine what they looked like: catching the light and magnifying it, piercing the darkness. Wild. Like the way he had studied me on my shift no more than a couple weeks ago. I shivered, convincing myself it was wholly alarm moving through me at his strange abilities, and certainly not intrigue.

Minutes passed, Abel standing perfectly immobile as he searched for threats. I knew, if I had been on my own, I wouldn't have thought to stop. I wouldn't have been as careful. And I would probably not have survived this long because of it.

Why are you trusting him? I questioned myself. Nothing about my situation made any sense. A small-town woman from inside Arberdon's walls runs away and meets an *Unnat* who guides her through the woods? Absurd!

But, despite the fact that he was more likely to hate me than help me, I did trust him. More than I was comfortable examining, really. Somehow it felt like I knew him already.

Clearly I was desperate and delusional. Maybe there was some validity to Dr. Kane's concerns, after all. My mouth twisted bitterly, refusing to let that thought take root.

Finally his left fist rose again in the air, and he opened his fingers to beckon me forward.

I was very aware, as I carefully picked my way through the dwindling underbrush, that I did *not* move like magic. I felt like a great, stomping Ursine sow, heavy and slow for a winter's sleep, and felt my cheeks heat with embarrassment. I settled into a crouch at Abel's side and waited for more instruction.

"Step *exactly* where I step. Do not speak unless you are dying." His words were more breath than sound and I found myself staring at his lips to make sure I understood each one. His spear was balanced, poised, in his right hand as he swiveled his eyes in my direction.

Whatever he was warning me about was serious. I knew, down to my bones, that the days leading up to this point had been easy and I was about to encounter one of those things in the wild that made civilizations live inside sturdy walls. I nodded once, swallowing nerves, and prayed I didn't get us killed.

He skulked forward a step, waiting for me to copy him. I cinched my pack's straps tighter to my shoulders, took a deep breath to calm my mind, and we broke from the dubious safety of the forest.

The slap and scratch of the ferns and brush that choked the spaces between the trees gave way to tall, whispering grass that clung like desperate fingers to the material of my pants as we moved. Long, slender blades covered the vast clearing like an ocean, with hulking shapes reaching up from the ground like Depth Beasts breaching waves.

And there in the distance, imposing with austere grace, loomed a ruined fortress.

I copied Abel's posture, hunching down into the chest-high grasses so we were mostly hidden. The grass *shh, shh'd* as we moved toward the building, Abel moving us forward when the wind blew softly, and stopping as soon as it died down. My knuckles paled against the straps of my pack, my pulse shuddering in the back of my mouth. I kept my gaze riveted to Abel's feet, his earlier warning a refrain coursing through my mind.

*Step **exactly** where I step.*
Do not speak unless you are dying.
*Step **exactly** where I step.*
Do not speak unless you are dying.
*Step **exactly** where I step.*
Do not speak unless you are dying.

I swallowed, choking down my fear, and let out a tremulous breath. Abel glanced over his shoulder and I gave him what I hoped was an encouraging smile, but was more likely to be a grimace. He narrowed his eyes, his lips thinning, before turning his attention to our path again.

You are breathing. You are alive. You are safe.
Stay quiet. Stay calm. Pay attention.

I made a conscious effort to slow my breaths, to relax my fingers. As long as I followed Abel's rules, we'd be safe from...whatever threat he knew was around here.

Oh, Pen, I thought, *why did you ever leave home?*

The new refrain redoubled, coursing insistently through my mind and crowding out my anxious thoughts.

You are breathing. You are alive. You are safe.

Stay quiet. Stay calm. Pay attention.

After what felt like an eternity, but also far sooner than I was ready for, we began easing up the huge steps of the fortress.

There were three tiers of stairs leading to an arched doorway that gaped like a hungry maw. I swallowed on a dry mouth and forced my gaze back down to my feet. I could worry about what was inside the building when we got there.

Abel scaled the ruined stone, careful not to disturb any loose pieces. Each step was painfully tall, the rises at least a foot and a half each between treads that were sturdy enough to stand on. Even Abel's muscles bunched and flexed with the effort, and my hips and legs were screaming for me to stop. I worked to ease my breathing, the thunder of my heart throbbing through my ears.

Each tier was made of forty steps, and the rises became steeper the higher we went as more and more steps were broken beyond use. We made it to the first landing unscathed and I carefully exhaled my profound relief. But we still had two more flights to climb.

The second flight of stairs was closer to two feet per step, the stone having crumbled away over years of abandonment. My quads quivered and shook unsteadily by the time we reached the landing. I braced my hands on my thighs, hanging my head and indulging in a moment's respite. I licked my lips and gazed upward. *Almost there.*

The third tier was made of steps that varied between two and three feet. Working to bring my foot up for the next step, and then the next, became an agony.

Come on, Pen, I gritted my teeth, *just a little farther...*

And then I tripped.

145

Chapter Eleven

The toe of my boot caught on the jagged edge of the second-to-last step and I pitched forward, my hands shooting out to catch me as a startled cry ripped out of my throat. My knee crashed into the rough rock of the stair just as Abel's hands clamped down roughly over the sleeves on my forearms.

He jerked my body upright, straining my shoulders, and whipped me onto the landing with him. I bit my mouth against my bark of pain, my eyes searching his face and not liking what I found there.

His burnished eyes were glued to mine, wider than they should have been. The lines of his face were harsh, pulled taught across his features. His mouth turned down sharply not in a scowl, but in dismay.

Abel was *afraid.*

My stomach dropped all the way down three flights of forsaken stairs and I wrapped my palms around his forearms, too.

Maybe it was my desperate touch against his burning skin that broke through to him, or maybe it was the way every sound that you hadn't noticed went suddenly and unmistakably silent. Whatever it was, Abel flung our hands away from each other, grabbed his spear, and shoved me toward the open archway.

"Run!" he snarled, and I didn't question. Without hesitating I sprinted toward the shadowy entry as an ominous groan swelled in the air.

The hall arched away into obscurity above me, passages branching off on either side. I ignored them, and the awful sound that seemed to suck the very air from my lungs, and charged blindly ahead. The echo of my boots reverberated around me until the sound of it blended with my sawing breath. Soon even that was drowned out by the harsh drone, building and building until it was all I could hear.

Don't stop! Whatever you do, don't stop!

Furious flapping sounded behind me, and the sound of something sharp scraping against stone. A flicker of movement to my left had me stumbling, but I pulled my attention back before I could turn my head. Something was clearly going to chase me. Something dangerous enough to scare Abel. Looking at it wouldn't save me, only distance would. I gritted my teeth against the panic and kept moving.

The groaning grew, expanded, stretched until it touched every corner of the ruin, pushed against every part of my body, filled the very air I breathed. I felt a scream coiling in my breast, trying to tear its way out of me.

Run! **Run!**

Dust rained down on my head to the rustling sound of flesh and scale, something large readjusting its position in the dark recesses above me. And still, and always, the groaning built.

A pale mass unfurled in the entry of another passage as I darted past; a vast, undefined shape of undulating forms.

Don't stop!

I pumped my arms, willing the movement to carry my legs faster. My muscles were burning, begging me to stop, to rest. But no, I couldn't. If I stopped, if I even slowed, I would die.

Ahead, a small light flickered enough to show me that the hall abruptly ended, two passages splitting off in either direction.

I banked my stride and turned sharply to the second path on the left, where the flicker seemed to come from. My arms wheeled out to keep my balance, pushing off of the stone walls to propel me forward again. My palms scraped against the rough surface, barking skin that burned with my sweat.

Some instinct tingled at the base of my neck and I dodged to the right, pressing myself against the wall. A big, pale, smooth shape hurtled past me. Lurching to a stop, I threw myself to the ground as the creature dove again. Its thick talons slashed the air just over my head before winging back into the darkness, large gusts of wind buffeting me. I clamored to my feet and kept running, scrabbling for a few precious seconds before I found purchase. I could barely see the outline of the pale thing descending again, and I knew it wouldn't miss a third strike.

And then Abel was there.

He seemed to materialize behind me, his powerful frame hurtling around the corner.

"Down!" He bellowed, and I dropped like a sack. He launched, powerful legs pressing him airborne, and used the solid wall beside me to kick toward the creature. His red tasseled spear aimed straight for its heart.

Then a number of things happened at once.

The spear sank in readily, almost eagerly, and the scream the thing let out rattled every bone in my body down to my very soul.

Abel rode the writhing body to the ground, burying the spear into its chest with his weight.

My guide, wild eyes burning out of the darkness at me, turned his head over his shoulder and screamed, "Run, Pen!"

I scrambled to my feet, oblivious to anything but the imperative to move. Abel wrestled his spear free and kept pace beside me, barely dodging the beasts that fell on the corpse behind us in a tangled, cannibalistic heap.

"Faster!" he demanded.

"Can't," I tried to say, but the sound came out broken and barely intelligible.

And still the groaning rent the air.

Abel growled, pushing me toward a path branching off to the right. I stumbled, righting myself as Abel grabbed my pack before I landed on my face.

"Off," he barked, and I managed to wriggle out of my straps. The relief I felt was short-lived as we charged toward a flight of stairs at the end of the hall, the sinewy creatures snapping and howling at our heels.

Fingers encasing the sleeve of my upper arm, Abel dragged me up the stairs. I clung to his arm for stability, bracing my free hand against the stone wall. He offered me a nasty snarl, but didn't shake me off.

You need to be lighter. Drift up the stairs. Skim the steps, don't land and stop on each one.

I gasped a manic laugh at the thought in my head. *Drift, riiight.*

My legs trembled under my weight. It was all I could do not to turn into a puddle in the stairwell and wait to greet our hosts.

"Come on!" Abel swung an arm across my back, taking most of my weight.

Finally the stairs ended and we spilled into a room. Windows ran the length of the far wall, letting in dim moonlight. Rows and rows of metal tables filled the space, covered with what looked to be mangled and discarded junk. Abel steered us between the tables and avoided piles of debris, his eyes frantically scanning the tables' contents. On the last table he reached out and snatched a fist-sized clump of metal from the mess.

"Abel!" I gasped as we charged toward the floor-to-ceiling windows. We weren't slowing down.

"Take a breath." The ambient groan was so loud I could hardly make out his words, but I could feel them as they rumbled out of his chest and into mine. I turned wide eyes to him, catching a mass of bodies cramming into the room in my periphery, as he hauled us over the window's edge.

And we fell.

I didn't have enough air to scream. Abel's arm, lashed about my middle, tightened. I clutched his neck, legs pin wheeling, as we hurtled toward the inky darkness of a lake. Abel managed to snag my legs with his, clamping us together into one straight line.

We broke through the surface of the water, sinking deep from the height of our fall. Somehow I'd remembered to inhale before submerging, but my shaking muscles and thundering heart demanded more than that paltry gasp. I clenched my teeth and eyes shut, clinging to Abel's shoulders while I ignored the way my lungs twitched inside my chest. He let us sink as low as we would, and when I would have struggled to the surface he kept my legs pinned between his own and forced us to go deeper still.

My lungs spasmed, the need to breathe clawing up my throat. I kicked my feet uselessly between Abel's calves, and he held me tighter as we drifted farther from the air I desperately needed. A little sob twisted in my chest, and I fought it. Fought the darkness that edged in around my vision, fought the effort of my mouth to open and swallow something, *anything,* to soothe the ache for a breath of air in my chest.

I strained, my neck reaching for the glimmer of moonlight above us. My hands were frantic as I pushed against Abel's face.

And, very suddenly, I couldn't fight it anymore. My mouth opened and water rushed in and down my throat. Water cut into my lungs, tore through my nose, ripped behind my eyes, roared in my ears. My body convulsed, recognizing how wrong it was, trying to eject it. But water was all there was; water in every pore and every part of my body.

Water.

Water.

Wat-

W-

***

I knew exactly where I was as my awareness returned to me. The Dark Room.

Though, this time, the room was significantly less dark, more dim or darkish. I attributed the change to the flame, which stood before me as a towering column of fire.

I slowly rolled from my back to my side, feeling groggy and...damp? I tucked my knees under my torso and eased myself upright.

"Hey again." I nodded to the blaze and tried to get my bearings. The flame throbbed, acknowledging me, and even though it soared up higher than my head in a brilliant pillar of light, the heat radiating from it wasn't unbearable. If anything it felt comforting and warm, like a hug from my Mother.

My breath caught in my throat at the thought of the woman I would give anything to see again, to be held by again, just one more time. "Oh, Momma." She would know how to untangle the mess my life had become.

The flame sighed and rippled, folding in on itself until it hovered in the air in front of my heart.

"I'm fine." I smiled, brushing at my eyes. "Just sneaks up on me sometimes, you know?"

I cleared my throat and took in my surroundings, making out vague shapes in the gloom. Branches and vines and large, old trees. A forest, then, but not one I was familiar with. A murmur drifted through the air, like soft voices from another room.

The burning orb darted in front of me, then slowly started backing away. When I turned away it did it again, and again, until I stopped trying to look around and gave it my full attention.

"Okay, what are we doing here?" The similarity between my question and the one I'd asked before trembled through me. Why was I here? What was the point of this place?

The fire started backing away again, pausing every few feet. I pursed my lips, analyzing my incendiary companion. "Alright." I shrugged and started after it.

As we moved through the murky forest the fireball picked up speed, darting from side to side, charging around corners so quickly I almost lost sight of it.

"Wait!" I wheezed, my lungs aching and my legs feeling heavy and sluggish, like I was trying to run with too much weight on my back. But the flame didn't slow down, only continued to dash and zip away from me until I was all but sprinting to keep sight of it.

Sweat poured from my already drenched temples, my damp clothes warming up from my effort. As we continued, the ambient light shifted toward the gray of dawn and more shapes became apparent. Evergreens, ash, aspen, hickory, birch, and more all flew past in a blur. And then I heard it.

"Pen? Pen! PEN!"

"It's Abel!" I said with surprise. I forgot about chasing my flame and turned toward his voice.

154

CHAPTER TWELVE

I came back to myself on a screeching gasp as a strange dream vanished, my chest heavy and bruised. Breathing *burned*. I was shoved to my side as a painful spasm gripped me, squeezing until my stomach kicked violently for freedom.

I hurled an ocean of water onto the ground.

Water gushed from my mouth and nose, my sight blurry and dim as I sputtered. Slowly I became aware of my body, sopping wet and weak. I was in a heap, my torso supported by someone, arms around my chest so I wouldn't fall into my sick.

My hands clutched at those arms, as though clinging hard enough would ensure my safety.

Abel's arms.

"Oh," I rasped, part apology, part alarm, and tried to scoot backward. He let me go quickly and I turned to face him, swiping water and snot off my face. My chest heaved, greedy for air.

He sat on his heels, unmoving, his arms and hands swaddled in what looked like every blanket and shirt he had in his pack. Sure enough, his pack was lying discarded on the swampy bank, contents scattered indiscriminately.

"I didn't realize," he croaked, pulling my bleary eyes back to him. "*I didn't realize.*" His voice, like the sharp features of his face, was tight. He held himself carefully, bundled arms sagging against his thighs, oblivious to the puddle I'd just made encroaching on his knees. As though any sudden movement might leave him manic, screaming.

I knew the posture of horror well.

I swallowed and tasted murky water on my lips, my raw throat appreciating it all the same, and took inventory. The marshy surroundings were dark, the moon hanging in the sky in about the same place I'd last seen it. Tall, sturdy stalks of some kind of thorny plant grew in clumps from yellowing mud that smelled of something long rotten. The quiet chirruping of night bugs, and the ever-present cicadas, filled the air.

I blinked and struggled to focus my eyes on Abel.

"The groaning?"

He nodded, still grim. "They're gone. The water—" he cut himself off abruptly and schooled his features.

So the groaners didn't like water; good to know.

"And here?" I asked, looking at the exposed sky above us.

He shook his head. "Can't stand the smell."

"Me either," I offered up a weak grin.

"Can you stand? Can you walk?"

"I don't know."

"I could—" he stopped and shook his head, glaring down at his protected limbs with barely contained disgust.

Right, I thought with a flicker of anger. *Wouldn't want to touch the dirty human!*

"No, no," I said with a venomous smile, struggling to my feet. "There's no need to touch me anymore, don't worry." I slogged toward my pack with heavy limbs.

The scowl he directed at his hands sharpened, growing downright murderous. "Don't pick that up," he snarled, never lifting his gaze.

I froze, mid-reach. "You're right," I braced on my thighs, not having the energy to maintain my ire. "Since *I'm* the one who almost died, *you* can carry the bags."

He uncoiled from the ground, roughly tearing cloth from his limbs as he squelched in my direction.

"Exactly." He ground out, snatching my pack. He settled on the ground a few feet away, roughly shoving his discordant supplies into his own pack. That task completed, he hefted our things onto his back, including my shotgun, thank the Stars, and speared me with a glance over his shoulder. "Come on, we need to make camp so you can rest."

I shuffled after him, his pace downright pedestrian, as we picked our way out of the swamp. My clothes oozed dirty water with every step, the smell lingering against my skin. Abel snatched his spear from the ground, the tassels muddy and matted, and didn't look back.

The air, putrid as it was, never tasted so good. I struggled to slow my breathing, feeling my heart pound in my chest despite the sedate pace of our walk. I struggled to keep my eyes open, to keep my feet pointed in the right direction, and hoped we didn't have far to go.

"Stay with me." Abel growled. And after a pause, quiet enough I almost missed it, "*Please.*"

I focused on the shoulders in front of me. Broad. Straight. Shifting under the bulging, weeping packs on his muscular back with each step. And then, when looking up became too hard, I focused on his feet. Booted. Large. Sinking into the mud just like me.

A smirk stretched slowly across my face. No matter how graceful or powerful or skilled at survival, *everyone* sank in smelly mud. It seemed like one of those universal truths you could cling to when your world was falling apart. A comfort of impartial facts when other comforts were scarce.

The sun would rise in the morning.

The forest would kill you.

Everyone would sink in mud.

Eventually the mud began to thicken and the elevation changed, lifting us out of the muck and onto sturdy ground. Abel kept an eye on me while scanning the sky, his hypervigilance almost inspiring me to watch for flying, groaning monsters, but it was all I could do to stay on my feet. We turned aside, moving toward and into a grove of bushy, thorny tree-things. He held back as much of the flora as he could, but we both wound up wincing and cursing by the time we stopped.

In the center of the grove, the bush-trees grew tall enough for us to crouch under the lowest branches. The ground was solid, but covered with discarded thorns and sharp, leathery leaves. Abel made quick work of dropping the packs, making a pallet of sodden blankets and furs, and telling me harshly, "Sit down, and don't move."

I didn't argue.

My legs felt as insubstantial as the mud we were slopping through before, and as heavy as stones. I tripped unceremoniously onto the ground and watched as Abel cleared lower branches so that we had enough space to move around without getting stabbed.

"You're tearing up your hands." I tiredly observed as he battled the greenery.

"Yes."

He set to his task with single-minded ferocity, piling the discarded limbs to the side of the clearing. My head felt so heavy. I wavered on my pallet.

"Don't sleep yet."

I snapped my eyes open, and Abel had already finished clearing and was digging through our packs, grumbling under his breath.

"Food's ruined. Everything's wet." He pitched sodden bread and jerky over his shoulder as he spoke. "We'll be hungry tonight. And we'll miss half a night's travel."

I watched him with weary eyes as he listed grievances. His voice, full of growl and agitation, was somehow soothing. Just having him nearby helped my mind relax.

"I'm glad I left."

Abel froze, gaze locked on my face, and I realized I had spoken out loud. I shrugged and looked away, shifting on my soggy pallet. "It would have been worse for me if I had stayed. And worse for my family. So I'm glad."

A startled sound barked out of his throat; a bitter and withered laugh. "We're soaked. Our supplies are soaked. You have no idea where you are, and you're traveling with *me*, who, if you recall, you tried to shoot a few days ago. Stars, I just almost *killed* you! And this is *better*?"

Surprise had me falling silent and holding his intense gaze.

"Are we having a conversation?"

The scowl on his face darkened his features, but he didn't look away. Didn't pull back to the way we had been before. I huffed, a smirk pulling at my lips.

Outside the walls of Arberdon, with Abel as my guide, had me feeling more myself than I had in a long time. Worrying about survival was still prominent in my mind, but it had nothing to do with Ben. The change was a revelation. And even though I had been terrified, Abel hadn't meant to harm me. His hands, though he was disgusted by the thought of touching me, didn't lie. I knew, like I knew the shape of my own body, that those hands worked to keep me safe. He might not be my friend, but I was starting to trust that he wasn't my enemy.

Like the satisfaction that came from reconstructing my shotgun after a cleaning, the rightness of my realization clicked solidly into place. I gazed back at him quietly, some of the anxious, tight energy that had been occupying my chest settling.

"Yes, this is better."

My reply had Abel leaning forward, bracing himself on one powerful arm, his burning eyes drinking in every nuance of my unguarded expression and all the things I couldn't bring myself to say.

"I'm glad you left, too." His soft words drifted across the space between us.

The air shifted between us, and for once it wasn't full of animosity or mere tolerance. Slowly, my breath softened. My heart slowed its gallop in my chest. And still his eyes held me.

I broke first, abruptly overwhelmed by his intense scrutiny, drawing my knees up and resting my forehead against them.

"Tired." I muttered to my pants.

Abel shifted, the sound telling me he was moving away. "I'll find something to eat. Get clean water. Toss the spoiled food."

I nodded against my knees.

"I'll be back."

"Uh-huh."

"Pen, you need to stay awake."

I sighed and looked up, leaning back on my hands. "I'll clean my gun."

Still he hesitated. "Pen, I'm coming back."

His words carried weight, like it was an important promise for me to understand. And, somehow, I did understand.

"I know."

I tugged my pack closer to me once he'd left and slung my shotgun across my lap, taking comfort from its familiar weight and grip. I took a deep breath, reveling in the tight, bruised feeling blooming across my chest.

"I'm alive," I reminded myself. "Being alive is a good feeling."

With no fire and no dry supplies, it would be a while before I could actually clean my gun. I set out what I would need for the task, pulling my rod and accessories from my leather apron and setting them on the pallet next to me in a neat row. Next came a small jar of oil. My cleaning and polishing rags were soaked, so I wrung them out and draped them over the branches around me, hoping the heat of a summer's night would be enough to get them functional. I pulled out the spare shells from my apron and checked them, placing them next to my rod. When my apron was empty, I untied it and draped it over a sturdy branch, thankful I had splurged and gotten brain-tanned leather instead of alum. The more thorough treatment of the hide meant I still had an apron, instead of a soggy slab of rawhide.

Hands shaking with the effort, I doffed the rest of my outer clothes, squeezing as much water out of them as I could and turning the small clearing into a laundry-line. Next came every blanket and piece of cloth from my bag. I paused to catch my breath as I studied my work. Fortunately, I wore my hair short, so it would dry quickly and without my needing to do anything to it.

I felt a little silly, clomping around in soggy boots and underwear, but I wasn't about to walk around barefoot. Or naked, for that matter. A spike of embarrassment surged under my skin, and I prayed something I could wear would be mostly dry before Abel got back.

My cleaning rags were still damp, so I considered what else I could do to pass the time and keep myself awake. My eyes fell onto Abel's bag, left across the clearing from me, and I pursed my lips as I considered it.

What was the protocol for hanging up someone else's stuff if they weren't around? And if you didn't really know that someone?

And if that someone was also an *Unnat*, who happened to have a temper problem, and was very good at killing groaning, flying monster-things?

I crossed my arms over my chest and jigged my leg nervously, feeling at odds with myself.

If it was Randall's things that had gotten soaked, I would have hung them up already.

If it was Ben's, I wouldn't touch anything without making sure it was okay. The thought sent a sour tendril of unease through my gut, and I pushed it down firmly. This wasn't Ben, this was Abel. An *Unnat*.

"How is that better, Pen?" I swung my arms impatiently, planting my hands on my hips. Somehow, it was better. Much better.

An *Unnat* who kept me alive.

I sucked another greedy breath into my lungs, refusing the panic attack that threatened me. *I am alive,* I exhaled slowly. *I am alive.*

Because of an *Unnat*. Multiple times over, actually. It shouldn't have been possible. According to the Executor training I'd taken, *Unnats* were vicious, rabid beasts that needed to be put down for the good of all people. *Unnats* were dangerous, unthinking vermin that threatened anyone outside of a walled city. Outside of an *Executor* city.

But Abel was nothing like that. Oh, he was unbelievably strong, fast...and irritable. But he was cautious and calculating. He was knowledgeable and calm and, surprisingly, thoughtful. He didn't kill a Canid because he knew it was a mother.

Death shouldn't be dealt lightly. His words echoed through my memory.

Decision made, I crouched on the ground and unpacked Abel's bag.

* * *

I was sitting on the pallet, draped in a slightly less damp tunic that hung down to my thighs, oiling the outside of my gun when Abel returned. He slipped into the clearing and paused, taking in the sight of his things strung up among the branches with my own.

"Thank you."

I nodded, returning my focus to my gun. There was a balance to strike between using too much oil, which was a discharge hazard, and too little, which would result in rust. A well maintained gun could save my life. A poorly maintained one would be more dangerous than it was worth to carry. I was heavy with fatigue, but it felt good to get lost in the rhythm of familiar work.

Abel came further into the clearing and snatched one of his shirts from above. Spreading it on the ground, he laid out the result of his excursion in front of me. I set my shotgun aside and folded my legs underneath me to get a better look. What followed was a detailed lesson in foraging that kept my attention rapt. Abel spent long minutes lecturing me on what to look for if I needed food, and what to definitely avoid. It was the most I'd ever heard him speak over the three days since we started traveling together. He had even brought examples of poisonous plants and toxic roots and berries, which he'd carried separately in his pockets, so I could better identify the differences.

"Some of these can be boiled to make them safe, but—"

"Since I don't know how to do that without a FlameStart, and I don't have a pot..." I finished for him. One corner of his mouth kicked up into a grin and he nodded.

"That's enough for now, I think." He leaned back, finishing his meager meal of edible roots and plants. I rolled the last of my berries around my palm before swallowing them.

"I appreciate it." I said, getting caught in the fire of his eyes. Those flaming orbs roamed my face before he ducked his chin and uncoiled to his feet.

"We'll help each other, right? That's the deal." There was something in his expression, some feeling I didn't know him well enough to place. Regret? Irritation? I rolled my eyes. Based on what I did know about him, there was a strong chance it was the latter.

"Well, I'm glad that I'm learning to take care of myself. I'll need to be able to travel on my own after we reach Terrah."

"Clearly I need to learn, too. Since I—" he cut himself off, tearing a blanket down from a branch in a shower of needles and thorns, but I heard the words anyway. *Since I almost killed you.*

"Why did we come here, anyway?" I asked, distracting him. "What was that place?"

Abel folded the blanket, covering the ground across the clearing and making an unnecessary fuss over it without looking in my direction.

"Payment."

I furrowed my brow. "That's...Abel, that's not an answer to either of my questions."

"How are you feeling?" he asked abruptly, his gaze on his folded arms.

"Uhm, I'm fine."

He turned sharply toward me, his eyes glowing in the dark. "*Fine?*"

I crossed my arms, mirroring his posture. "I'm sore. It hurts to inhale, but not enough to worry me."

"Could be a broken rib."

"It's not a broken rib. I know what that feels like." His gaze, those eyes that always saw too much of me, were glued to my face. "I'm *tired* and I want to go to sleep."

"Not yet." He shook his head decisively. "Nausea? Rash? Fever?"

I took inventory of myself and shook my head. "No."

The tension melted off of him, his hands dropping to his sides as he folded his powerful frame onto the blanket. His shoulders slumped as he rubbed his face.

"Good. Then we just have to keep you awake until dawn."

"Why?"

"Just to make sure there aren't any complications, no delayed reactions." He ducked his head, picking at a loose thread on his shirt. "Sometimes that can happen."

"So answer my question." I said, making an effort to push thoughts of my mortality aside. "Why did we come here? You clearly knew it was dangerous, you knew about those *things*—"

"Howlers."

I nodded, logging away the name he used. "So why come? What was so special about that hunk of metal?"

His brows lifted and a lopsided smirk appeared. "You noticed?"

"I'm observant." I replied, definitely not preening.

Abel dug into a pocket and produced the dull block. He tossed it in the palm of his hand, considering it as he considered his answer.

"The ruins are from an old facility. It was, in name, a place to research problems and then experiment with creating solutions. In practice it wasn't as cut and dry as that."

"What does that mean?"

He shrugged, a line appearing between his brows. "I don't know the full scope, but I do know that they manufactured inanimate weapons. And attempted to create animated ones."

I stared at him incredulously, a laugh threatening to bubble out of my throat. "*Animated* weapons? How does that work?"

He tilted his head, turning the block over and over with long fingers. "Take a natural predator, tweak a little here, splice a little there..." His voice trailed off.

"That sounds like a make-believe story. A fable, not reality."

A deep breath rolled his shoulders. "It does. But facilities like that one are scattered all over. I've seen a few of them myself, gone exploring inside." He shuddered. "I'm convinced, at least."

"Say it's real then. That sounds like genetic manipulation. Who would do that?"

His gaze lit on mine for a moment. "No guesses?"

My mouth opened, getting ready to say I had no idea. But that wasn't true. And as soon as the thought formed in my mind, I couldn't shake it. I swallowed, and it felt like I was trying to fit that chunk of metal down my throat.

"Executors."

He nodded once, tossing and catching his prize out of the air. "Before the Great War, so they had a different name. Not that it matters what they call themselves." The growl in his throat scraped against my ears.

Cicadas and gnat-stingers buzzed while I absorbed the information. A powerful organization with connections all across the continent. Careful, piece-meal communication that made it easier to work on controversial projects without oversight. Even the Executors in Arberdon tightly controlled the release of information, communications, and maps. Was it that much of a stretch to believe his story?

"The Howlers," I started, and he nodded.

"Rumor has it they started as one of those experiments. And then took the place over as their roost. Leaving the facility to ruin, and the surroundings a place best-avoided."

"But you didn't avoid it. *You* knew about them, and how to get through alive." I shook my head and studied my travel companion, who was apparently more than a nomad. "How?"

His expression closed off and he placed the metal down in front of him with precise movements.

"I have my resources. But *that*," he nodded at the object, "was why we came. For you to use as payment in Terrah."

"Terrah." I repeated dumbly. "What, *exactly*, is the task I'm doing?"

H M DuVal

CHAPTER THIRTEEN

Between running for my life, sleeping like the dead between long nights of forced marches, and then almost drowning in a lake while being chased by Howlers, I had completely forgotten about the task I would do for Abel in Terrah. The task *in exchange* for him guiding me through the wilds and depositing me safely at the city's gates.

Because he's **not** *your friend, Pen!* I reminded myself harshly, and frowned at the bitter feeling that thought left behind.

I was to navigate into the city before curfew without being noticed by the gate guards, since I had no papers and was actively wanted by the Executors, then find my way to a leisure den called *Penance*. Once there, I was to get an audience with someone known as "The Chemist" and offer up the hunk of metal that almost cost my life in exchange for...a message.

I was then to leave the den as quickly as I could, without attracting attention, and get past the gate guards to give the message to Abel outside the city. Then get back inside the city and find a place to hunker down for curfew without getting caught.

And at that point I would be on my own.

I shifted on my pallet, my seat still soggy. "I can't imagine how this could possibly go wrong."

Abel shot me a sour look.

"This seems like a lot of risk for a message."

The sour look got sourer.

"And I'm assuming you need me to memorize this message—"

"It should be written down on something," he muttered under his breath.

"Oh a *written* message! That's even more special, considering no one gets paper mail except Executors—"

"This is *not* mail," he hissed between his teeth. I pressed on, pretending not to hear him.

"What do you think it will be written on? Plastic? Metal? Maybe the skin of my corpse?"

"Pen," he growled.

"Call me crazy, but this sounds like more than a simple errand. I'm thinking you left out some details about how important this is. Like, 'matter of life and death' important—"

"It is!" He shouted, the sound ripping from his chest. He took a deep breath. "It is." He repeated, his eyes pressing closed. He shook his head and muttered, "Forget about it."

"Oh." I leaned back on my hands, pressing my lips closed around any other sarcastic remarks I had, and let myself really *look* at him.

His tight, hunched shoulders.

His tense, thin lips.

His fist, flexing and releasing on his knee.

It would be easier to just *forget about it*, as Abel suggested. To use him for safe transport to Terrah and then forget I ever met and traveled with an *Unnat* in the wilds. Let the memory fade like a dream and get on with building a new life inside of a new city, surrounded by my own people and the rules I knew.

But the thought of doing that sank heavily in my chest. Maybe it was my desire to be different from the person I had evolved into in Arberdon, only thinking as far as the next day and what that meant for my self-preservation. Maybe it was the kinship I felt unfolding between me and my unlikely companion, the way I recognized his bitterness and isolation. Or maybe it was a compulsion to even the scale between us, to feel empowered to save him the way he kept stepping into the space between me and danger.

Whatever the reason, and despite my misgivings about his plan, I knew I had to get him that message. Or at the very least try.

"Well then. I'll do my best."

Abel's eyes snapped open and he looked at me with such unguarded hope and gratitude it stole my breath.

"Thank you."

I nodded, something in my chest twisting uncomfortably, and turned away. *What was his story?* The thought whispered through me and I fought the urge to look back at him. *What could the message possibly be about?*

I didn't ask him. I didn't *want* to care about him or what brought us to this arrangement, two unlikely partners on an impossible quest. I shifted again, the air thick with all the unspoken life between us. But I didn't say anything because I didn't know if I wanted to be any more connected with Abel. And, apparently, neither did he.

"Sun's rising."

I looked up, noting the pale blue and gold tint to the pockets of sky I could see high above the thicket. The stars were fading, and the first enthusiastic members of the forest were rustling about, *chirrup*ing to a new day.

"Get some sleep. I'll keep watch."

I swallowed, ignoring the way my gut clenched. Without the distraction of conversation, worry over Abel's earlier words wormed through my mind. What sort of complications did he mean? Was there a chance that I was more injured than I realized? *What if I didn't wake up?*

"Pen," Abel said sternly, and I met his gaze. He studied my face for a time. Then, softly, "I'll watch over you. Get some sleep."

There was something about his voice and the way he held my gaze. Familiarity washed over me, soothing my deep ache for home, and I decided to lean into it just this once instead of questioning it. I laid down on my pallet and watched the *Unnat* with tired eyes as he moved quietly around our campsite, letting all other thoughts become distant and muddled. Before long he sat down across from me and I felt something inside me settle. I drifted off to the sound of his breath.

* * *

*It wasn't surprising that I fell into a deep sleep on the damp, lumpy ground. I was exhausted and recovering from my horrific encounter with the Howlers. It **was** surprising that I didn't dream of the Dark Room.*

Instead, I dreamed of a lush, green forest drenched in sunshine so pure it was almost white. The smell of damp, healthy forest hung in the air and I drew it into my lungs hungrily. I could hear a creek burbling ahead of me, could barely make out its rocky bank through the trees. I thought of reaching out to brush branches out of my way and I was suddenly corporeal.

My fingertips trailed along the buds of new growth that dotted the arms of saplings, gently bending them aside for me to pass. Rowan trees, I thought, and appreciated the soft fronds of more mature leaves that tickled my palms. Brilliant sunlight dappled me, feeling like the warmth of a familiar caress. I closed my eyes and sighed as the sensation soaked into my soul.

"Yes," I murmured and felt myself relax. This was exactly where I needed to be. Concern about another voice finding me in the forest flitted through my mind, but I pressed it away. I wanted peace, not panic. I wanted what was barely visible up ahead.

Soft moss and violets cushioned my steps as I eased closer to the sound of a burbling creek. I hesitated, suddenly not wanting to be anywhere near water. A memory choked me; murky water all around, chaotic limbs churning in a desperate attempt to survive.

A flock of birds the color of fire erupted from the undergrowth, pulling me back into the dream. My misgivings floated away and I stepped forward, the rich earth giving way to gritty shoal and larger rocks. Boulders of varying sizes dotted the shore. And off to my right, on top of the largest rock with a flat surface, was a man.

He was stillness and power embodied, standing with his hands pressed together in front of his heart. He bent at his hip, stretching his arms forward. Slowly he eased farther into the fold, bringing his hands down onto the stone and ending in a position that made me very aware of my lack of flexibility. The muscles of his back tensed as he shifted his weight forward, his gaze steady on the rock between his hands, and lifted his legs to point at the sky in a perfectly balanced line.

I tried to swallow, but my mouth had gone suspiciously dry. The beat of my heart felt heavy and loud. My hand drifted to the upstart organ, tracing over the fabric there absent-mindedly. I knew that form well, had memorized its breadth and angles. I had been following it for days.

Abel.

Heat whispered through me along with his name. In the dream I felt powerless to deny the growing attraction I harbored for him.

His dark hair fell from the crown of his head to trace over the backs of his hands. It was wavy and thick unbound, and the gentle breeze tossed the strands in a way that made me wonder what it would feel like to twist my fingers into it.

I clenched my wayward hands into fists, forcing my arms to my sides and digging my nails into my palms. I should not be having thoughts like that about Abel. And yet I couldn't look away.

He tucked his legs toward his chest, pulling in on himself until his knees rested on the backs of his bent arms. He hovered there, his nose inches from the rock, before his legs shot behind him into a plank. He lowered his body, grazing along the stone's surface. His muscles bunched with the effort, a tantalizing sheen of sweat glistening against his uncovered torso.

A flush rushed up my neck and face. I hadn't had one of **those** dreams in quite a while. I licked my lips and definitely did not let myself think about what it would be like to run my mouth over that sweaty skin. I did not think about how the salt would coat my lips, how it would taste on my tongue. I did not wonder about how the smell of him, coated with fresh air, effort, and sunshine, would coax me into tasting him again.

I closed my eyes, trying to get a handle on myself and stop the slow coiling deep in my belly. Just a minute more, I thought, and then I would figure out how to wake up.

I sucked in a breath as my eyes opened again. Abel lifted his face to the sun, strong arms supporting a torso corded with lean muscle. He folded his body, stretching the backs of his legs, before stepping one foot forward. His arms reached toward the sky, his chin tilting back to greet the sun. His expression was so peaceful it was almost unrecognizable. I felt like I was really seeing him for the first time and he was...

Beautiful. I caught the swell of my lower lip between my teeth as I gave up and allowed myself to appreciate his body.

Powerful. My heart pounded uncomfortably in my chest, taking up too much space between my lungs. I couldn't seem to take a deep enough breath.

Striking. I swallowed awkwardly.

Desirable. I forgot all about my need to wake up and thought only about taking a step closer.

The rocks beneath me shifted and I tripped, coming down hard on my hands and my knees.

"Oof!"

"What are you doing here?" Abel's sharp question ripped through me. I looked up to where he was suddenly standing over me.

"Stars! Scare me to death," I muttered to myself and clamored to my feet, dusting off the front of my pants. I'd somehow transported myself onto his rock. "Weird."

"Are you really here?"

"What kind of question is that?" I snapped, unsettled by how real he felt and the yearning in his eyes.

Those eyes narrowed, lips pressing into a firm line. Any vulnerability from before was quickly hidden, locked away like it had never been. Still glowering at me, he roughed the length of his hair into its customary knot.

I turned in a slow circle while he was dealing with his hair, trying to make sense of the dream.

"Very weird," I muttered, edging away from the sound of rushing water, and turned back to the irritated Unnat beside me.

Cross-hatching scars danced over his exposed skin, a map of the life he lived outside the walls. I traced the marks with my eyes, wondering why I would add that kind of detail to my dream. And wondering why my fingers ached to touch them.

Abel scowled, crossing his arms rigidly in front of his chest. "Where is my shirt?" He growled.

"Well, my dream-brain certainly has you down pat."

That furrow between his brows that I often saw turned into a full-on trench. "What is that supposed to mean, Pen?" Anger or hurt vibrated off of every word, though he held himself perfectly still.

"I don't know!" I threw my arms up, refusing to feel guilty toward a figment of my imagination. Refusing to be cowed in my own dream.

"I want you to leave."

"Excuse me? This is my *dream!"*

"I can't leave, thanks to you! You're the one just traipsing—"

"Traipsing!"

"—around wherever you please, consequences be damned!"

"This is rich. My own subconscious doesn't want me around." I rubbed my temples, trying to stop the burn behind my eyes. "I really thought I wasn't crazy. I thought I was better now! I thought that by being away from Arberdon, away from...No, no, I don't want to think about that right now. Dammit!" I buried my face in my hands, tugged the hair on my head, tried to shake out the unwanted thoughts and memories. Failed miserably.

"Pen,"

Rough hands.

Sharp words.

"Pen, can you hear me?"

And my body, Stars Above, my body that wasn't mine.

Lies I told to try to save face, to try to hide the ugliness from the ones I loved best.

"Pen?"

And deeper than all of the pain was the shame and loathing I felt for myself.

For allowing it to happen.

For being too blind to prevent it, and too weak to stop it.

"Pen!"

The wind screamed past my ears, ripping Abel's voice away from me.

"I didn't stop it!" I tore my hands from my scalp and shouted at dream-Abel. "And that's the part I hate the most. I hate it!" My teeth chattered, my fist crashing against my sternum. If I could only break through, I could dig out that nasty feeling and throw it away.

The wind roared, tugging at my clothes and tossing Abel's hair loose again. Spray plumed over the edges of the rock, shockingly cold. I looked past Abel to what was supposed to be a quiet creek and stared in horror at the raging river that was advancing on the boulder, pressing impatiently against its banks.

"Pen," Abel finally caught my attention, his fingers dragging his unkempt hair out of his face. "Shit, Pen!"

My feet shuffled a few inches closer to Abel, but I couldn't pull my gaze away from all that water.

"It was a creek, just a creek!"

With a scream the wind raced past, buffeting me toward the edge of the boulder again. Tree branches snapped and cracked behind me, the sky dark and angry. A torrent of leaves scattered through the air and the clouds erupted, throwing rain like spears toward the ground.

"Pen, what are you doing?" The edge of panic in Abel's voice brought my own fear into sharp focus.

"Nothing!" I carded my fingers into the roots of my hair, palms slick in the downpour. The river surged over the banks, its depths growing murky and clouded. Water coursed down my temples, puddled under my boots. The surface of the boulder was getting slippery, and was it just me or had it started to tilt toward the river? I swallowed against the answering surge of my stomach.

"I need to wake up now. I need to wake up!"

Abel's sharp eyes darted between me and the river below. "You need to relax," he cried in a voice as tense as his posture.

"Relax?" I shrieked, gesturing all around us, water slinging from my fingertips. A manic laugh tumbled out of my mouth. "You know, I used to have this whole calming routine that I did." I pressed my eyes closed, refusing to watch the waves that plowed over the rocky shore and surrounded our boulder. Panic flexed in my chest and I forced my words out haltingly. "A sort of...meditation that let me access this...peaceful place I'd built inside myself. So I could visit it whenever life got...too ugly for me to look at."

Like some dam had broken, all the emotions I had been avoiding for years rushed through me. Pain. Fear. Loss. Loneliness. Loathing. Desperation. I gasped around it all, desperately trying to drag air into lungs already flooded. I strained my eyes open, like that would open the fist that clenched my chest too tightly, shuddering when I saw that the land in every direction was swallowed up, the trees half consumed by dark swells of water that stank of rot. I felt Abel's gaze taking me in, but he said nothing so I kept going in a rush.

"And doesn't that say something about me? Instead of making my life something I could actually be happy with, or even just survive, I opted to check out of reality entirely. I thought if I could pretend it was fine, eventually it would be." I shook my head in disgust. "Such an idiot."

"You're not—"

"So this whole calming thing I did?" I cut him off with an impatient sweep of my arm. "The thing that helped me keep going, literally helped me stay alive *the past five years?" I turned, needing to feel connected to something for this confession, and found his eyes studying me intently. "I'm afraid to do it now."*

His lips parted in confusion and I took a deep breath, clenching my fists at my sides as the water rose around us. My palms squelched.

"It was water." The confession cracked my voice, and I saw recognition flare in his eyes. I wrapped my arms around myself, crowding the center of the rock surface with Abel. "I would imagine water. Coursing all over me." I hiccupped, bracing against the murky memory of dirty water in my mouth, in my lungs.

"Let's try together." Abel's voice stroked over me, soothing some of the fear. "That's it, Pen." His voice brushed against me again. Softly. Tenderly. "Open to me."

I exhaled a breath I hadn't realized I was holding, the embers of his eyes entrancing me.

He folded gracefully onto the surface of the rock, holding my gaze, and gestured for me to sit across from him, ignoring the water that lapped toward his fingers. I sank down, hugging my knees tightly to my chest.

I didn't understand how he could sit calmly with the water crashing around us, the spray reaching up on top of the boulder where we sat. We were soaked to the bone already, but the rain kept pounding and the river kept rising. Much more and the water would surge over the rock, would rush around us and away with us, and then...and then...

"Teach me." His voice pushed through me, bringing my attention back to his face, to his calm, to his eyes. "Teach me." He urged again when I hesitated, his voice sinking into me like an anchor and settling me.

I felt myself drifting into his eyes, my mind spinning slowly until all I could see was Abel. I drifted, like I was falling asleep inside my dream. But I didn't mind; it promised to be restful as the panic and the pain and everything else faded to the back of my mind.

"There was this pitcher of water on my dresser back home. And when I'd wake up at night to start my shift, I'd go to the dresser and look into the mirror right above it. I'd stare into my own eyes and tell myself I was fine."

"Tell me about the pitcher." His voice caressed me, intimate and familiar, brushing down the hackles of my anxiety. I felt my shoulders drop, my brow soften.

"It was white, with a crack on the left side that ran from the rim to the swell of the basin," my hand lifted, tracing the shape of it in the air between us. "The crack was big enough to collect dirt and be noticed, but it never leaked water. I'd never seen anything like it; that pitcher was so fragile, and yet it held together with that crack running through it. It was Mother's," my voice trailed away.

Abel nodded, his understanding of that importance filling the intense stare between us. "What then?"

"Then I'd pour the water over my head and imagine it washing away my fear. My anxiety and panic. The water would take everything bad away from me and carry it down to the floor and, eventually, the earth. Where it would be buried and I wouldn't have to feel it again."

"And it helped." It wasn't a question, but I answered anyway.

"Yes."

"How?"

I closed my eyes, thinking back to the sensation I relied on mere days ago. Had it really only been that long?

"I would bring all of my attention to the feeling of the water touching me. How it tunneled through my hair like...fingers." My own fingers pressed through the damp curls at my temples of their own volition, mimicking the soft caress as I explained. "The water always took a different path, so I had to quiet my mind and pay attention. Maybe it would brush my lips," the pads of my fingers traced my mouth. "Or trail down my neck, or rush down the length of my spine." My hands pulled at my tunic, tracing past my collarbones and snagging against the fabric below. "It made me aware of my body, centered me into one spot, and I would remember that I was still whole. I was still alive and, like my Mother's pitcher, I wouldn't shatter."

I let out a long breath, feeling myself relax as my hands dropped from their gentle exploration into my lap. I felt calm, like the creek that gurgled happily nearby. My lashes fluttered open and I looked in amazement across the boulder to Abel.

Our eyes met and I froze, adrenaline of a different sort surging from my chest. I recognized the hunger in his gaze, the deep longing, the pull of a shared connection. I felt it, too. I was kindling, anticipating the heat of a nearby match. Waiting to be consumed, and maybe even wanting it. I breathed in the thick tension between us, swallowing it down into my core.

"Pen," he breathed harshly, looking conflicted.

I parted my lips to speak, aware of how Abel tracked the small movement.

"What—" I started, just as a column of fire roared to life between us and engulfed us both.

* * *

I sucked in a breath and sat up, almost running into Abel as he lurched to his feet.

"What—"

"Be *careful!*" Abel snarled, springing away from me.

"Sorry, I must've rolled over here while I was sleeping," I rubbed my eyes groggily, wondering at how I'd managed to roll across the prickly clearing without waking up. "I wasn't trying to crowd you." Heat surged up my neck as broken memories of my dream came back to me.

Abel's blue-tinted skin, glistening with sweat in the sunlight.

The quiet strength of limbs that I wanted to test with my teeth, with my tongue.

Thick hair begging for my fingers.

I sucked in a breath as awareness of Abel's body skittered over me, sending tendrils of excitement coursing through my limbs.

I tamped that shit down like it was on fire.

"You can't do that!" Abel growled, waving his arms in my direction in a clear loss for words. "You can't!"

"*Stars*, Abel, I said I was sorry! I didn't mean to roll over here." I eased to my feet, feeling stiff, and rolled my eyes. "I guess we're back to snapping at each other."

In the growing darkness, Abel started grabbing his things and angrily packing his bag. "I'm serious, Pen!"

I snatched my unused blanket off of the ground and shook it out, snapping it into folds and shoving it into the bottom of my pack. "So am I! I swear it's like you think I *like* pissing you off or something! Believe me, I'm not *trying* to make this whole arrangement more awful!" I threw my pack down and whirled around, marching over to Abel and planting myself right in front of him. "I'm at least trying! I'm trying to learn, trying to be considerate, trying to work together!" I punctuated every statement by jabbing a finger in the air beneath his arrogant, straight nose and relished the way he stumbled back away from me.

"Pen—"

"I'm not done!" I advanced. "I'm trying and not always succeeding, I know, but at least I'm *trying*! Would it kill you to *try* not to be a complete ass?"

"Don't *touch* me!" He yelled, dodging away to the other side of the clearing.

Chests heaving, we studied each other. The angles of his face pulled harsher with anger and something else. Fear? Could he be that repulsed by my nearness?

"Well," I muttered, pulling back. "I guess that answers my question."

We finished packing in tense silence, the incessant drone of the cicadas and night creatures filling the charged air between us.

As we lined up to make our way out of the bramble, Abel paused and glanced at me over his shoulder. "Pen, I—"

"Don't bother." I cut him off, never moving my gaze from the middle of his pack. Thankfully, he didn't. And I didn't analyze why that disappointed me so much.

184

Chapter Fourteen

We walked in silence for hours, each stewing in our own thoughts. Or maybe I was the only one stewing and Abel was unaffected because he was a complete ass and had no need for other people and their inconvenient habit of *existing*.

Except, he did need me. At least to fetch a message for him. And risk my life while doing it. Was it so much to ask for a little civility?

Right; stewing.

I heaved a heavy sigh and readjusted the straps of my pack. The pace we maintained was sedate out of consideration for my recovering lungs. Though breathing still felt raw and I fatigued quickly, there didn't seem to be any other complications. I hadn't developed a wet cough or heart palpitations. I wasn't sure what rashes or nausea had to do with near-drowning, but Abel asked after any of those symptoms incessantly. He informed me that if I seemed fine after 24 hours, I was probably in the clear. The comfort that statement brought was dubious at best, though I felt better after my strange dream than I had before I'd gone to sleep. It was something about my Mother's pitcher back home and how water was soothing...I grasped for the tatters of the dream, but nothing else was there.

There was less light to see by as the moon continued to wane, and a light cloud cover drifted over its face periodically. Still, my eyes had grown accustomed to darkness and I could see shapes well enough.

Thickets and brambles grew sparser and more sporadic until we left them behind us altogether. Gently undulating hills of completely overgrown blade-grasses and shrubs stretched out in all directions, broken up by islands of granite or some other veined stone surging up from the ground. My legs cramped from the awkward crouch we used to shuffle across the spaces between these rocky protrusions, thankful every time we came to a stop for Abel to scour the distance.

I set my pack down quietly at one of these formations, leaning back until I felt my spine crack. Relief had me groaning, and I dug my fists into my hips, shifting from side to side to try and relieve the tension there. I stretched my neck and shook out my hands before grabbing my pack and hauling it onto my shoulders again.

When I turned, Abel was only inches away. We both froze, startled. He must have leaned closer to say something, just as I had been about to, but all thoughts scattered from my mind. How was it that I could travel beside him for days, but still get caught off guard when I really *looked* at him? Stubble darkened his jaw, a narrow scar bisected the corner of his lip. His eyes, cataloging my face just like I was searching his, held flecks of umber and smoke.

He licked his lip, the tip of his tongue brushing against that narrow scar I'd noticed, and I fought the attraction that twitched under my ribs.

"Are you ready?"

I sucked in a breath. "Yeah."

We kept on. My shoulders had raw patches from hauling my pack every night for hours on end, but the stinging pain in my elbow from breaking Ben's nose was just a ghost. And as the bruises that had branded my body faded to nothing, I felt the fear that had held me in its fist begin to loosen and unfurl. It was like I was growing a new body. Eventually, I'd have a body that he would never touch, never control. A fierce smile pulled at my lips. I was grateful for the burn in my thighs and the cuts on my arms from the sharp grasses. Grateful for the distance between where I was and where I came from.

I still missed home, and worried about my family, especially Missy, but I knew deep down that I was doing what I had to for them to be safe, sheltering them from my fallout. I just hoped they saw it that way and could forgive me for how I left.

The earth opened and pushed more rocks skyward across the landscape until we traversed like Tusk-goats, scampering from rock to rock on nimble feet. Well, Abel was nimble and I managed to not fall down. I felt stronger than I had in Arberdon, but also completely exhausted. Only the memory of what happened with the Howlers the last time I stumbled kept my feet sure. That, and the fact that I let myself be much slower than Abel.

As I skidded down one rocky slope, I noticed him waiting for me near a crevice in the ground. The sound of trickling water reached my ears as I drew closer and my mouth watered. I could just imagine how cool it would feel coursing over my skin and across my tongue. Abel reached out one of his large, scarred hands as I skip-stepped the last few feet to where he was standing.

"Water?"

I handed my canteen over without a word, dropping my pack to give my shoulders another break.

He sank onto his haunches, leaning down into the crevice to fill my bottle and providing me with a glorious view of his—

I abruptly turned around and walked away to stretch my legs, biting my lips against the wave of embarrassment that crashed over me. What was I *thinking* ogling him like that? Wasn't I mad at him? And we weren't even compatible species...were we? Wait, no, that didn't matter. It was just the adrenaline of being stuck out in the wild together combined with my *almost* erotic dream. The stress of the situation was enough to make anyone look for a little distraction.

"Here."

I startled at his voice, directly behind me, and turned slowly, willing myself to act normally. Abel stood close, much closer than was necessary, and held my canteen out to me by its strap.

My heart pulsed thickly in my chest as I held his intense gaze, grasping the bottle with two hands and pulling it to my sternum. The strap pulled tight before he released it, letting his hand fall slowly to his side.

"Thank you." Stars Above, was that *my* breathy voice?

He nodded once and took a step back, rubbing his hand over the back of his neck. I licked my lips and shook my head. The heat crawling up my neck had to be from exhaustion.

Unscrewing the lid to my water, I allowed myself a long drink, relishing the way it shocked my tongue and teeth with its coolness. I swallowed, feeling it slide like ice all the way down to my middle. The chill suffused my body, a small shiver racing down my limbs. Not wanting to waste the opportunity to immediately refill my canteen, I gave into impulse and tipped some across my neck, gasping at the damp cold. Feeling awake and giddy, I joined Abel by the crevice to top off the canteen, my body humming with awareness at his nearness.

He'd already hefted his pack but waited for me as I lingered, staring into the darkness of the crack in the earth and listening to the jump and crash of the water.

"Pen, about earlier. I should—"

"Stars, I almost wish I could—"

Our words crashed over each other. I snorted, looking up into his eyes with amusement.

"I guess we're talking now?"

"Ah, you go first." His palm found the back of his neck again, his gaze darting down and away.

I shrugged, taking a breath and letting it out. It felt good to break the stalemate between us, if I was being honest.

"I was just going to say I wish I could climb in there, get cleaned off." I picked at my smelly clothes. "You know, I think it might be nice to swim while not running for my life. No offense."

His lips twitched to the side, his eyes warming gently, before we started walking again.

"That would be a relief. I'm surprised you'd be interested, though."

"Why's that?"

A considering hum rumbled out of his chest. "Figured you'd still be hesitant around water, especially after that dream." He shuddered dramatically and I chuckled.

We had only gone a few feet when I stopped.

"Abel, how did you know about my dream?"

He turned to me and shrugged. "You shared it with me, remember?"

I shook my head. "I wasn't speaking to you earlier."

Abel's lips pressed into a firm line, that wrinkle between his brows becoming more pronounced. He studied me, cataloging every aspect of my face. His eyes narrowed, tense concern pulling at his mouth.

"Abel?"

I was getting uncomfortable under his scrutiny when his lips twitched to the side again, serrated teeth flashing briefly.

"I'd be scared after almost drowning." He said lightly.

I frowned at his rapid change. Would I be able to tell if he were lying to me? Something felt...odd about this conversation. Had we talked about me being afraid of water? Why did that feel so familiar? I stared into those brilliant eyes and tried to read them the way he seemed able to read my features, my thoughts. My head felt funny, sort of like I was listing to the side, spinning into a foggy oblivion that promised to be restful.

Let it go.

"Well," I said, shaking off my unease and trying for equal flippancy, "I was starting to think you weren't scared of anything."

"I'm scared of plenty."

"Like what? Other than drowning. I don't recommend it, by the way."

"Don't joke about that, please." He shot me a look through narrowed eyes.

I moved up beside him as we started up another rocky slope, using his staff to help when he offered it. He seemed more cautious around me, awkward in a way he had never been before.

Maybe he was actually giving some thought to what I said in our argument. If so, good; he didn't need to snap at me for every blunder I made. Though, to be fair, it had been pretty jarring to wake up so close together. Especially after that dream...I shook my head abruptly, dismissing the heat that gathered at my cheeks. *Don't go there, Pen,* I cautioned myself. Better to pay attention to our surroundings anyway.

The night was calm and beautiful, full of distant stars scattered across an impossibly vast sky. I smiled to myself, feeling appreciation for the nocturnal wilds that I had never expected before leaving Arberdon. I turned to mention it to Abel, catching him staring at me again.

"What?"

"Ah, nothing." He turned away abruptly and hustled a few steps forward, effectively cutting off any conversation I might have started. I frowned after him, but decided not to let it ruin my enjoyment of the night.

There was a slight breeze, bringing with it the smell of ripe plants and pollen. Before long, that scent would shift toward drying leaves and decay as the end of the growing season came, but for now it was spicy and full of heat. I inhaled, pulling that familiar smell into my lungs, and the ache for home wasn't as raw as before. Insects and small creatures scurried and chittered among the fields around us, growing quiet where we walked and swelling as we passed. My eyes longed for color, for light, but there was something soothing about the dark. Like walking in a cocoon.

We managed another four miles of brutal hiking before making camp, nestling into a crevice of craggy rock toward the top of a rise, the sky close enough to touch. I dropped my pack enthusiastically as I scrambled onto the ledge behind Abel. Gritty sand coated the stone, sticking to the sweat on my palms.

I leaned back, kicking my tired feet out in front of me, and looked out over the landscape in amazement. The flat lands of grass and shrubs seemed so far away! The trees in the far distance looked like indistinct fuzz against the horizon. I drank in what details I could see as the edge of the sky began to lighten and blush with the dawn.

So, I thought as I used the arriving sun's position to get my bearings, *that way is South.*

Somewhere out there, past the stretches of grass and through the thick of the forest, stood Arberdon. Somewhere out there, my family was waking up and starting their day.

Father would be striking out toward the fields with Dale and Rena. Or had the two apprentices moved on already?

The night watch would be heading home. Was Randall working? How was Randa faring?

Grandfather and Missy would be checking fences for the livestock and tending to the courtyard crops.

And Ben...even though I didn't regret standing up for myself, it was hard not to be concerned. I hadn't intended to kill him, hadn't been thinking at all. But intentions didn't matter if he ended up dying anyway. Was he still in the hospital, or was I a murderer on top of defecting? Had the Executors expanded the search for me? Was I already a fugitive?

Abel unpacked a heavy gray blanket and started wedging it across the opening of the crevice, blocking my view and bringing me back to reality. None of those concerns mattered more than survival. I turned my attention to my own pack, pulling out the plants and nuts we'd collected along the night's travel. When he finished, Abel claimed the small pile I'd set aside for him and eased to the floor, being careful not to touch me at all, and picked at his food while studying his handiwork.

"Problem?" I asked, following his gaze.

He shook his head, then shrugged. "The cover here isn't very good. We'll be vulnerable during the day." Weariness hung heavily from his shoulders and he rubbed a large hand across his face.

I twisted some minty leaves between my fingers before chewing thoughtfully. "We should take shifts. No, really," I cut off his argument when he started to speak. "I've been resting all day long this whole time, and thank you for that. But I need to pull my weight. I need to help."

"You'll help at Terrah."

"And I'll help now. I'm a trained guard, Abel."

"But there's," he caught himself staring at me again and ducked his head. "We need to—I need—"

"To sleep. You need to sleep. You're exhausted."

He looked like he would argue more, but I held my ground.

"You'll note I can arch my brow as well as you can." I gestured to my face, using the expression I had cultivated to keep Missy in line as a child.

He chuckled, then nodded with a self-deprecating twist of his lips. "Fine. We'll talk when I'm actually rested. First shift?"

* * *

Two thousand three hundred fifty four times two, I thought as I shifted my seat on the hard stone, *is four thousand seven hundred eight.*

I sat near the blanket covering our ledge, my faithful shotgun resting under my palms across my lap. If we were discovered, my shotgun wouldn't do much good before the Executors were on top of us. But at least it would slow them down.

Sweat cascaded down the bends in my elbows, the middle of my chest. My upper lip was dotted with salt. My eyes hurt from squinting into the bright light of day through the small gap I pressed my nose to. Blinking, I turned to smirk over my shoulder.

It took a few moments for my eyes to adjust before I could make out Abel's shape in the gloom. He sprawled on his back, one solid arm flung across his face.

Snoring.

I rolled my eyes and shifted again, wishing I could move around and work the kinks out of my limbs, but there just wasn't enough room. Pressing the back of my head into the rock supporting me, I sighed and closed my eyes for a minute. It was just past the middle of the day, when we were supposed to switch shifts, but I lingered a bit longer. I was enjoying looking at the colors of daytime, devouring the landscape with my eyes like I was starving, and Abel seemed in serious need of sleep. I could last a little while yet. Stars Above only knew when he'd last taken a full rest, and meanwhile I'd been blissfully unaware and trusting him to keep us safe. The absurdity of that fact was not lost on me.

I hadn't seen more than a small herd of Tusk-goats pass through the area, their four-pronged faces nosing the loose rocks aside to find plants. Plenty of Stone-hoppers scrabbled around, bifurcated heads looking in two directions at once. I still didn't know how to make a cooking fire, so killing any of the small lizards seemed an unnecessary waste. We weren't that hard pressed for food yet, despite losing our supplies the night we encountered the Howlers.

I smiled as I remembered Abel's proclamation from our first day traveling together. Death should not be dealt lightly, indeed.

The drone from the cicadas faded up the rocky slope, barely even registering to my ears up in our camp. Without plants to climb in, they stayed mainly south of us. The quiet was a unique noise of its own, almost louder than the clamor I was accustomed to. It made more space for the commotion in my head, which I was avoiding at all costs. Thoughts about where we were going, and what I was going to do when we got there. What I was going to do once I was *completely on my own.*

I shifted again, trying to shake the thick, sinking feeling of sleep from my limbs. Just a little longer, and then I would wake Abel. I spared another glance out of the make-shift curtain, but nothing had changed. Heat waves danced up from the ground, blurring my vision, and not a soul to see. Lazy wisps of white clouds drifted high across a sky of brilliant blue, wheeling with some kind of carrion hawk, traveling quickly toward the coast on a breeze we wouldn't feel down here on land. The smell of the brown, sun-warmed stones tickled my nose.

I dropped the edge of the blanket again, closing my eyes just for a minute to adjust to the dark. That same sucking feeling pulled at the edges of my body, enticing me into relaxation. I felt my body shifting sideways, my head falling toward the back of the shadowy cavern we'd created. I sighed, feeling the brush of a cool breeze across my skin. A breeze thick with the scent of forest and rain.

* * *

"Penelope," that hated voice slithered through my mind, seeking me out among the trees. "Where are you, Penelope?"

I clenched my jaw and breathed out slowly to steady my pounding heart. For once it wasn't overwhelming terror that gripped me when I heard Ben's voice in my dream. He couldn't find me if I didn't let him. No, it wasn't terror, but it was anger. My lips twisted into a grimace. I would move further into the woods, farther away from the places I recognized. I would be swift and silent, leaving no trace. I would float like the wind.

The reminder of the thought I had while running for my life with Abel by my side had an unfamiliar warmth rushing up through my chest. The flutter swelled, pattering against my ribs before bursting forth into brilliant light. As I followed my flame through the forest, Ben's voice faded away behind me.

Reality shifted strangely as I walked; I got the sense that I had been in the Dark Room forever, and also that no time had passed at all. We passed groves of trees, many different species twining together to make an impossibly lush wilderness. We crossed valleys dotted with spindly new saplings and wove around thick trunks that amazed me with their sheer size. A moment or an interminable amount of time later I stood at the edge of a large clearing, amazement overtaking me as I stumbled to a stop.

A massive oak tree dominated the space, its roots rippling the ground and mighty branches holding up the unseen sky. The tree shimmered with the light of thousands of flames, maybe tens of thousands, that drifted and darted and sighed all over the space like lightning-flies. The flames flowed over and into the tree, making it incandescent in the gloom.

A soft, lilting wind whispered through the branches while those flames eddied to and fro as if the passage of time meant nothing. My eyes adjusted to the glow of the clearing, picking out the shapes of a vast number of smaller trees growing within its circle, each one simply dwarfed by the magnitude of the oak.

An aspen tree caught my eye and I moved toward it, brushing my fingertips over bone-white branches. The contact sizzled through my skin and straight to my heart, the sound of my steady pulse filling my ears. The beat vibrated back to me from the aspen tree, its tender branches shaking ever so slightly.

A young rowan tree grew close by, bent and broken at a strange angle. I took a step toward it, feeling an inexplicable pull.

My flame danced nearby to get my attention, coaxing me closer to the giant oak. I craned my neck, gazing up to where the huge branches faded into obscurity high above me. Its trunk was enormous, easily bigger around than the center of Arberdon, and covered in thick, scarred bark. This tree had been around for an eternity, had seen more than I could imagine. I sucked a sharp breath as that gravity settled on me.

Hesitating only a moment, I ambled over the ground where its roots surged and swelled. I pressed my hands against the rough surface of the bark, feeling the answering heat of life press back against me.

The tree's name reverberated through me as we connected. Truthfully there were many names for the tree, as many as I had drops of blood in my veins, and they all coursed through me with a heavy pulse, but there was only one that spoke to me, only one that I could translate into something I could say.

"Yeshua," I greeted her.

I closed my eyes and took a deep breath to center myself, sinking down into my peaceful place. I pressed my brow against her and felt a tingling sensation, an invitation to reach outside of myself. I followed it and my head lightened; I felt stretched thin and drifting, my mind spiraling into the sky above with Yeshua's farthest leaves while my feet remained rooted beside her in the earth. I focused on the pulse thrumming through my being, the sound swelling within me as I touched her, and tilted my head to better listen. Warmth swelled in my middle, just below my ribcage.

*Behind my closed eyes, I saw fire burning inside Yeshua. She **was** light and fire. Her radiance coursed into the air, following her branches, and into the ground with her roots. She showed me the path she tunneled, how she touched every plant and tree and rock in this place. And she showed me the rowan tree that I had noticed before, connected to her and pulsing with its own beat.*

Eyes still closed, I turned and followed her fire to the rowan tree. I slipped down the rippling earth, following Yeshua's roots. As I came closer, a new beat pulsed through me from the ground. The life vibrating through it shook my bones and rattled my core. Leaning toward the young tree, pressing my hands against the warm bark, I listened to the steady pulse more closely, each beat sharing insight with me.

Discipline.

Focus.

Hypervigilance.

Guilt.

Shame.

"It feels familiar. Safe."

My flame compressed itself smaller, becoming little more than a lightning-fly, and circled around a wound in the tree that oozed red. The wound was on the main trunk of the rowan tree, bending it at an angle, with the branches above it struggling to support the small buds that dotted its arms.

A lesson my mother had taught me echoed through my mind: "Burdens, when carried well, create strength. Burdens, when carried poorly, create wounds. Wounds not healed will fester, blocking you from growth." She had reached out to me, pressing on the space between the flares of my ribs, and smiled gently. "Growth cannot take root if you are blocked."

Instinct had me looking back at the rowan tree, swallowing my apprehension, and reaching out. My flame settled against me, engulfing my fingers, but I didn't burn. Together we pressed my palm against the wound.

"Teach me," I invited the tree, using words I'd heard Abel say in a dream. The red oozed over my knuckles. "Show me."

In an instant my vision clouded, black smoke rushing in from all sides to choke out the clearing. I would have panicked if I hadn't still been able to see my flame, wrapping around my hand where I held it pressed against a tree I could no longer see.

With a sound like an agonized gasp, the smoke snaked back the way it had come, leaving a new landscape before me.

"What the—" I turned, my arm dropping to my side. The rowan tree, and everything else from the clearing, was gone.

I stood in a settlement of some kind, one that definitely didn't have a wall. The modest-sized houses, maybe a couple dozen in all, were well-built and faced the wide swatch of hardened ground I was standing on. The forest around them seemed to be embracing them, arms of brown and green reaching between each building. Each home was built on risers of some kind, short legs of gear-work that held them above the ground.

I shifted a glance over my shoulder at one structure in particular, fighting the urge to brush off my arms. The house swallowed my attention, consuming my awareness of anything else. A single door stood in the middle of its stern face, beckoning darkly. Its empty windows, one on either side, gaped.

I sucked in a desperate breath, tearing my eyes away from the house. My shaking hands wrapped around my arms, trying to chafe away chills that had nothing to do with the weather. Heavy clouds rushed in, shrouding the space in gloom. No fires burned. The absolute stillness of my surroundings burrowed under my skin like maggots on a corpse.

Unwillingly, my gaze returned to the one house. Was it somehow closer to me than before? A shiver crept up my spine and I turned to face it fully.

The building itself was innocuous. Logs of wood lashed together formed the walls. The two windows that flanked the door were draped with heavy fabric, some sort of dark jewel tone, probably homespun and dyed by the owner. The roof sloped in a long line away from the center of the settlement, giving it the appearance of a long rectangle.

Unease cascaded over me like rising water, a cold sweat prickling under my arms and down my back.

The walk leading up to it was the same length as the rest, but as I watched space seemed to stretch and snap between us. The gravity of the house grew, reaching toward me and dragging at my senses, pulling at my limbs. Dread coiled deep in my belly, holding my insides tightly. Whatever the reason was for my being in the clearing, I knew the way out was through that house. Swallowing bile, I forced my feet to start the slow progression up the path.

Instinct had my shoulders rising and curling tight around my chest, my left shoulder leading since I had a stronger punch with my right cross. My tingling fingers reminded me to relax my hands. A loose fist was a more effective fist.

My eyes scanned for any movement, anything in this eerie place. The overwhelming silence hung like a sodden blanket, tainting every breath.

The front door swung violently inward, slamming against the wall and startling a scream from me.

The threshold loomed, restraining the darkness beyond, denser than it had any right to be. I was only inches away, but could see nothing through the portal.

Adrenaline danced across my skin.

I had to physically cross the threshold if I wanted to see what was inside.

"Okay," I shook out my fingers again. "Okay, I can do this. I asked to be shown."

I took that last step, pressing my foot through the doorway. An icy chill surged up my leg, flowing over me and sucking at the rest of me to follow. My left arm submerged into the empty space next, my body breaking out in shivers. The darkness was viscous, clinging to me. I gasped one last breath and pressed my face into the void.

Crossing the threshold took effort. My lungs burned for a breath, my eyes pressed tightly closed. I pushed forward, breaking free to stumble into the room beyond.

"Oh," I gagged, clamping a hand across my mouth and nose.

The smell of fresh death, coppery and warm, clung to the roof of my mouth. The tang of a gut wound, the sweetened stench of rot. Blood-splattered walls undulated and shuddered at the edges of my vision, the sound of a pulse echoing faintly from the logs. Whimsical pictures of flowers and animals danced under drops and splotches of gore.

A trampled table.

A broken lantern, leaking fuel.

Shattered plates.

Four corpses of Executor officers, three men and a woman, sprawled across the center of the room.

Ignoring my need to run, I tucked the lower portion of my face into my shirt to filter the stench as best I could, and moved closer to the carnage. I blinked quickly, trying to clear my vision and force the walls to be still. The sound of that pulse gushed throughout the room.

Dark stains bloomed. Two chest wounds, one vicious gut wound, and one slit throat. Their eyes, glassy and dull, gaped in surprise at the ceiling. I skirted around dark puddles where I could, ignoring the squish of my steps where I couldn't.

Roving patrol, based on their uniforms, an exact match to the style Randall wore when he was sent with a team outside the walls. Their job was to patrol the surrounding area to ensure safety. They escorted people into protected cities where they would be safe, or looked for lost travelers. This was someone's home. Why...?

I came across a fifth officer toward the back of the room. He was face-down in his own vomit, the air around him thick with the acidic smell, but there was no blood around him. I held my breath and crouched down. The loose tails of his belt were just visible on either side of his body. His face was battered, blistered with rash, the pustules breaking open and releasing sludge to seep down his ravaged skin even in death.

I gagged and stood back up, choking on my nausea. The fifth officer had his right arm stretched out across the floor, his head tilted in the same direction. I followed his lead and looked.

Slumped on the other side of the wall, hidden mostly in the shadow of a hallway, was another body. I stepped over the last officer. A heavy hush fell over the house as I moved toward the hall at a dream-thick pace. The walls froze and I felt myself holding my breath with them.

She would have been beautiful in life, I decided, more because of the kindness pressed into her skin over the years than her features. She had dark hair that rumpled in waves over her shoulders, matted in places by blood. Her eyes, which sloped slightly at their corners, were framed by laugh lines. Half of her face was scarred and swollen, her lips split and dripping brilliantly red blood down her chin. The blood pooled against her breastbone, soaking into the heavily mended tunic she wore. Two daggers lay forgotten at her sides, sitting in a pool of red from a gaping hole in her middle. Multiple gunshot wounds, close-range. Her legs stretched out in front of her, one twisted oddly and sitting in its own bright pool of blood.

I knelt beside her. Confusion and rage burned in my gut. A Roving Patrol should not have come here. Their job was reconnaissance, and rescue when needed. I could only imagine how she would have felt, one woman with two daggers against five trained Executors with guns. How she managed to survive long enough to take them out with her should have been a mystery. But it wasn't.

Under the gray pallor of death, her skin was tinted blue.

"Oh, Stars." I bit the back of my fist.

She had looked toward the back of the house when she died, an almost peaceful expression on her damaged face. I turned to see what she had been gazing at.

A door stood open, framing the broken limbs of the trees beyond.

I pressed my lids closed, trying to shake my clamoring thoughts free as the sound of a heartbeat again filled my ears, easing out from the walls of the house.

Thrum.

Thrum.

Thrum.

"I am so sorry," I told the woman. "They shouldn't have been here."

Thrum.

Thrum.

Thrum.
"I don't understand. They should not *have been here."*
Thrum.
Thrum.
Thrum.

* * *

I became aware of a sticky warmth on the side of my face and licked my lips with a dry tongue. Slowly more awareness creeped into my groggy mind.

I was sitting at a horrible angle, my hips pressed uncomfortably into a stone surface.

My cheek was wet where I had started drooling.

There was a heartbeat under my ear.

My eyes popped open. Sure enough, a vast plane of pectoral perfection greeted me. I stiffened and held my breath, careful not to move suddenly and wake Abel.

Abel.

Here I was, face planted and drooling a dark circle onto Abel's shirt. *Don't-ever-touch-me-Pen-I'm-serious* Abel. And if that wasn't bad enough, I was supposed to be on guard!

I exhaled quietly and eased my hands to the ground, pressing away from him slowly. I was counting my lucky stars that he was too exhausted to notice my intrusion. After the last time we woke up near each other I could only imagine how upset he'd be.

And rightfully so! I offered myself another serving of shame. He didn't want to be touched, and I would respect his boundaries even if I didn't understand them.

I managed good progress, levering up so I could get my knees beneath me. Sliding away from his body, I watched him for any sign that he was waking. His chest rose and fell steadily, his face shadowed with beard growth and sleep. His full lips parted slightly. My stomach fluttered and I clamped my teeth down on my bottom lip before I was abruptly stopped.

Abel's arm.

Stars Above, Abel's arm was *around my shoulders*. His grip tightened gently in the hair at the back of my head, sending a bolt of awareness low in my belly. I hovered, studying his sleeping face from a dangerous few inches while that awareness coiled tighter. And left me feeling vile for taking advantage of him.

"Don't," he muttered, his voice a deep growl in sleep.

I tightened, my breath seizing in my lungs. Want shivered through me, and I hastily ignored it. I took a measured breath, pushing my weight carefully back into my knees. I hoped that the gravity of his arm would make him let go. Preferably before it woke him up.

Incrementally I dragged my body backward, careful to breathe *just so* as not to disturb him. The fingers that twisted into my hair squeezed once more before releasing and he rolled onto his side. I scrambled back as far as I could, retrieving my gun and peeking outside the gray blanket. I exhaled my relief when I realized the sun was still in the same place as the last time I checked. At least my epic lapse was a short-lived one.

I studied the landscape for any changes, using the task to help ground myself.

I'd fallen asleep on Abel. And, Stars help me, it had felt good.

Chapter Fifteen

I woke Abel once I was sure I had my embarrassment under control. And instead of taking my turn to sleep, I insisted we got moving immediately. Abel looked like he wanted to protest, but could probably sense my reluctance to do any interacting at all. Whatever the deciding factor that prevented him from arguing with me, I was grateful for it. The shock I felt at waking up practically sprawled on top of him had rattled the drowsiness right out of me and I was eager for some distance.

The terrain offered up rocks, rocks, and more rocks in every direction, though by the time the sun slipped away from its zenith the ground leveled out again. The horizon taunted, still looking simultaneously impossibly far and tantalizingly close after hours of hiking. Massive columns of rock pointed to the sky periodically, with strange stick-like plants and thorn-covered blobs growing out of the sun-burned ground in between.

The land was painted in various shades of brown and red. The earth cracked, parched, much like my throat. My tongue felt fat when I tried to swallow, dancing heat blurring my vision and refusing to be blinked away.

Living in Arberdon my whole life, I thought I understood heat and drought. I thought I understood discomfort when sweat coated me, pooling and puddling in inconvenient places.

Discomfort was *not* sweating, not even having water in the air when you breathed. Discomfort was hard grains of dust and sand coating your teeth, blowing into your eyes and ears and nose.

The heat was oppressive. There were no trees to help hold water to the ground, no clouds to hold water to the air. Each inhale stole more moisture from me, leaving me wrung-out, as cracked as the ground coughing up red dust under my boots.

As we walked, we took spare tunics out of our packs, spooling them around our heads and faces. Hot wind breathed across the plain, falling in merciless waves.

I drank water carefully, not willing to lose any and not sure when we would have the chance to refill our canteens. Still, my head felt less woozy with regular swallows. I figured it was better to survive long enough to get to a freshwater source, instead of passing out from dehydration. We moved steadily and silently, neither one of us having the energy to spare for talking.

As the sun finished dragging itself across the sky, spilling brilliant color across the horizon, I breathed a sigh of relief. Long shadows reached across the ground and a chill danced down my spine.

"I'm glad we didn't get started any earlier today," I croaked, breaking our silence after a brief rest as twilight settled quietly around us. "I don't think I could have kept going much longer in that heat." My heart beat quickly as it was, like I had spent the afternoon running instead of walking.

Abel nodded, his brilliant eyes looking a bit dazed as he palmed his canteen.

"We need shelter," he growled, his voice rough. My eyes traced the cracks in his lips as he spoke, the burned skin across his cheeks and down his nose.

I turned in a slow circle, taking in the expanse. The ground stretched out in every direction, punctuated by clusters of rock. The sky darkened drastically as we stood there, brilliant stars winking into existence.

"Where? There's nothing out here but rock and sand."

Abel rubbed the back of his hand across his mouth with a grimace before replacing the cap on his water. The growth of a few days' beard rasped under his knuckles. His gaze skipped over the land, considering and discarding options.

"Somewhere high."

"On one of those rock pillars?" I suggested, looking where he was.

He nodded, extending a lean arm to point. "That one has a ledge we can use to trap our heat in. We're going to get cold soon."

I noticed the drop in temperature, too, and agreed.

Knowing that we would be making camp soon was the only motivation that got my feet moving toward the indicated pillar. We spent the better part of another hour hiking toward it as more and more stars ignited the sky. I shivered, chilled without the heat from the sun, and refrained from licking my painfully dry lips.

We didn't speak, the muffled cadence of our steps filling the comfortable space between us. I longed for the sweet bliss of getting off my feet, my head heavy upon my aching shoulders. In the distance, Dune Canids called hauntingly to each other. I wasn't sure how far away they were, or if they felt like enjoying a fugitive Arberdon guard and a grumpy *Unnat* for dinner, but I pushed myself toward the pillar with renewed determination.

Abel had insisted on taking both of our packs before we started to climb, and I was aware of my physical limitations enough to acquiesce with thanks and no argument. My shoulders burned with the unfamiliar activity, my fingers clumsy with fatigue. I tore the pads of a few open against the pillar's rough texture, ignoring the sting. Hand over hand, we had to reach the platform.

Darkness fell, vast as the stars above, and had my eyes straining for each next handhold. I relied on touch more than anything, praying I didn't stumble upon a Rock-snake or Flesh-beetle, and progress was slow.

Abel followed and, though I was moving at a glacial pace, offered no complaints. I was thankful for his reassuring presence behind me. He was temperamental and snarled a lot, but he had proved himself over our days of traveling together. More than simply not wishing me harm, he actively protected me, using his own body as a shield between me and danger on more than one occasion.

Because he needs your help with something, I scolded myself, trying to squash that insistent flutter in my belly that seemed to spring to life whenever I started thinking there was some tangible connection between us. *It's transactional, Pen, not because he li–*

My tired fingers slipped, scattering sand across my face. I sputtered, instinctively recoiling from the burn in my eyes, and lost one of my foot holds. Before I could even register panic, the heat of his body was there pushing against me, bracing between me and my inevitable fall.

"Easy," he murmured, his own voice tight and quiet. "Easy, I've got you."

Adrenaline crashed through me, heightening my awareness. Without sight, my other senses amplified. The burn of the coarse sand beneath my grip, the tremble of my muscles. I could feel his heart pounding in his chest, echoing across the skin of my back. Every inhale brought him into my mouth, his scent of forest and heat and sweat. The hard strength of the leg he wedged beneath me, and the coiling low in my belly. The caress of his breath as it danced down my neck, the sharp edge of his jaw as he tilted his mouth toward my ear.

"Are you okay?"

"Yes." I lied, my voice low.

I swallowed another shiver, swallowed my inconvenient reaction to the man behind me. What *was* the draw I felt for him, the inexplicable attraction that tangled me in its grip? I'd never lost my head over a man before, not even at the beginning when Ben stated his interest in me. It had felt like a logical move, like security and an offer I would be a fool to refuse.

But *this*, this visceral reaction, the way my whole body lit up with his proximity even though my mind balked, the way his scent tasted like a memory I wan—

No, no I couldn't think that way. He was a stranger, a thoughtful and imposing stranger I encountered when I was vulnerable, and I was imagining things. I shook my head firmly, blinking grit out of my eyes, and forced my muscles to carry me upward.

Minutes later, we pulled ourselves on top of the ledge and I stretched out my abused fingers. My heart crashed inside my chest, speeding along at a frantic pace. I chose to blame it entirely on the difficult climb and my fear of falling, chose to ignore the awareness of him that still trembled in my veins. Still shook me to my very core.

I peered over the edge cautiously; we were uncomfortably high above the ground. Maybe not enough to kill but certainly enough to be seriously injured from a fall. With a slow breath I subsided, tilting my head back to gaze at the sky. Somehow bigger and closer at the same time, it took my breath away. Layers of stars twinkled along with the light of the waning moon, the unfathomable vastness reminding me of something from a dream.

"How much water do you have left?" Abel's question brought me back to my senses and pushed thoughts of dreams aside. I took out my canteen and shook it, testing its weight.

"Maybe a quarter."

He nodded, the worry on his face mirroring my own. "We should be through this section of The Sands with another day or two of walking, but it'll be tight. We won't have as much time for traveling; we'll need shelter during the heat of the day, as well as in the coolest hours of night."

"I didn't realize we were at The Sands," I said with as much surprise as my exhaustion could muster. I'd read about The Sands in one of my contraband books. Read about it when it was just an arid climate, before the Great War.

I smoothed the gritty surface of our rock ledge, tracing what I remembered from various books of maps with my finger tip. I placed Arberdon on the Southern horn, East Elm Bay just above it on the Southeastern coast. Wrinkling my brow, I tried to recall where Terrah was situated; I placed it inland and toward the middle.

As I worked, Abel leaned back beside me, watching me over my shoulder. It should have felt intrusive or uncomfortable, but it didn't. It felt...*Familiar. Safe.* Something else from a forgotten dream fluttered through my mind. I was too tired to chase after it, though, so I just shook my head and finished filling in my map as best as I could remember.

"That's very good," Abel murmured when I wrapped my arms around my drawn up knees, fighting the urge to lean into his space.

I shrugged. "It's outdated, since it was printed before the Great War. But I must have read all of the books in my parent's house dozens of times, including stuffy old books of maps."

"Incredible. How many books do you have?"

"I have no idea." I rubbed my chin against my knee. "Not as many as there used to be. I made the mistake of trusting the wrong person, ended up having to destroy a bunch."

"May I?"

At my nod, he reached out and gently dusted away a couple of smaller cities from my map and expanded the boundaries of The Sands. The barren land stretched in an undulating ribbon from West to East across the entire continent, isolating the Southern horn from the Northern bulk. The Dead Grove took a large section of land just outside of Arberdon, consuming the edges of East Elm Bay. He left the other major cities where they were; Jatora in the Western Ridges, Evereen along the North Eastern coast just past the Hacknor Mountains, and Yeven far to the North.

"We're here." He indicated a spot in the thinnest section of The Sands. I let my eyes roam the sketch, getting my bearings.

"How do you know?" I gestured to our drawing. "I haven't seen an updated map of the continent. In Arberdon that was Executor property, only issued out in sections to Roving Patrols with strict rules not to copy or share."

Abel's expression grew strained and he pulled his hand back. "I told you. I have my resources."

I frowned and huddled into myself more tightly, the chill in the air taking on a sharper edge.

"This is all for the errand you're on?" I guessed. I knew I was right when his glowing eyes cut in my direction and quickly away. "Will you tell me anything more about it?"

"You deliver a message to me. That's all."

I blinked. "Deliver a message. Are you even listening to yourself? Might I remind you of the entire, dare I say *dangerous* and *faulty*, plan that leads to me retrieving this message?"

"It's just a—"

"It's *not* just a message!" I snapped, shifting around on our little ledge to face him fully. "Come on, Abel, you've got to tell me the truth after everything we've been through. You have access to current *Executor* maps. You know the history of former *Executor* projects." He held the challenge in my gaze without flinching. "What in the Stars are you involved in? What am *I* getting involved in?"

The echo of my shout slithered off into The Sands, the mournful cry of a Dune Canid joining it.

Harsh wind buffeted against our ledge. The reality that I had only known Abel for a handful of days settled uncomfortably in my chest. I had put my life in his hands without fully understanding his motivations.

He could be about to betray me. He could be leading me anywhere, to any fate.

Yet that didn't sit right. My gut told me I could trust him, that I somehow *knew* him. He might not be a friend, but he didn't feel like an enemy, either.

Finally he dropped his face into his palms with a snarled curse. He rubbed his sunburned face roughly, ripping his fingers through the loose pieces of his hair.

"I need to apologize."

My stomach dropped, a queasy dread spreading inside me. I clenched my jaw and waited, hoping what he said next would ease the anxiety tightening its grip on me.

"We are heading to Terrah. The Chemist has information that is desperately important to me. I need your help to get it."

I offered him a jerky nod; I already knew that.

"But you were right that morning outside Arberdon, Pen." He looked at me, studying me cautiously. "I wasn't chasing you, not exactly. But I had been following you."

A quick inhale pierced my lungs. I was abruptly aware of how little space there was on our ledge. How The Sands stretched all around, not another soul for miles. How his powerful body blocked the only way down. My fingers dug into my arms.

"I came to Arberdon to find you."

My heart stuttered in my chest.

"I'd been shadowing you for weeks."

"Weeks." My lips felt numb around the word.

He nodded once, still holding me prisoner with that impossible gaze. "Why?"

"Because you called me to you."

The air was too thin to breathe. My knuckles ached as my nails bit through my sleeves and into my skin.

"You called. And I came."

"I don't understand," I shook my head, convinced I was misunderstanding him. "I didn't call you."

He dropped his hands into his lap.

"You did. But you didn't know what you were doing. I realized that last night."

"What are you talking about?"

"Your dreams, Pen." He curled his fingers into his palms, glaring at them while I stared at him. "You're blessed. You're a Dream Walker."

My hand connected with my chest, like I could remove the weight that made it hard to breathe. Like I could stop the recognition that resounded through my every cell.

"I don't know what you're talking about."

He took a deep breath, his lips pressed into a firm line while he considered his words. "Spirits need space to stretch and grow, instead of staying trapped inside a body all the time. Spirits that stay trapped become stagnant, and if you're stagnant," he tapped his chest with his fingers, "you can't grow. At least, that's what my mother told me."

He cleared his throat after a moment and continued. "That's what dreams are for. When a person dreams, their spirit leaves their body and travels to another place. A spirit plane. Everyone goes there, but some people can go farther. Deeper. Can send and receive messages."

"You think *I* can do that?" A harsh laugh shot out of my throat. "No, that's *insane*! The kind of madness that Dr. Kane was talking about. I'm not crazy, I'm *not*!"

I pressed my spine into the rough pillar behind me, willing myself to melt away.

"It started months ago." Abel continued like I hadn't said anything. "I was meditating, and suddenly there was this voice at the edge of my mind. '*Help*,' it said, over and over. So I answered." He shrugged, a stiff gesture that had him flinching away from my stare. "I had been on my own for a while, and it felt good to hear you. Felt right."

"You were just having a dream, Abel. That has nothing to do with me!"

"You're right, I didn't know if it was just a dream or not. Not at first. But—I don't know how to explain. It didn't *feel* like a normal dream. So I decided to try to talk to you, figure out where you were and what you needed. You didn't answer, but I could hear you so clearly. And I *felt*," he balled up a fist, wrenched it against his chest. My own sternum felt cracked and raw. "And then I was alone again. I kept searching, though, listening for that voice. For *your* voice. Eventually it paid off."

I forced myself to take another breath, crushing the cuts on my palms until they burned. I didn't want to hear this story, didn't want my reality to tilt and shift yet again. But at the same time I was riveted, frozen in terrified curiosity as he continued.

"I was sleeping the next time I heard you, a couple weeks later. Faint at first, muttering about feeling trapped. About wanting to escape and be free." He moved again, lifting and dropping one broad shoulder. "It resonated with me. So I *reached* back to you, encouraged you to open up to me."

A memory of Abel and I sitting on a rock together blitzed through my mind, made my heart pound. *'That's it, Pen. Open to me.'*

"And you did. You showed me where you were. You told me about *him*." A feral snarl ripped out of his chest, and I was grateful he wasn't looking at me.

He knew. Stars Above, he *knew*.

Dismay settled heavily on me. Old guilt and shame burned through my veins, curdling in my gut. He knew about Ben, about what he'd done to me. About what I'd done trying to appease him, trying to survive. The last few months in Arberdon had been the most brutal, the most demeaning, the most...

I swallowed hard and tried to shut that mental door. *Right here, right now, I am alright,* I reminded myself. *Right now I am safe.*

"Your voice was so clear, I followed it straight to Arberdon and waited for you. And the whole time we stayed in contact. Or, at least, I *thought* we had." A bitter laugh coughed out of him. "I thought we were friends."

"We're not friends." The words I'd been repeating to myself shot out of my mouth and filled the space between us. His eyes locked on mine and I flinched away from what I saw there.

"I know." The resignation in those two words settled between us like a mantle.

He kept talking, his mouth moving over words I couldn't comprehend. Behind unseeing eyes my mind reeled.

My memories. My humiliation. My pain. My anger. My *pathetic* existence. Abel had seen it all. How much had he seen? How much had he taken from me?

The sound of his voice filtered in as panic bloomed to rage.

"And then, when I finally found you, you *shot* at me. Which is what I deserve—"

"*Shit!*"

"Pen?"

"No!" I barked, drawing my knees in tighter. "No, you don't get to call me that. Why did you even start calling me that?"

His usually stoic expression crumbled, revealing an openness so raw it was painful.

"Answer me!"

"From you, P– I got it from you. It's what you call yourself." He tapped his temple, in case I didn't understand.

Some inarticulate sound clawed out of my throat. I pressed my head into my knees, tunneling my hands through my hair and pulling hard.

That was *my* life story, to choose to share or not. Indignation throbbed in my chest. How he must see me: the poor, stupid, beleaguered girl from Arberdon, not even enough sense to survive *inside* the walls.

And, dammit all, why did that bother me so much?

"Why have I never heard of this?" I demanded, latching onto something I could stand to talk about. "Spirit expansion and dream whatevers?"

"Everyone who dreams visits the spirit plane. Most people just forget on the way back into their bodies."

"Of course they do. So you believe everyone is just, what? Having conversations with strangers while they sleep?" I scoffed, leaning into the anger.

"No." He frowned in my direction but took my tone in stride. "Being blessed to Dream Walk, it's not common, even among my people."

"But you do the dream thing," I accused.

"No," he shook his head. "No, I can't go into other people's dreams."

"See—"

"Minds are better defended the farther into the spirit plane they are." He took a deep breath, turned so I could see his face better. My protests died in my mouth. "I'm not a Dream Walker, but I can *skim* the surface of an open mind. And nudge a thought or two. I'm a Persuader."

Realization came over me slowly, and I wasn't sure if I wanted to laugh or cry or scream.

"When I finally confronted Ben. And ran away." I snarled, my voice low. *And other times.* Every time my mind felt cloudy, every time I felt disconnected or fuzzy. "*Stars,* Abel, have you been controlling me?" The words curdled, my arm clamping over my folded middle.

"No! No, I can't control anyone, and I don't want to control you."

"But you *nudged* my decisions. You *nudged* me to do things that helped *you.*"

"I thought you knew I was there! I thought you had invited me!"

"What difference does that make?"

"I thought we were talking, not that I was Persuading!"

"You!" I stabbed at the air between us, unable to articulate any further. "*You.*"

"I'm sorry—"

"Just stop."

"I never wanted to hurt you."

"Actions have consequences!" I spat, hating that I used his words as soon as I said them. Hating the pain I saw etched on his face in response, but unable to stop. "Whether or not you meant to hurt me, you did. My entire life is in shambles, I'm a fugitive on the run, and *you* are responsible!"

I swiped my hand across my cheek, hating the dampness there. Doubts crowded in my mind like carrion hawks around a carcass. What were my own decisions? What was real? How could I trust—

"Last night I asked you how you knew about my dream."

Abel bowed his chin to his chest and clenched his fists in his lap.

"You knew because you *were* there!"

He nodded, never raising his gaze. "Your mind entwined mine, pulled me in with you. It was really dangerous; what happens in the spirit plane has physical consequences. We could have both died."

Which explained his volatile reaction when he woke up. I shook my head, getting back to my point.

"I asked you how you knew. And you said it wasn't a big deal." Another tear tumbled across my lips and I swatted at it angrily. "You Persuaded me, didn't you?

"I—"

"*Didn't you!*"

"Yes, I did."

"Why the hell would you do that?" The words scalded my throat, ripped at my heart.

"I panicked! I realized you didn't know me, that I had everything wrong about us, and I didn't know what to do!"

"That's an excuse, and you know it!"

"I'm sorry,"

"I don't want to hear that! *Stars*, I can't even stand to look at you." I wrapped my arms around me as tight as I could, the torn pads of my fingers digging into my shoulders, and buried my face against my knees. My breath hitched and I bit the inside of my cheek as hard as I could stand.

I was such a fool. Such an idiot for trusting that I knew what was real, that I understood what was happening around me. No doubt Dr. Kane would catalog it as more evidence of my mental instability. Yet again I'd miscalculated and blindly followed when I should have made different choices, should have remembered that I couldn't trust anyone but myself.

I hated the salty tears that refused to stay inside, the damp breaths that marked my weakness. Holding myself rigidly, I waited for the storm to pass, waited until I had a tether on my roiling emotions. Until my ragged breathing was under control again.

When I looked up, Abel had moved to the edge, one long leg hanging down the side of the pillar. He held his spear in his left hand, his right hand clenched in a fist on a drawn up knee. His back was stiff as he smothered the sound of his own grief.

And I don't care, I insisted, rolling onto my side so I faced the rock pillar. I tore a blanket from my pack, pulling it up over my head. Eventually exhaustion took me.

* * *

I opened my eyes in the Dark Room. My flame wriggled free of my chest and hovered nearby, flickering faintly.

I didn't bother getting up.

"Go away."

The flame dashed frantically around my head, leaving light spots in my vision. I gritted my teeth and swatted at it.

"Go. Away." I turned my back and closed my eyes again, and darkness embraced me.

Chapter Sixteen

We got moving again hours later, when I couldn't find any more rest and before the sun rose. We moved in silence, my mind feeling like one of the dried out plant husks periodically tossed across the ground by the wind. Rootless. Drifting. Lost.

I had nothing to say to Abel, and he wisely kept his mouth shut. Despite our jarring confrontation, nothing had really changed. I needed a guide to help me survive the wilds, and Abel needed help collecting his message. We would use each other and go our separate ways. We were not friends.

I rubbed a fist over my chest, willing its incessant ache away. The sky above The Sands stretched for miles in all directions, bending down to kiss distant horizons. Rivers of twinkling stars, twisting and winding across a backdrop of black, reminded me of my flame, of the Yeshua tree that I remembered from strange dreams. And it made me bitter.

I refused to be controlled; by Ben, by Abel, by some mystical flame entity in a spirit plane.

I heaved a frustrated sigh and readjusted my pack on my shoulders, my skin still raw and sensitive. I embraced the physical pain, letting it pull me out of the thoughts pacing in my mind.

The chill night air licked at my fingers, tunneling under my nails and leaving fissures along my knuckles. The wind ripped through my clothes and burned my skin. Each breath was a stabbing pain in my throat. The shivers down my spine almost made me long for the heat that would come with the sun.

We ran out of water sometime in the night, the end of the desert nowhere in sight. My lips were cracked, my throat sticking to itself. I didn't even have enough spit to swallow and soothe my tongue.

My feet were heavy, my boots dragging trenches into the ground. My eyes, no doubt bloodshot, blinked blearily against the gritty air. It was fatigue that made them ache, exhaustion that still pounded through my sinuses. It had nothing to do with all the crying I'd done when my world crumbled yet again. Nothing at all to do with the grief that was still lodged in my chest.

Abel's spear stretched across his shoulders, held in place by a limp wrist on each end. He scanned as we trudged, scenting the air across his tongue.

I scowled when my chest tightened, that Stars-forsaken attraction still pulling at me, and dropped my gaze to my feet.

Hours passed, the sky growing lighter as dawn crept closer, and all thought concentrated down to my desperation for water. Just a drop on my tongue. Just something wet in my mouth. Dear Stars, just something to swallow.

The sky looked the same. The landscape looked the same. The Sands stretched on forever; there was no escaping.

"Hang in there." Abel's raw voice cracked. I didn't reply, just continued dragging myself after him when he tilted his head and turned aside.

My temples were pounding, my heart pulsing sluggishly under my tongue. I was exhausted, shivering, and desperately thirsty. My entire body was one throbbing mass of pain and I just wanted to lie down and let it end.

Abel dropped clumsily to his knees in front of me, wrestling his arms free of his pack. Stabbing his spear into the ground nearby, he started to dig with single-minded determination. I circled to face him, squinting weary eyes, watching his powerful shoulders pounding into the sand over and over. I wiped my lips with a dry tongue, tasting sand.

After a minute I dropped my pack and painfully got on the ground in front of him. He flicked a glance in my direction.

"Don't touch me," he rasped, never breaking rhythm. I didn't even have the energy to be offended.

I worked in with his pace, diving my hands into the ground while he was pulling back. The sky blossomed in bruises, purple and blue, as the sun finally began to rise. Color erupted from the horizon, and with it came the merciless heat of the sun. My skin prickled, trying to sweat, as warm wind ripped past my ears and tunneled under my shirt. My hands were raw, grains of sand embedded under my nails, by the time Abel moved.

"Stay back now," Abel warned, grabbing his spear to poise over our trench. The gold of his eyes could rival the sun, burning with intensity, as he stared into the hole and waited. The wind buffeted by as I rested on my heels, my arms hanging limply across my thighs.

Something moved inside the hole, the sand shifting ever so slightly. But it was enough.

Lightning fast, Abel plunged his spear into the ground and wrestled out a Rock-snake. He lifted it high, impaling it on the blade, as its thick length coiled in pain. Three sets of short, clawed feet spun, scratching for purchase at the air.

"I see your sacrifice." Abel murmured to the creature before jerking it sharply and tossing the head with its venomous glands aside. Taking the carcass from the spear, he plunged his mouth into the bloody wound of its neck and swallowed.

I gaped. It took a moment for coherent thought to filter into my brain.

So *this* was a brutal *Unnat*. Filthy, blue-tinted skin, blood in his teeth. Awesome in power and violence. Before me was a display of my people's worst nightmare.

"Here," Abel turned to me, silhouetted by the blinding dawn, blood dripping from his beard. Sharp eyes fixed on mine.

I reached out and took what he offered.

The blood did not taste good, but it was wet. I was equal parts relief and revulsion, but I knew that without fluids I would die. After a few pulls the neck was dry. I handed the snake back to Abel when he reached for it and forced my stomach to submit.

Abel sliced another section off the muscular length, passing it back to me. Back and forth we went, slicing medallions off and removing organs as needed, sucking the meat dry. I grew accustomed to the sharp tang of the blood, the thick heat of it sliding down my throat. I licked my sandy fingers, not willing to waste a single drop.

I see your sacrifice, I thought, looking at the pile of Rock-snake Abel was collecting on one of his tunics. Shifting my eyes to him, I took in his haggard appearance. Blood coated his face, spattered the front of his shirt. His hands were dark with it.

But instead of being horrified, I felt something far more compelling. Something that furrowed my brow and made me want to soften the grim line of his mouth. And once I let myself feel it, once I got out of my own head enough to realize, I couldn't *not* feel it. I was worried about him. Concerned how my harsh rejection, made out of fear and meant to protect me, might actually harm him.

Something tight and toxic loosened its grip inside my chest. The simmering fire of my anger sputtered as the sun continued to rise, as I finally let go of my own limited perspective.

Would I have done anything different without Abel's encouragement? I had already known I was in danger in Arberdon, with Ben hounding my every act and word. The reality that I had to escape him somehow was apparent long before I took action. Regardless of how I did it, there would have been consequences. The fact remained that running away was the decision that I would have made anyway; it was the decision that protected my family from the fallout.

Had Abel wronged me? Or had he responded to my request for help, even though I hadn't known I was asking?

"Your hair's growing." I commented, noticing how the scars decorating his scalp stood out. He looked at me like I'd startled him, a palm running over the fuzz across his cheek and onto his head.

He let his hand drop as our eyes met. We studied each other quietly as I collected my thoughts. I had to get this right because, as much as I wanted to cling to my anger and the defense it provided, I knew we couldn't keep traveling together without clearing the air. And if I was being honest with myself, I didn't like the dissonance between us.

"I'm mad at you." I said finally.

"Yes."

"Not for me being here, because it was my choice to run away. *Mine.* I own that. But you lied to me, manipulated me, when you knew it was wrong. If we're going to work together, you can't break my trust like that. Don't get in my head again."

"I won't," he replied quickly. "Not unless you ask me to."

"I won't ask, but I don't know when I'm doing it. So if it happens again, you can't try to hide it from me."

"You're right."

I nodded, struggling to my feet. "Let's go before we start attracting Flesh-beetles."

Relief, a brief smile, lifted the corner of his mouth as he bundled up the Rock-snake remains and we got into our packs.

We walked through the early hours of a new day, collecting whatever sticks or plant husks we came across as the sun climbed the sky. The apprehension I felt toward Abel the night before was gone, my mind catching up on the fact that every other part of me recognized him as an ally. I couldn't deny that his presence felt comfortable and familiar. Safe. It was hard to maintain the distance I felt should be between two strangers on an unlikely journey together.

Except no, we weren't strangers. It was a disconcerting realization, like I was stepping into a friendship formed between two other people. Would I ever remember those months we spent together on the dream plane? Or were those memories lost to me forever? Did he recognize me as the friend he knew, or did he now feel like I was an imposter wearing his friend's face? While I felt like I'd had pieces of my narrative taken away, he'd clearly lost a friendship that was as important to him as it was confusing.

Rock pillars scattered across the land, giving a reprieve to the monotony of the landscape, but nothing could distract from the increasing heat. Not even the middle of the day, and already my skin felt drawn tight, my eyes struggling to focus through heat waves that shimmered up from the ground. The only sensible option was to make camp at the first opportunity, which had us veering off our steadily Northward path to hole up inside one of the rock pillars.

The huge pillar, buffed smooth from years of wind and sand, had a fissure along its side just big enough for a person to squeeze into. Abel paused at the opening, scenting the air. When he was sure we wouldn't be stumbling into danger, we moved inside.

The air was warm and stagnant, but the shade was enough to have me tripping forward in relief. I closed my eyes so they could adjust, letting my fingertips trail along the walls to guide me. The rock was as smooth as polished wood, and cool to my touch in the shade. When the walls opened up wide enough to pull away from my fingers, I opened my eyes.

"Oh my." I breathed.

Shades of red, yellow, and gold swirled across the walls in glittering layers of rock. Pockets of sunlight drifted down from the unseen sky high above us, radiating like beams from a lantern. The sand floor was smooth and cool, only our steps disturbing its surface.

"What is this place?"

"I don't know. But I'm grateful."

Abel moved to one of the undulating walls and ran his palm across its curved surface. I wrapped my arms around myself as I watched him, smoothing a hand down my ribs, my feelings a confused jumble in my chest.

But sorting through them would have to wait. We had more urgent things to worry about, like surviving The Sands. Mentally I shook myself, moving farther inside to gratefully drop my pack and stretch my legs. Sitting down against the wall practically had me groaning in appreciation as I pushed my fingers into the soft sand.

Weariness pressed against me with insistence, and I surrendered without fighting. My eyes closed as I listened to Abel move through the large, twisting rock room, trying to track him by sound alone. The shift of his weight. The rustle of his clothes. I reconstructed him in my mind, giving life to every edge and slope and scar. A feeling low in my belly started to coil.

Listening that carefully, and without the pressing need to travel or immediately drop to sleep, had my attention right back on that messy knot of emotions. There were the obvious ones, like residual anger and shame that my private history wasn't as private as I had thought. Embarrassment and guilt for not recognizing Abel when he clearly put a great deal of value on our friendship.

But there were also ones with less bite and more thrill, like curiosity and amazement. I could hardly believe how far I'd made it from Arberdon, in no small part thanks to Abel. There was solid gratitude and unformed hope for what I'd make of my future. I didn't have names for all the subtle, soft things I felt for Abel. Things that felt like a full breath on a fresh day. The tight squeeze of your belly right before you start to laugh from your soul. The vibrating, intimidating energy of looking down from a great height.

"Tell me something." I blurted.

"Hmm?" He was circling slowly to my left.

I shrugged, picturing his movements. Trying to differentiate which foot he was on helped distract me from a flutter of embarrassment.

"Something about you. Something you don't share with anyone."

The flutter was threatening to turn into a whole flock of embarrassment inside me, but I held myself still. I wouldn't take the question back. I wouldn't apologize.

Once the idea of our shared history settled into my mind, I couldn't ignore how it changed everything between us. Recounting our interactions since we 'met' in person had me cringing; how much of our animosity was fueled by hurt feelings, confusion, and misunderstanding? I tried to imagine what it would be like if Randall didn't recognize me; worse, if he treated me like an enemy the next time we met.

Well, I could start again. I *would* start again. If I wanted to grow a new body and a new life outside Arberdon, why not a new mind while I was at it? I wouldn't remain ignorant of Abel. He knew about me. It was time for me to put aside my prejudice and learn about him.

His steps slowed. Stopped. I didn't hear him move for long moments, so I opened my eyes and found him staring at me.

The blood all over him was brown and caked with grit, as neither one of us had cleaned it off yet. He'd lost weight over the past week of traveling, the veins along his arms standing out against harshly defined muscles.

His features softened slightly and he nodded to himself, laying his spear down on the sand. Keeping some distance between us, he used the wall to lower himself to the ground, stifling a groan of his own as he did.

I studied him as he leaned his head back, propping his forearms on his updrawn knees.

"I never knew my father," he began like he was retelling a story. "He died before I was born. Didn't just die; he was killed. He'd gone too far from the clan, left the safety of the deep forest. He should have known better."

"Executors." I murmured when he fell silent. He sucked a deep breath and continued.

"My mother died when I was fifteen. And it was my fault." He cleared his throat, his voice raw. "I killed my mother as surely as if I'd pulled the trigger."

"Abel," I gasped, shocked and honored that he chose to give me what were clearly his most painful memories. Because he knew he carried mine. As much as our unique partnership confused and frustrated me, decisions like that proved he still counted me as an ally, respected me enough to make himself vulnerable. Even if our friendship was vastly different from when I'd been dreaming. "That can't be."

"Yes. *Yes* I did." He gritted his teeth, his lips pulling back in a snarl. "I'd gone too far from the clan. I should have known better." His voice caught. "And then I killed her."

One of those nameless, soft feelings twisted inside my chest as I watched him. The lost, guilty look on his face reminded me so much of Missy when she was younger and learned how Mother had died. She'd blamed herself for taking Grandfather's daughter, taking Father's bride. Even though she never knew the woman herself, she felt her absence by the empty space in our family.

I never left Missy alone in those vulnerable moments, never let that self-hatred take root. I made sure she knew how much Mother loved her, how much we all loved her. That no one blamed her, least of all our Mother.

And even though I knew better, even though he had made his position on touching abundantly clear, I leaned toward Abel, my hand reaching out instinctively.

"Stay away from me!" Abel shouted, stumbling to his feet.

My hand fell back to the ground heavily as I stared at him.

Traitorous appendage.

Confusing emotions.

Ungrateful Abel.

"I'm sorry." I muttered, fisting my fingers in the sand beside my hips. "I'm not trying to make you uncomfortable. I wasn't thinking—"

"No, you weren't!" He cut me off with a snarl. "How many times have I asked you not to touch me?"

"None! All you do is shout at me!"

"Because you don't seem to get it—"

"I don't get it!" I snapped back, staggering to my feet. "I don't. You say we were friends, but you don't act like it. How can you consider me a friend if the *thought* of me is so repulsive to you?"

He drew up, firming his lips and looking down his nose at me.

"Nothing else to say?"

An expression I couldn't name flickered across his features before he glowered at his palms. Turning abruptly, he pounded a fist against the stone wall and escaped to some other place I couldn't see in the winding rock enclosure.

I wanted to charge after him, fume and fury at him. I wanted to wrap my anger around me like a shield, keep him at a distance while we traveled, and then be done with him. But the thoughts soured in my gut as soon as they formed.

His behavior was completely wrong for someone who claimed to be a friend. Someone who traveled to Arberdon because I asked for help, someone who waited around and kept me as safe as he could *after* I'd tried to shoot him. If I paid attention, and let go of my own hurt feelings long enough to consider his perspective, I might be able to figure out what his deal was.

Knowing that was the better path, the *friendly* thing to do, didn't soothe my hurt feelings, though.

I scrubbed the blood off my skin with sand until I was raw.

CHAPTER SEVENTEEN

I'd gotten myself clean, or as clean as I was going to get, and changed into different clothes, bundling up the bloody ones to be laundered later. Assuming we ever made it out of The Sands. Then, brimming with exhaustion and more complicated feelings than I knew what to do with, I'd taken a blessedly dreamless nap.

When I woke, I felt him before I saw him. His presence seemed to charge the space, electrify the air. The skin along my neck and arms prickled, awareness sizzling through me to flutter in my belly. I cracked my eyes open and saw Abel seated across from me, his spear leaning casually against the wall beside him. He'd gotten cleaned up, too, though he still hadn't shaved. His head was bowed as he leaned against the wall, his dark hair loose and tumbling around his shoulders.

As though he sensed me watching him, his golden eyes flicked in my direction. I thought I saw his gaze heat, his lips part on an inhale. Like he was tasting me on the air. An answering burn ignited inside me, a tight reeling in my chest that would have the power to draw us both—

He cleared his throat abruptly. "Are you okay?" The wall above my head became incredibly interesting.

I closed my eyes and pushed myself upright, using the time to collect my thoughts, remind myself that my resolve to be a friend wasn't affected by whatever attraction was trying to grow in me, fueled by stress and dependency. His form was appealing. There, I'd admitted it to myself.

That was all. There wasn't, there *couldn't be*, anything else. The thought of touching me horrified him, for Star's sake. Not that that would ever happen, even given the opportunity. The point was, I could be a friend without needing to touch him. And that started with communicating better.

"I'll be honest, it hurts when you snap at me like you did earlier. It's like every time I try to be decent to you, you have to explode and act all revolted. *'Don't touch me'* this, *'stay away from me'* that."

His eyes widened, his mouth opening. I raised a hand and plowed forward, figuring it was better to air it all at once.

"I'm not looking for an apology or anything, because I think you should only apologize for accidents, or things that you won't do again. And clearly you're not going to change, so—"

"Physically," his strangled voice reached my ears. "I meant physically."

I barked a laugh, shame burning up my cheeks. *Stop trying. We're not friends,* I worked at convincing myself, *no matter what happened between us while I was dreaming.*

"I'm fine. An idiot, but fine. You?"

I looked up and caught a mix of expressions before he shuttered himself away behind a calm façade.

"Fine." He nodded. "I'm glad you're *fine*. I...forget myself around you sometimes. And earlier, with the Rock-snake, I—" he growled and spun his hair into a knot on top of his head, packing away whatever he was going to say. "I'm really glad you're okay."

I shrugged, digging into my pack for a length of cloth binding. I wrapped it around my head to press my hair back from my face. It was getting voluminous enough to tickle my ears and pester my eyes, stiff with sweat, dirt, sand, and Stars only knew what else. I couldn't wait to shear it off again.

"I'm glad you thought of blood. I would be dead or dying out there somewhere otherwise," I waved a hand toward the exit. "It wasn't so bad." I pulled my lips into a smile as I tied off the end of my binding.

He rubbed at some dried blood stubbornly clinging to the cracks on his fingers, his mouth pressed into a thoughtful line.

"Want to learn to make a fire?"

"Yes." I said, my smile becoming genuine. I knew a peace offering when I saw one. "Yes I do."

We separated out the sticks and brush we'd collected based on type. Smaller sticks we broke into hand lengths, and some we shredded into a loose pile.

"Make your pyramid here," Abel instructed as he dug out a shallow pit in the sand floor. I put some loose material on the bottom, followed by the smaller sticks and brush, and the larger ones on top. It wasn't very big, but it would have to do.

Abel took some of the loose material and bunched it in his fist before putting it under a flat, thin piece of wood. He took a rock from the ground and notched a small divot in the wood. Then he got a long, narrow stick from the pyramid I built and pressed one end into the divot, right on top of the nest of loose material.

"Hold the flat piece still, and drill the stick like you're trying to get to the nest." He showed me what he meant. "You do it." He carefully handed me the sticks, mindful of keeping his fingers away from mine, and set the nest in front of me.

I got started with enthusiasm, sliding my palms over the stick as fast as I could. If I could start a fire without a Flame-start, I would be better able to care for myself. I would be able to make my own heat, cook my own food. I wouldn't need to use Executor tools inside Executor cities just to survive. It felt like a step toward my new life, like hope.

It wasn't long before the shine wore off.

"This is impossible." I declared, cursing at yet another splinter while my palms flew back and forth over the stick.

"You're making progress," Abel chuckled.

"Sure, laugh at me, Abel." I scowled without heat, which only made him laugh harder.

"You're really doing well. If I can do it, you can."

"I'm half convinced that you *can't* do it, and just think this is a fun joke or something." I muttered.

"Hand it over and I'll do it, then." He challenged.

"No!" I snapped, moving my hands faster even though he hadn't moved to take anything from me. "No, dammit, I'm going to do it."

"Go ahead then."

"Stuff it, Abel."

"Today, maybe?"

"You!" I looked up at him sternly. Light lines crinkled at his eyes and softened his mouth. I definitely didn't pay attention. "Hush."

He raised his hands in surrender and kept quiet, watching me with a curious, exciting light in his eyes.

Don't go there, Pen, I scolded myself. *It's just infatuation. There's no light for you in his eyes, it's just that strange glow they always have.*

I turned my attention back to starting a fire, and fortunately Abel let me. Or maybe unfortunately, since without his distraction I became increasingly aware of my own discomfort.

My palms burned with friction. My neck and shoulders burned from the awkward position. My entire world narrowed down to the sticks in front of me.

Then suddenly, "It's smoking!" I could be embarrassed by my squealing later.

"Yes!" Abel crawled a little closer, edging into the space beside my right leg. Gently he added his breath to the smoke. "Keep going!"

More smoke spiraled up from the sticks until I broke through the flat piece into the nest beyond.

"Perfect!" Abel grinned. "Now bring it to life."

I cupped the loose material in my hands, blowing gently on the smoking embers. Color bloomed, red and orange curling around the loose material. *Just a little more,* I thought, tempering my breath so I wouldn't blow it out. Finally a bright lick of yellow fire sprang up from the cluster and I pressed it to the nest of material under my pyramid. A few more moments of blowing gently into the nest and the first sticks caught.

"I did it!" I leaned back triumphantly and smiled so brightly my face hurt.

"You did!" Abel agreed, a broad smile that showed his sharp teeth stretching across his face. "Yes, you did."

The beaming smile on my face faded as we regarded each other, morphing into something more tender. The air between us felt comfortable, like settling back into a familiar rhythm. I could have basked in that feeling longer, but the meager fire needed our attention if we were going to make use of it.

The smell of Rock-snake searing over the small fire made my stomach cramp painfully with hunger. It was burned to charcoal on the outside, barely cooked on the inside, and I was fairly certain I'd never had anything more appetizing. I ate quickly, the juices burning my tongue and fingers, but I wasn't willing to wait for it to cool.

Abel was already collecting his pack while I savored the fading light in the fissure after our meal. The colorful swirls shifted from vibrant hues to dull gray as the sun began to set.

Maybe it was not knowing where the path outside would lead, or maybe it was the truce that Abel and I seemed to have found in the cavern, but I didn't want to leave.

Doesn't matter what you want, I scolded myself as I scrubbed my hands clean with sand and smothered the smoldering remains of the fire. *The only way is forward.*

We shrugged into our packs and reluctantly headed back out into The Sands.

The sun hung low and heavy in the West. There were a couple hours of daylight left, but the worst heat of the day had passed. Unsated thirst clawed at the back of my throat, but we were fed and as rested as we could be. It would have to be enough. We walked side by side, Abel scanning the horizons and scenting the air as we went. Reminding myself that friends didn't stare, I let myself take in the unreal colors around me.

The sky shifted from blinding blue to gold before the Western horizon erupted in a blaze of molten orange. As the sun slipped down, yielding to the coming night, dark pink and azure stretched across the sky, pulling along a blanket of dark gray silk.

Twilight fell swiftly across The Sands, spilling diamonds in the sky and a chill in the air. It wasn't long before full night came, a scythe moon cutting slowly across the twinkling expanse. Wind whipped across the dunes, sand stinging into my cheeks. Thirst plagued my every thought, my breath rasping over chapped lips. I knew better than to lick at them, but the temptation was strong as the temperature continued to drop.

Onward we walked, heading due North as far as I could tell. Abel pointed out the Guide Star we followed; the one that would lead us out of The Sands. Its brilliance shimmered in the night, my neck craning to take in as much of the vast sky as I could. Despite the inhospitality, I had to admit that the desert was beautiful. Hostile, but beautiful.

Weariness was a quiet song in the back of my mind; I knew it was there, chorusing over and over, but I could ignore it as we hiked across the expanse. I did long for the sturdier ground of the forest, however; each step I took felt half wasted as we trudged.

Abel motioned for me to slow as we came to a rise, intensity burning in his gaze as he flattened himself and looked below. I followed his example and settled on my belly beside him, my heart hammering.

Look, he mouthed beside me, directing my attention to the dunes below.

It took a moment for my eyes to adjust, but when they did I couldn't help the delighted smile that crept up my cheeks.

A pack of Dune Canids, smaller but no less dangerous than their mountain cousins, danced in the weak light of the waning moon. Quiet yips and huffs of their laughter drifted up the rise to where we hid. My chest constricted in wonder and terror as we watched them. Wild abandon and power...*playing.* They leaped into the air, twisting around and prancing, massive paws swiping at each other. Sharp teeth latched onto necks, shaking mightily before darting off to start the game again. They were deadly. They were joyous.

My eyes wandered to Abel's face, to the unguarded pleasure that melted the harsh lines I'd memorized. To the dark brows that so often held a furrow; to the high cheekbones cradling slight lines by his slanted eyes; to the corners of his full lips that pulled up to reveal serrated teeth.

Like he was pulled by the weight of my gaze, he turned to face me. That reel in my chest started pulling again, a tight coil winding in my middle. I pushed my fingers into the sand beneath my chin, the texture shifting intoxicatingly. What *was* this longing that dug under my ribs and refused to be moved?

One side of his smile kicked up into a boyish grin, and my lips moved to copy him, not even fear of my reaction to him, fear of *myself*, able to resist. He tilted his head to the side, indicating we'd have to divert around the Canids. We backed down the rise and continued on.

I kept my hands wrapped on my straps, my eyes drinking in the vibrant bands of stars. I was *so far* from home, so far from anything I was used to. So far outside of my comfort zone.

It was mind-bending.

It was confusing.

It was amazing.

Some part of me still didn't think I was anything more than an isolated guard from Arberdon. The part that clung to the certainty of life behind the walls of my city, the part that quietly let others decide the right path. Carrying on with the already established status quo was comfortable.

But it wasn't satisfying. Certainly not now that I'd done the impossible. Now that I'd seen so much more of the world around me. I'd lived a life, however short thus far, *outside* of Arberdon's walls and expectations. And now, looking back, I could see them for the limitations that they were, however well intentioned. Limitations I had put upon myself, and then allowed Ben to layer more on top.

Maybe it had to do with getting acquainted with my own mortality so intimately. Or the boggling sensation of walking on the threshold between the sand and the sky. Whatever the reason, the thin edge of a choice became as clear as the stars that shimmered above me. If I was going to survive outside of Arberdon, as I had every intention of doing, I had to let go of that part of myself. I had to intentionally remove that isolated guard from my mind, amputate her doubts and leave them in The Sands. I had no idea what the right path was, but I knew with certainty that I had no hope of finding it if I kept thinking like a limited woman.

* * *

The night was still deep when we started looking for another place to camp. There was no water to be found, and I knew Abel was growing increasingly concerned. He glanced over his shoulder at me again.

"Sorry I'm so slow." I'd meant it as a joke but my voice fell flat. Everything about me felt flat, deflated under the oppressive thirst and fatigue that wrapped tight around me.

"I didn't say anything," he shook his head wearily. "How are you?"

I offered him a wilted smile. "Are you worrying about me, Abel?"

"Not just you," he grimly replied.

There were no other rock pillars to climb, just mounds and mounds of endless sand. My head throbbed while I crunched the grains of sand that had nestled between my teeth.

One more step, I urged my cramping muscles. *Just one more.*

My legs felt thick and heavy, unwieldy in the sand. Twice I slipped making my way down a dune, barely managing to keep my feet under me. After that Abel kept a firm grasp on my pack while we walked. That only worked until he started stumbling, too.

My body felt hot and uncomfortable, but I shivered with every gust of wind that chased us across the desert. I readjusted my pack again, trying to shake some awareness back into my mind. Beside me, Abel was muttering to himself.

"What did you say?" I slurred.

"It's got to be here, it should be here,"

"What should?"

"Wind-break. From before."

I squinted at his profile as we trudged toward Guide Star. "You came through The Sands before?"

He nodded once, his throat making a clicking sound as he swallowed.

"How?" It wasn't my most eloquent question, but fortunately he knew how to interpret it.

"Rover."

An inarticulate sound crawled out of my throat as I slipped in the sand. My muscles seized, incapable of reacting quickly, and I crashed to my knees. Abel, who was still clinging to my pack, tumbled in a heap right next to me. Dazed, and exhausted, we both stayed where we were.

"Why," I managed around the new sand in my mouth, "did we not bring the Rover?"

Abel pushed himself to his side, his hand disappearing into the sand. I felt like we were swimming in it.

"No gas."

I groaned, pressing a fist to my forehead. Which I immediately regretted as it poured more sand on my face.

"Could we not have gotten more?"

He leaned back, uncaring of the sand that was no doubt burrowing into his hair, and shook his head.

"Only runs on a special type. From the Chemist."

We lay there quietly for a time, looking up at the stars and trying to convince ourselves to move. The thought of pulling myself back up, of resettling my pack against my shoulders and trudging forward in the night, made me want to cry. I breathed through the impulse slowly, my brain finally processing what Abel had said.

"Wait, the Chemist?" I forced myself to sit up so I could study Abel's face. "You came from Terrah?"

"Not far from." He cracked one eye open and fixed it on me.

"Abel," I stared at him in bewildered confusion. What was he doing on the South side of The Sands if he came from Terrah?

He watched me, his gaze touching my features with weight I could almost feel against my skin. He shrugged a shoulder, looking away again.

Because I called.

He risked his life, crossed The Sands, moved into the woods outside my city and waited for me...because I called.

Guilt tugged at me, but I knew it was misplaced. Even if I had known that I was calling to Abel in my dreams, he made a choice to find me. He made a choice to leave his home, leave the place with answers desperately important to him, sacrifice his rover...for me.

"Abel," I said again, at a complete loss for words. "Why?"

My chest constricted, flexing with raw emotions that I didn't have the ability to process. I wanted to reach out and touch him, to see if I could make that tether between us real and tangible. But no, he wouldn't invite that. So I dug my fingers into the sand beside my knees and returned his stare.

"We need to move." He finally said, closing his expression and pulling himself to his feet. I sighed, not quite sure what had just passed between us, and struggled to my feet.

On we marched, the sand spilling into the cracks of my boots with every step, chasing after the Guide Star. Distant sounds haunted the dunes, drifting and dancing in the wind. The howls of Canids, the call of moon-birds.

What if we never made it—no, I wouldn't let that thought form. I focused instead on moving my leaden feet, pressing up one more dune and then on to the next one. Just as light began to touch the sky, just as I was about to give up hope of ever making it to the other side of The Sands—

"*There!*" Abel exclaimed with palpable relief.

I looked where he indicated, barely able to see the sharp edges of a structure nestled among the sloping dunes. I had never been so glad to see such an ugly building. We stumbled our way to the door and I helped Abel dig the sand away from the threshold. He didn't even remind me not to touch him, though I respected his space. Once cleared, Abel strained against the old metal door, forcing it open inch by inch.

The air inside was stale, the walls stained brown from sand. We slipped inside the small room, an observatory of sorts, and he shut the door behind us, wedging his spear through the handles to lock it shut.

Immediately I fell upon the shelves that lined the back wall, searching for anything that might be water. Jars and containers covered the surface, but none held any liquid. I trailed my fingers over old writing utensils, marveled over what used to be a pile of papers, and finally turned to Abel in defeat.

"No water."

"No," he agreed apologetically. "Didn't think to leave any. I was faster crossing the first time, with the rover."

"Right." I rolled my dry tongue around my mouth.

"Having shelter is good enough."

I grimaced, not saying anything. It had been over a day since either of us had had anything to drink. Shelter would not be good enough for long.

I finished my visual inspection of the room, noting the broken desk and chair that sat in front of a blackened screen.

"Is that a computer?"

"Just a monitor, and it's broken." Abel sighed, taking my pack from my shoulders and setting it next to his by the door. "Not worth moving it to sell for parts."

"What was this place?"

"Similar to the place we went before, with the Howlers."

"What?" I exclaimed, instinctively moving closer to him.

"There's nothing left living here," he was quick to assure me. "As far as I can tell."

"Comforting," I muttered, brushing off my arms. The corner of his mouth kicked up again. "Well, let's rest while we can."

He nodded. "We should make it out of The Sands the next time we travel."

"We better." I muttered, making my pallet and lying down.

Chapter Eighteen

I noticed the scent first; damp and verdant and alive. I pulled it into my lungs greedily, my hands sliding over the roots that cradled me. I cracked my eyes open and took in the shape of a towering trunk that disappeared into the darkness above. Tiny lights drifted around me, spots of living flame in the midst of the Dark Room.

With a gasp I bolted upright and scrambled back from the massive oak.

From Yeshua, my mind corrected instantly, the name full of fear and longing and awe.

"I'm not here," I muttered, wrapping my arms tight around my middle. "I'm not here, I'm asleep."

I didn't want to be a Dream Walker, but here I was again, traipsing like Abel had accused before, consequences be damned. How was I supposed to stop Dream Walking if I didn't even understand how I was doing it in the first place?

My heart slammed against my ribs, jolting from side to side before my own flame wriggled free to hover before me.

"No," I turned away and squeezed my eyes closed again. "I don't see you. I'm not here."

Voices whispered, wrapping around me and tugging at me, coaxing me toward Yeshua's trunk.

"No." I planted my feet, ignoring the hum that swelled as the voices continued. Ignoring the light that flashed behind my eyes. Fisting my clammy hands, I tucked them tight under my arms and tried to force myself awake.

I wasn't terribly surprised when, the next time I peeked at my surroundings, nothing had changed.

"Fine," I grumbled. "If I can't wake up, I'll just go somewhere else."

Decided, I picked a direction and struck out, jogging away from the clearing where Yeshua stood. Ducking into the density of the forest, I distracted myself by identifying what species I could.

Locust.

Maple.

Myrtle.

Aspen.

Rowan.

My steps slowed as I studied the last, some memory tickling the back of my mind. I felt drawn to the tree, moving close enough for the leaves to caress my face. Close enough to touch the bark.

A pulse pushed through my body, echoing up my arm and into my soul. Startled, I jerked my hand backward and turned—

Turned to face Yeshua, standing before me in the sacred clearing.

"What? No!"

I picked a different direction this time, running faster than before. No distractions, I warned myself. If I kept running long enough I was sure to wake up.

Weaving through the trees, I swatted branches out of the way. The limbs scratched at my skin and snagged my hair, but I wouldn't stop. Not until I'd found a way back to reality and out of the dream plane.

The small lights that drifted through the air swirled in my wake like dust motes, twirling haphazardly before settling again. The area brightened as they condensed, more and more of the mysterious living flames filling the air as I burst through a line of trees–

And stood face to face with Yeshua again.

"Argh!" I curled away reflexively, panic grabbing hold of my spine and flinging me in yet another direction.

I hadn't minded being in the Dark Room previously, but that was before I knew that it was real. That my soul had stretched so far outside my resting body that I was touching the minds of others. That I was communing with what could only be described as divine.

Sweat coated me, terror flushing my skin. I wasn't meant to be a Dream Walker. I was a farmer's daughter from a dusty southern city. Arberdon was all I knew, small and insignificant on the grand scale. I was a pathetic woman trying to run from her problems, just like I'd run away from—

"Penelope," the whip-crack of his voice cut through the trees. Instinct took over and I dashed behind a boulder, clamping a hand across my mouth.

His voice shifted through the trees as he continued calling my name, circling me and wrapping tight like a noose. I clasped a hand against my throat, assuring myself that I could still breathe. That I wasn't trapped in Arberdon.

"This isn't real," I assured myself. "This is just a dream."

Except that I was walking through a dream, possibly tangling my mind with the actual real, live Ben, and the things that happened to me in my dreams had repercussions in the physical world. My mind spun, fear tightening its grip on me.

What if he found me? What if he was also a Dream Walker? What if he overpowered me? What if—

"There you are."

"Ben?" His name strangled me, all other thoughts fleeing from my head.

"Penelope. I've missed you. Come here." Ben eased closer to me, his outline translucent and flickering. Like he wasn't fully present, or fully on my plane? He smiled, reaching both hands toward me. It was an offering.

It was a trap.

"No." I swallowed and pushed away from the tree. Put some more space between us. *"No, I'm not going anywhere with you."*

For a moment, he didn't move. Then the smile slowly faded from his face. His arms dropped to his sides. I shivered, a familiar knot forming in my gut.

"You think I don't see your games, how you twist things in your head?"

My breath hitched, those familiar words haunting me.

"Look what you make me do!"

I shook my head, backing away.

"Why aren't you wearing my ring?"

I couldn't inhale, my vision tunneling down to the fury on his face.

"Please," I gasped. "Stop it."

"Stop it!" He mocked, plowing through the underbrush after me. I shivered, memories accosting me. The smell of the barn, the taste of the dust in the air. The sharp edge of the workbench pressing into my belly.

"No!" I shouted, turning to run in the opposite direction. Maybe if I could get back to the clearing, get back to Yeshua—

I tripped and fell, tumbling in a heap to the ground.

"Give it up, Penelope." He laughed. "You can't hide from me. You know where you belong."

The words cut me, tore my horror out where I could see it. I clutched at it, the realization heavy and real and the anchor I needed. I couldn't go back, I wouldn't go back to the way I had been living before.

Be different, *I pleaded with myself, wiping my palms down my thighs.* You're not that woman anymore. You *can't* be her anymore.

Maybe I was just having a nightmare, built on fear and amplified by my memories. A dream inside of a Dream Walk. Whether Ben's mind was attempting to connect to mine or not, it was my *dream. All I had to do was change its outcome.*

How often had I told myself that if I stopped something much worse from happening, it would be okay? How often had I swallowed my words and protests, swallowed and swallowed until there was nothing left of me?

But I wasn't that person anymore, was I? I didn't want to be Penelope, Benjamin Joshen's property. I wanted to be...me. And for the first time in my life, I was going to figure out who that was.

"Go away." I said through gritted teeth, pushing away from the ground. "Leave me alone!"

"No," he snarled.

"Go. Away." I repeated, standing up on trembling legs.

"You're going to regret that." His sharp features, looks I once considered handsome, twisted with rage.

I pivoted to face him, forcing my shoulders back despite my pounding heart.

I ran away from home with nothing but the pack on my back and the belief that I could keep my family safe.

I braved the wilds, traversed The Sands, with the hope that I could have a different future.

I had survived Canids, Howlers, and almost drowning. I drank the blood of a Rock-snake and made fire with my hands.

I took the hard steps, would continue to take the hard steps, because I knew they were leading me somewhere better.

"Leave me alone." I repeated, curling my fingers into my palms.

His response was a snarl, but he hesitated. His image flickered.

A sharp laugh rang out of my throat, cut through the air between us, adrenaline giddy in my chest.

"How did I not realize?"

Benjamin Joshen wielded influence like a bludgeon in Arberdon. I let him control me for a while, for far too long of a while, but it was time to sever the cord. Take the lessons in perseverance and build something new.

Because, to a power-hungry man who needed to feel control, there was only one thing worthy of obsession.

"You're threatened by me."

I looked up at him and something in my face made him shift back a step.

He opened his mouth, ready to spew more hate, but I had heard enough. Hurt and rage and regret and hope boiled up inside me and I unleashed it, let it rip through me, pouring every ounce of who I was and who I would become into one massive mental push.

"Enough!" I flung out my arms, envisioning a door slamming shut and locking with him on the other side.

Blinding light seared my eyes, the whole world shaking with my voice. Every cell in my body hummed with resonance, vibrating with the energy that coalesced in the air. My bones shook, teeth rattling, throat tightening over the unbelievable power that swirled like a torrent. Power that wasn't mine, exactly, but I'd somehow channeled.

Eventually my breathing settled and my heart slowed as my vision came back into focus. The echo of my voice drifted and morphed, softening and changing into a thousand different unrecognizable voices that spoke as one.

Enough.

I turned, finding Yeshua looming behind me.

Whatever I'd done to shove Ben out of my dream plane took every ounce of energy I possessed. My legs quivered, finally giving out and depositing me at the base of the tree.

I let out a slow breath. Yes, it was enough. Enough running, enough hiding.

I looked up at Yeshua, at the fire that moved through and around her. I took in her impossible size and felt very small.

"Okay." I said, not sure what I was agreeing to but feeling relief at my acceptance all the same.

My fire came back to hover beside me, pulsing with waves of affection and assurance. I closed my eyes and welcomed the heat of it suffusing my limbs as it pressed back through my ribs. I laid my head down against the roots of Yeshua and finally, finally let go of who I used to be.

* * *

I peeled my dry eyes open, my tongue fused to the top of my mouth. Even breathing took a painful amount of effort. My whole body throbbed, my skin stretched too tight across my limbs. My stomach kicked, squeezing against nothing, had bile crawling at the back of my thick tongue. I tried swallowing, but there was nothing to swallow. Dismay cracked out of my throat.

I lifted my head slowly, my neck at an uncomfortable angle, and folded my legs beneath me. Just that slight movement made my head spin and my vision darken.

Abel was still sleeping, curled around the space I used to occupy. Close, but not touching. Something gentle struggled to bloom in my chest. I leaned in, nudging his boot.

"Abel." I croaked.

His lashes fluttered, molten eyes peering up at me without focus. For an instant his features softened as he took in my face, as his chapped lips wrapped quietly around my name.

"Pen."

My heart fluttered at the sound of my preferred name, my most intimate name, coming from him even as I steeled myself against inevitable loss. I had no business feeling the things he made me feel. I had no business being curious about what he tasted like. I had no business longing for the memories of him I'd lost.

But long for them I did, and I wouldn't hide from it any longer. It couldn't mean anything, but I let myself feel it all the same. Feel it, and then try to let it go.

He blinked, pushing back to a safer distance and rubbing his hands over his face.

"We need to find water." I stated the obvious, worried by how slowly he was moving.

"Right, yes." He pulled himself to his feet, staggering with a hand pressed to his temple.

"Go slow," I cautioned, fumbling to my own feet and lurching after him. *Stars,* even my eyes felt dry inside my head. I opened my canteen, licking the inner rim for any condensation that had collected. The slight dampness only left me more desperate.

Abel moved our packs and took his spear from the door, pushing it open against the sand that had collected at the threshold. Late afternoon sun slanted inside.

I took a shirt from my pack to use as a sun shield, preparing to head back out into The Sands. We didn't waste energy speaking as we gathered our things or as I rummaged through the items on the shelves one last time for anything useful. Of course there was nothing. When there were no other excuses to delay, I took a deep breath and we forced the door the rest of the way open.

The heat shimmied up from the ground, reflecting the sun's intensity. My muscles ached at the abuse, but there was no other option. It was either walk to water or die. A harsh wind skated over the dunes, making the heat more bearable. At some point my knuckles cracked and began to bleed. Progress was slow, exhaustion digging its claws into the both of us. A lone carrion bird twirled in the air high above, following us for a time. I grit my teeth and forced my legs to hold me upright.

Twilight painted the world in deep purples and golds. Ribbons of color bathed the sky, interrupted by broad swaths of the first stars of night. The temperature began dropping as we passed strange plants, their husks shrunken and cracked and covered with thorns. I could only hope it was a sign that we were making our way out of the belly of The Sands as we moved past them.

The Guide Star shone brilliantly as the day faded to deeper night, prompting a slight course correction. I didn't have the energy to worry about how easily we'd veered off course, only prayed we'd find more landmarks before the night ended. I moved a bit closer to Abel as we pushed forward, his grim determination no doubt mirroring my own. We both knew that there would be no stopping until we found water.

Over time, the plants grew a little bigger, a little more robust, and we could see where they started bunching together in desperate clusters in the distance. My feet moved faster, my muscles trembling with the effort.

Sand gave way to rock-riddled clay. My heart started to speed up in anticipation, both of us increasing our speed until, at the crest of the next rise, Abel turned to me with exaltation.

"Pen!" His eyes glowed in the darkness around us, and I embraced the happiness that bloomed in me when he slipped and used my chosen name again. "I smell water!"

I could have jumped in the air and hugged him, but remembered myself in time. Instead I did some goofy dance that startled a laugh out of Abel and left me breathless and smiling like an idiot.

We charged into the valley, skidding over loose stones. I forgot all about the sores on my shoulders and my tired muscles as we surged up the next rise, scrabbling with our hands when we needed to. The sound of crashing water reached my ears and I thought I would cry. I pulled myself up the last stretch, looking down into a rocky basin dotted with thorny trees. In the middle rested a dark pool, fed by a stream that burbled free of one of the rock walls before tumbling over a series of natural shelves and, eventually, into the pool.

I dropped my pack and scrambled down to the nearest rock shelf, landing hard on my hands and knees as I pressed my face into the puddle glossing its surface and sucked greedily. The damp seeped through my clothes, chilling me, making me feel alive again. My tongue rejoiced, my lips finally finding relief as I scraped the water into my hands and painted my face with it. I was barely aware of Abel bringing both of our packs down to a lower, drier ledge.

We did it! Giddiness and relief condensed in my chest into a ball of energy. My cheeks pulled up painfully, my chapped lips cracking at the expression, but I couldn't stop if I tried. A laugh bubbled out of my chest as I rocked back on my heels, flinging my arms wide. I didn't know if I felt like laughing or crying in relief, or dancing and jumping, but I had to do something with the energy buzzing inside me. Taking a deep breath, I shouted it out to the stars, basking in their glow.

"Here," Abel held out the blunt end of his spear, a smile in his eyes. I took his offered help to get down the slippery ledges. The inane happiness I felt was reflected on his face, and by the time I'd closed the distance between us I felt breathless and reckless.

"Thanks," I beamed, before jerking the spear away from him, spinning it and using the blunt end to push him into the water.

The startled protest he made before the water swallowed him was immensely satisfying. I laughed so hard my sides hurt and I thought my cheeks would crack.

But he didn't come back up.

And the night was very dark.

"Abel?"

I crept closer to the edge of the pool, cursing my stupid impulse. I looked for ripples, bubbles, anything to tell me where he might be. A string of curses left my mouth as I waded in, testing the depth with his spear. The bottom dropped off quickly and was too dark for me to see anything. I bent over, squinting my weak, human eyes.

What was I *thinking* pushing him into the water? There could be some water creature that *ate* large men in a single gulp, or a frenzy of blood-slugs to drag him to the bottom and suck him dry!

"Abel?" My voice shook with the horror of what I'd done. Cool water poured over the tops of my boots, drenching my feet. The ground under my treads was slick as I edged out a little farther, the water coming up past my knees.

"Abel!" I fought the rising panic, trying to think logically. He was strong and healthy. He was fine; he *had* to be fine.

But walking this far had taken a lot out of each of us. He'd lost weight and was dehydrated. And I held his weapon in my hands. Maybe he couldn't fight off whatever creatures were in the water. Maybe he hit his head when I pushed him and he was dead.

"Abel!" I screamed, not caring about what other dangers could be hearing me and heading my way. I had to go in after him.

I pushed the spear out a little farther, feeling the edge where the ground dropped off into black water. I pressed the spear down, trying to find the bottom, but there was none. Being careful of the tasseled end near my face, I pulled back to prepare to dive. My muscles strained, but the spear was stuck fast.

"What the—" I leaned forward, trying to see what I'd gotten snagged on.

My only warning was brilliant, burning eyes opening underwater right in front of me. A long, blue arm snaked out and snatched the gaping front of my tunic and I was airborne.

Water closed over my head just as I had the wits to scream, bubbles catching the sound and floating it away. Just as quickly, I was dragged back to the surface and took a deep breath.

"I've got you," Abel laughed as I blinked water out of my eyes. "Don't worry, I've got you."

His hands steadied the spear I still clutched, his legs treading water for us both until I could get my bearings.

I gave him a soggy glower and a dark chuckle vibrated out of his chest. Heat bloomed in my middle, surged over my cheeks, pooled in my core. We were very close, his legs churning with mine beneath the water's surface. My tongue slipped out, catching drops off of my lips. He tracked the movement, a deep hum rumbling out of his chest. His eyes were happy and intense as he searched my face.

"Are you alright?"

"Yes." I said petulantly, then laughed. "I asked for that." I released the spear and pushed back to float a bit.

"Yes." He laughed again, drifting closer, and I smiled at the stars.

We climbed out and made camp for the night on the edge of the oasis. Eventually. We had to have a water fight first.

H M DuVal

Chapter Nineteen

My boots were still wet and would no doubt rub blisters into my heels when we continued hiking north. I scolded myself again for pushing Abel into the water, but I couldn't help the smile that tugged at the corner of my mouth. Playing like that had been irresponsible, dangerous, and *fun*.

A flicker of excitement pattered under my ribs and I slid my eyes to Abel's profile. We were slowly drying, sitting near each other by the pool of water that saved our lives, as he used the careful application of a blade to scrape the hair from his face and the sides of his head. He didn't have a mirror or use the pool's warped reflection, just closed his eyes and knew his way by touch. Which gave me an irresistible chance to watch him.

There was nothing particularly interesting about watching a man shave, but I was enthralled. I hadn't had the opportunity, or cared to take the opportunity, to study him closely before. But now, well...

He sat barefoot with his pants rolled up his shins to wrap around muscular calves. His shirt was off so it could dry, the muscles of his shoulders and arms bunching and rolling as he rasped the short blade over his skin. I pinched my lower lip between my teeth, aware of the heat that crept up my neck.

His torso was littered with scars, including the healing welts from the Mountain Canid. Some were faint, thin lines like the ones that danced down his forearms. Others were gnarled masses of reconstructed skin, like the one that pulled taut over his right hip bone, or the one that capped the back of his left shoulder. I grimaced to think of how he must have gotten them, the pain they must have caused. Abel had clearly encountered death a lot in his life, and managed to escape it. It enhanced the respect for him I already carried.

The scars highlighted his strength and ferocity, but there was something undeniably graceful about him, too. The way his hands moved with confidence across the contours of his skin. It made me wonder what it would be like to have someone's hands move across my body with that kind of soft confidence. What it would be like to have *his* hands—

I clenched my fists and gave my head a good shake. I was exhausted, anxious, and relying on Abel to keep me alive. I wasn't naive enough to become blind to those factors. Recognizing that I found him attractive was one thing, but fantasizing was another. Any feelings I had didn't have to mean anything.

Couldn't mean anything.

"Do you ever get tired of doing your hair like that?" I asked to distract myself.

Abel looked up, golden eyes catching me and squeezing my chest for a moment. He'd finished with his shave and was wrapping the longer section up into a sloppy knot that flopped to one side. I grimaced and he laughed, shaking his head to make the mess wobble around precariously.

"Is that why you keep yours short? Because you got tired of dealing with it?"

I ran a hand across the top of my head, pressing into the springy curls as they dried.

"Nah. I like it short, but it does need to be cut pretty regularly or else I end up looking fuzzy. Like now, actually."

"You don't look fuzzy," he smiled as he took me in.

"And you don't sound like you're answering my question," I smirked, ducking my eyes from that gaze. *Doesn't mean anything,* I staunchly reminded myself. "Don't change the subject."

A considering hum vibrated in his chest. He took a deep breath, searched the stars for something, and finally pinned me with his eyes again.

"I don't know how to do anything else." He shrugged, turning his attention to cleaning his blade.

"That's not true, you had it braided before."

"If that's what you want to call it,"

"I never said it was a *good* braid."

We both chuckled.

"Well it was my first time," he defended, his skin flushing to a warmer color. I arched my brows suggestively, startling another laugh out of him.

"In that case, you needed to weave it tighter at the base. When I was younger I kept my hair long, and my mother would braid it. She told me it was like pulling yourself together at the beginning of each day—"

"—body, mind, and spirit." We finished together.

Water trickled over the rocky shelves into the pool, gentle ripples edging toward us on the shore. The stars glittered overhead, cool wind whispering through the thorny trees that bravely grew on the edge of The Sands.

And in that stillness, with the dark making the inches between us intimate and safe, I realized.

I had taught him how to braid. In a dream I didn't remember, I had shared memories of my childhood, of my Mother, with Abel. Which meant he carried the memory of my Mother with him, too.

Warmth swelled my chest, taking up more room than air. I sucked in a breath, watching his profile as he studied the sky.

"Abel," I crooned softly, savoring the way he closed his eyes with a flushed smile. "Were you trying to impress me?"

I'd meant it as a joke, but his skin warmed more across his cheeks and the bridge of his nose.

"No," he smirked. "Maybe. Seemed like the thing to do. Like a sign."

"A sign of what?"

He shrugged. "That I was listening."

It can't mean anything, I repeated to myself as that longing took root in me again, pulling at my middle and making me shiver. *He doesn't mean it like that.*

"Thank you for listening."

He smiled, without the bitterness that I had grown accustomed to, and settled back on his arms.

Maybe I wasn't the only one who had been smelted into something new by The Sands. The crossing had cost a great deal from us both, had almost cost our lives. But maybe that sacrifice just helped make space for something new to take root.

I took a deep breath, wrapping my arms around my knees for warmth. As we stared at the night sky the peaceful oblivion of my mind gave rise to an impossible thought. A terrible, immensely bad idea that I knew in my bones I was nonetheless going to pursue.

"I could teach you again." I murmured, knowing he would hear me.

He tensed, no doubt priming to snarl and move away.

"I'm not going to tackle you, Abel, relax." I carefully kept my eyes on the sky, like I wasn't watching his every move in my periphery. "I won't do anything you're not comfortable with. This is a no-pressure offer."

He was staring at me, eyes wide and conflicted. I was just about to rescind my offer, tell him to pretend I hadn't suggested it, when he spoke.

"You can't touch me." He whispered, the phrase lacking its usual vehemence. It sounded more like he was reminding himself. More like a plea.

I turned my head to study him, laying my cheek against my knees. His words were at odds with everything in his expression.

"What are you afraid of?" I whispered back.

Hunger. Fear. Indecision. They all occupied his features in turn.

"I could wrap my hands. Would that make you more comfortable?"

His chest moved on an inhale, his jaw working.

"And if you tell me to stop, I will. You know I will."

Finally he nodded once, decisively. I fought the urge to jump to my pack before he changed his mind, a thrill of excitement charging through me. Instead I took a breath, and then another.

"Okay, so I'm going to wrap my hands and braid your hair. Right?"

Another nod, this time with tight fists.

"Right?" I prompted again.

"Right." He parroted, eyes anxious as he took me in.

I dug out my cleanest pair of socks, though that wasn't saying much, pulling them over my hands like gloves. By the time I turned back to Abel he had two of his own shirts on and was about as comfortable as someone being sent to the Executor judicial court.

"Why don't you lean against this rock and I can sit above you on the ledge?"

We rearranged ourselves, me with my legs folded beneath me and Abel on the ground below. I picked the leather tie out of his damp hair, my hands shaking and compounding the difficulty the socks presented.

Get it together, Pen, I scolded myself. *You're teaching a friend to braid hair. It doesn't mean anything. It can't.*

Except I didn't do much teaching as I sectioned his hair into thirds, running the length between my palms and wishing I could feel it against my skin. As my focus narrowed in on making the weave uniform and smooth. As the silence stretched between us, full of my fondest memories of my Mother and wonder at the man sitting at my feet, and morphing the space between us into something far more profound than an attraction had any right to be.

I tied off the tail of his braid, stroking one hand lightly down the length of it that rested against my knees.

"There." I breathed. "That's how it's done."

He roused himself, sitting straighter and rubbing his hand across his face before studying my work.

"Thanks, Pen." His deep voice rumbled, and my pulse jumped.

"Anytime. I'll take first watch."

* * *

Leaving the pool of water the following night was hard, but we were both cleaned up and rested, though I still had sand in unfortunate places. I palmed my canteen to make sure it was still full, assuring myself that finding water again wouldn't be nearly as hard after leaving The Sands. It was time to move on.

The ground sloped steadily upward, becoming darker and rockier as we left the transition zone from the desert. After the flatness of The Sands my thighs were complaining, but the rest of me was thankful for hard ground to walk on and enough moisture in the air that I was sweating again.

Small, hearty trees and shrubs dotted the area, surging up from cracks in rocks and poor soil. Their leaves were small and thin, their branches covered in long thorns. Their presence indicated that the ground held more water than had been in The Sands...but not much. In the distance, under a murky haze of fog, the hulking gray shapes of the Hacknor Mountains cut off the horizon.

"Do we have to go over those?" I asked, frowning.

Abel shook his head with a chuckle at my tone. "Terrah is in the foothills just before them. Thankfully."

I nodded in thoughtful silence, my mind churning over where we were headed and what would happen next.

*Get into Terrah undetected. Blend in with the locals. Find the Chemist and make the trade for a message. Get the message to Abel. Go to ground for curfew and...**then** what?* We were only days from Terrah, and I still didn't have a solid plan. I wasn't ready for the changes that were coming, didn't feel remotely prepared. Giving up the security I had found traveling with Abel seemed impossible, even if it meant going back inside the familiar walls of a haven city.

Arberdon seemed so long ago, like a whole lifetime had passed since I tried to shoot Abel during my shift. I cringed every time I thought of it, and thanked the Stars and all of Yeshua's light that his reaction time was better than mine. My path had seemed so obvious then, but now I didn't know what I wanted.

Did I want to get lost in Terrah? What about heading back to Arberdon once enough time had passed that it was safe for me again? Could I even make the trip on my own?

I stole a glance at Abel, appreciating the braid that traced the back of his proud shoulders. Flexing my fingers against the urge to wrap it around my fist. Abel came from just outside Terrah; would he return there after I delivered the message? Would he be willing to escort me back to Arberdon? But what then? It wasn't like he could move into town. It wasn't like I could venture out to visit my...friend. I was likely experiencing the last days I'd ever be in contact with him.

Unless I opened myself to the idea of Dream Walking on purpose. But more often than not, entering the dream plane had me confronting Ben, or at least a specter of him. Maybe it was just nightmares born of memory. Or maybe he knew what I was and somehow hunted me while I slept. I shivered, pulling my sleeves a little tighter around my hands. I wasn't ready to analyze the repercussions of that possibility. Not to mention, Dream Walking seemed far too dangerous and complex to use merely for a social call. Especially since I hardly knew how I did it in the first place.

The stars began to fade as the sun came closer to rising. My mind was mushy after chasing my questions all night. And still I had no good answers, just an increasing melancholy as we came closer to the end with every step. My eyes were scratchy, lids threatening to stay closed with every blink.

"How much farther?" I gave into the weight on my eyelids, praying my feet kept moving in a straight line.

"Not much." Abel answered. "We need to get as close as we can to the forest before dawn."

I looked in the distance to the dark, fuzzy mass that blanketed the foothills of the Hacknor Mountains. The forest seemed impossibly far away.

"We're not going to make it. Well, *you* might," I corrected wryly, "But I'm not going to make it there before dawn."

He rubbed a palm across the smooth side of his head, scars crosshatching the skin. Not for the first time, I wondered how he had survived despite them all.

"We need shelter then. We're too exposed out here."

"Because there'll be more Executors the closer we get to Terrah." I finished for him, nodding to myself.

"That's one reason." Abel growled, quickly dropping his hand and saying nothing further. I didn't push him.

The land didn't offer up much in the way of shelter, so our only choice was to keep heading toward the trees as the sky began to blush eagerly, then surge with brilliant blue. My body hummed with fatigue as time doggedly passed. I lowered my lids again, peering at the ground periodically beneath my lashes, my mind drifting.

My breath deepened, my feet getting harder to pick up. Rocks skittered across the ground, knocked loose by my dragging toes, but I managed to keep moving forward.

My vision grew hazy, a dream spinning out of my mind and superimposing on the world around me. Somewhere in the back of my brain, I clamored that I shouldn't be dreaming, that it was dangerous and I needed to be careful...but the notion was little more than a flutter of awareness. It was soon smothered by the cocooning weight of exhaustion.

I saw trees in my waking-dream first and assumed I'd been pulled into the Dark Room again. The image was painted in gray, as insubstantial as the distant fog, save for one thing: brilliant orange light.

I focused on the four flames, small as matchsticks, and the images around them grew clearer: four bodies coalescing around the flickering lights. They crouched behind trees, peering around their cover to watch something intently. I willed myself to see what they saw, what danger they nervously gestured to each other about.

The dream shifted accommodatingly, zipping across space to show me two other faint flames drifting across a rock-laden field. I waited, somehow knowing my eyes would etch the shapes I was missing if I were patient enough. Slowly two more bodies formed: one tall and powerful, and one shorter with its flame trailing along behind it.

My foot caught on a stone and I stumbled, slamming back into my body with enough force to steal my breath.

Abel reached for me as I righted myself, stopping himself abruptly and clenching his hand into a fist. "Are you alright?"

"Yes," I managed, adrenaline making my heart gallop uncomfortably in my chest. "We're being watched," I hissed.

Abel took on a predatory stillness, only his eyes shifting to look for threats.

"Where?" His lips barely moved.

"I don't know." I said, copying him. "Somewhere with big trees."

He looked to the forest in the distance that was supposed to be our haven and he growled a curse. "Keep walking."

I moved up beside him, keeping my pace deliberately slow. "What are we going to do?"

"I'm working on it." He muttered absently, his brow furrowed tightly as he considered and discarded options.

The sparse, rocky plane leading to the forest didn't have any place to hide. In front of us stood the forest, and the scouts who had spotted us. Behind us stretched The Sands.

Abel cursed again.

We needed a plan. I made myself stumble on the rocks, throwing myself onto my hands and knees again. Abel crouched beside me as I maneuvered to sit with my back to the forest, using the opportunity to secure the knots on my boot laces.

"Maybe I'm just being paranoid," I shook my head, hardly believing myself. "I'm not really sure what happened. I could've been imagining things. Daydreaming."

Abel scoured the edge of the forest over my shoulder. "Let's assume you're right, regardless."

"We *can't* go back to The Sands." The emphatic words tumbled out of my mouth on an exhale. I sighed in relief when Abel agreed, but that didn't solve our immediate problem. I thought back to the wisps of the waking dream, the details fading like fog in sunlight.

"They weren't right in front of us. They have an angle on our position, somewhere to the east."

Abel's lips pursed. "How many?"

"Four." I rubbed my temples roughly, wondering at how Abel could take me seriously. I felt ridiculous, but couldn't shake the urgency pounding through my veins. "Scouts, probably."

"We'll go in the opposite direction. Try to get lost in the forest before they can report back and mobilize in force."

"Won't work." My stomach tied in knots as I cinched the ties on my boots. "Standard scout protocol to send two back, and leave two to keep following us."

"It's our only option." He said grimly.

That was true enough and I didn't have any better ideas, so I pushed to my feet and we kept moving.

As we drew closer, the forest stretched out to greet us in a crescent shape. We veered to the west, forcing whatever scouts were watching us to break cover across the open field, or take the long route through the woods to keep following us.

Exhaustion evaporated as adrenaline clamored through me, making it hard to maintain the same pace we had set before. The back of my neck prickled with awareness and I struggled not to turn and scan for the scouts among the trees. Was it a standard Roving patrol, or something else? My hands were greedy for my shotgun, itching to take it down from where I'd stored it on top of my pack. But one shotgun and one glorified sharp stick with tassels wouldn't do much against an Executor patrol. And I didn't relish the thought of adding murder to my growing list of criminal charges. I grimaced and twisted my fingers in the straps of my pack, keeping my eyes glued on Abel in my periphery.

Rocks crunched underfoot, the dirt between them dark gray in color. The air smelled a little heavy, a little damp, and carried a tang on the breeze. Birdsong swelled as we approached the trees. And bringing an unexpected pang, cicada screams cut through the air, the constant drone seeming to lift up out of the forest and carry me all the way back to Arberdon.

What was I even doing out here, so far from the walls of my city? Who did I think I was, tromping across the continent? I never would have gotten in this situation if I'd never left home. I never would have had to suck blood out of a dead Rock-snake, or almost drown while being chased by monsters, or learn about being a Dream Walker.

You never would have survived, either, I reprimanded myself, squashing the useless self-pity before it could take root. *Right here, right now.* I set my jaw and put one foot in front of the other.

Sweat coated my palms and I wiped them down the front of my tunic. If I understood what I had done in that strange almost-dreaming state, I could keep an eye on the people following us. But no matter how deeply I took a breath, or how I chanted *peace* or *sleep* or *calm* over and over in my mind, I couldn't slip back into that waking dream.

I gritted my teeth and exhaled, trying again while tremors shook my fingers. My heart felt jittery, a band of fear clamping around my chest and squeezing tight.

"Steady." Abel murmured, sliding a glance my way.

"This is killing me." Not knowing where they were. Not knowing what they were planning. I couldn't anticipate them, couldn't prepare myself to respond, couldn't control the variables. A familiar feeling of being trapped coursed through me, and I hated it all the more.

The forest loomed as we crossed the distance, deep shadows weaving between the trees and promising a respite from the heat that continued to climb with the sun. Chills danced down my arms even as sweat streaked from my temples. My mouth was dry and my throat clammy.

"Almost." Abel whispered, reading my anticipation. I inhaled slowly and forced my feet to maintain our leisurely pace.

Individual trees became visible, separating out from the mass of the forest. The trees were a deep green, almost blue, and covered in needles from pointed tops to flared bases. The undergrowth looked scraggly and sparse, very little sunlight capable of reaching the forest floor. It would make for easier running.

"Glancing blows from the trees will scrape, but don't run straight at a tree."

"Thanks for that sage advice,"

"We'll have to climb one once we have a safe lead, but I'll help you," he continued, ignoring me.

I nodded, tightening my shoulder straps.

"Move in front of me. Don't look back."

I scraped my tongue across my teeth, forcing myself to swallow. I shrugged my shoulders, resettling the weight of my pack.

I passed him as we stepped into the young, outermost reaches of the forest, nudging long fronds of tree branches out of my path. Most of the needles were soft, but underneath the foliage true thorns grew close to the skeleton of the tree. I smarted my fingers a couple of times before I figured out the trick of gently pressing the branches aside. Abel's warning about the trees started to make a lot more sense.

"Get ready," his low voice rumbled, keen eyes searching around us. We strode on like we hadn't a care in the world as the trees began to grow larger. "Wait until the trees are thick enough to hide us."

I kept my eyes trained ahead, picking out the path I would take. The air became cooler, the sound of cicadas more insistent. The ground became softer, our steps cushioned by discarded needles and other gently rotting detritus. I tugged my straps a little tighter, just for good measure.

"*Now!*" Abel hissed, and I was already flying.

Unnatural

274

CHAPTER TWENTY

I danced between boughs, trying to avoid direct impact with any of the branches. The hidden thorns scratched and tugged at my clothes and pack, but I tore through the trees like I was running for my life.

Which I likely was.

The trees pressed together, long boughs squeezing in on me as I plunged further into the woods. I hunkered down, turning away from the thorns as best I could, and plowed on.

I was aware of Abel cutting a blunt route behind me with his staff, leaving a more obvious path to attract the scout's attention.

"Keep going," he tossed at me before veering off and leaving me on my own. My heart seized and I had to remind myself that he usually traveled by himself. It made sense for us to split up; he could travel faster, lay a false trail for the scouts, and catch up with me after. It would be fine. He would find me.

The sharp burn of shallow cuts coated my skin, but I didn't bother checking the damage. I couldn't afford to go any slower, and the only path through was the one I made with my body.

Light filtered through the trees eerily, making me see shapes in the long shadows they cast. My arms pumping, thighs burning, I kept my eyes glued on the path ahead and pressed on.

The trees matured as I crashed toward the heart of the wood. Huge trunks surged out of the ground, the lower branches shrinking before fading away entirely. The branches from above, feathered with needles and thorns, blocked out enough light to stunt the younger growth. It was good, because I could run freely without cutting myself. It was terrible because I had no cover.

I ran, praying Abel's plan would work to distract the scouts. Praying I could find a place to take cover before I was discovered. Praying he would return to me soon.

Sweat burned in the shallow cuts on my exposed skin. My muscles burned with acid. My lungs burned for more air. I was desperately ablaze.

A flicker of light off to the side caught my attention, there and then gone again. A glimmer of something warm and bright coming from the dark of shadow.

A flame.

I turned toward it, not allowing myself to second-guess the impulse, and dodged fallen branches and ancient, moss-covered husks of wood. In front of me stood one of the largest trees I'd ever seen, almost as wide at its base as...

Yeshua! My heart surged with each thundering pulse. *Yeshua! Yeshua! Yeshua!*

A chill snaked down my spine as I ran toward the dancing spark. Yeshua had roots even here, when I was awake? Was this even real, or some elaborate dream-scape that any minute I'd lurch upright from and quickly forget about?

Did it matter?

Around the far side of the massive tree, the trunk split open to reveal a chasm large enough for me to hide inside. Without stopping to think, I plunged into the darkness after the flame.

Abruptly the spark vanished and I careened blindly in the sudden dark, catching myself against the heartwood of the tree. My palms scraped against the tiny, soft thorns that sprang out from the tree even here, injecting a tingling sensation into my skin. I didn't have time to worry about that, however.

"Where did she go?"

I glanced around as a new wave of adrenaline kicked into my blood. The scouts! I couldn't leave the tree without being spotted, and it was only a matter of time before they stumbled upon the crack in the trunk where I hid. Somehow I had to disappear.

I looked up, to where an abyss loomed above me.

Gritting my teeth, I stretched my arms out and pressed my palms firmly against the wood. Almost instantly, a shock surged down to my elbows. My shoulders strained, lifting my body until I could press my boots against the walls as well.

It was hard, painful progress, but I forced my way higher into the tree. The sides of the fissure came closer together the higher I went, making it easier to wedge myself in. I moved carefully, taking particular care of where I placed my hands. I had long since lost feeling in them.

"Did you check in here?"

The voice was louder, nearby, just outside of the tree. I froze, locking my arms and legs in place and praying that it was enough, that I had gotten high enough and wouldn't be seen.

Below me, footsteps approached. I didn't dare look down, hardly dared to breathe. The sound of the steps changed slightly, paused, and then moved on.

"I don't see anything." The voice got quieter. "We can't check all the..." The one sided conversation trailed away.

I held myself still, my arms trembling with effort though I couldn't feel a thing below my shoulders. Waves of burning numbness surged over my skin and down to my bones. I was thankful for the thick soles of my boots; at least I had one set of limbs I could feel.

I slowed my breathing, counting breaths until a minute had passed. Then two. The tingling absence of sensation was becoming painful, curling over my shoulders and into my neck. Deciding to get down before I fell down, I prepared to descend.

A shock of pain lanced my hands when I pulled them free from the wood. I clamped my teeth over the gasp, smashing my lips together and forcing myself to continue breathing slowly. I managed to straighten my fingers, crushing them against the tree again before I could think too much about it.

The shock that sliced through my hands each time I moved had me thinking of the time I'd gotten too close to the cook surface of the stove when I was younger, the sharp cut of pain that borrowed under my skin. It had only been for a few chaotic moments, but the pain had continued long after I scrambled to the sink to dunk my palm in tepid water. The damage from such a relatively mild burn lingered for days.

I pushed the memory away. Worrying about the state of my hands would have to wait until I got back on the ground. Focusing on my breathing, I moved my hands again. Pressed into the tree again. Again. And again.

Getting down took more effort than getting up had. The numbness tickled the base of my ears, made my throat feel strangely uncoordinated when I tried to swallow. My back was ice and fire, my arms were dancing with pins and needles, and my *hands*. My hands were agony.

I whimpered with relief when my boots touched the ground and cradled my palms to my chest. Moving to the faint glimmer of light that came from the crack in the trunk, I forced myself to look at the damage.

Blood.

Thick, red ribbons wept down my wrists and between my fingers. The meat looked like something from the butcher's counter. Thorns clung to my flesh, were embedded in the webbing at the base of my knuckles. I'd lost a nail at some point.

"Okay," I breathed out slowly to control my stomach. "Okay."

I didn't have time for nausea. Pushing back the panic and bile that threatened to climb up my throat, I focused on what I could control. The thorns had to come out, but I couldn't use either hand. Pulling my lips back from my teeth, I brought the palm of one hand to my mouth.

The taste and smell of my own blood roiled my stomach. Sticky sweet sap mingled with the gore, and I worked slowly and carefully. Who knew what would happen if I swallowed the stuff.

Pull. Spit. Curse. Repeat. My awareness narrowed until all that existed was the pattern and the pain. By the time I finished I was shaking and sweating. Rubbing my face against the shoulder of my shirt to remove the blood, I tested my fingers. Another curse ripped out of my throat and I stopped trying. My hands had become rigid, locking into claws.

I nudged my canteen with my elbow until I managed to knock it out of its holster against my leg and onto the ground. My arms were heavy and slow to respond, but at least I could still move them. I crouched, holding the canteen upright between my feet and using friction from my forearms to unscrew the cap. I filled my mouth, holding the metal container between my tingling forearms, and spat a stream of water across each palm until the worst of the blood had washed away.

My hands would be useless for at least a couple of days, and tender longer than that. I wrapped my brain around that limitation and tried to maintain my calm. I wouldn't be able to use my gun. I wouldn't be able to climb. Feeding myself would be difficult. Foraging. Getting into my pack. Changing clothes.

Stars Above, how was I supposed to stop infection?

I exhaled another curse and closed my eyes against their burning.

It would be okay. I'd made it this far. I wasn't going to let a hand injury prevent me from making it to Terrah. To whatever life I would make for myself after. This was a temporary setback.

I hoped.

I managed to knock the cap back on my canteen with my forearms and screw it on tight enough, but getting it back into my leg holster was a different story. I wasn't about to waste precious time on an impossible task, and I would absolutely not leave my water behind, so I folded my body awkwardly on the ground, balancing between my knees and one elbow. I scooped the canteen to the side of my breast and held it in place with the underside of my arm, the muscles of my shoulders tingling sharply in protest. It would have to do.

The scouts were still searching the surrounding forest for us, so staying in the tree that they'd already passed over might have been the safer bet, but I needed to find Abel. *Urgently*, I grimaced, making a heroic effort to stop looking at my hands.

I took a deep breath and peered out into the forest, scanning for movement and listening for any sounds. Nothing seemed out of the ordinary, birds and bugs singing their songs around me, so I eased out of my shelter. I oriented myself with the weak light that filtered through the trees, pointing myself north toward Terrah. I would head in that direction and hope that Abel would be able to find me along the way.

Progress was slow as I picked my way carefully through the foliage, trying to leave a minimal trail. I was thankful to the mature forest with its high branches. At least I could walk without brushing up against any more of the awful dagger-trees.

I hunched over my hands, doing my best to ignore them, and listened for anything large enough to be a threat. Cicada screams sawed through the air, blending into an audio haze as a prickle of numbness closed over my throat. I swallowed compulsively, just to make sure I still could. A bird screeched as it exploded into flight nearby, the rustle of its feathers sounding far away.

Ferns and other shade plants blanketed the ground, unfurling from the rich earth. Their soft fronds reached up my legs, stroking at my wobbly knees. The pungent scent of crushed leaves and conifer needles filled my nose. Earth and forest and damp. It reminded me of Abel and I pressed my eyes closed against their prickling burn. I couldn't afford to stop. I forced my thighs to lift my heavy feet, trudging forward through the underbrush. My chest hurt and I sucked a shaking breath into my lungs.

My body felt unwieldy, my feet heavier, harder to pick up and move. I stumbled, the world spinning in a confusion of color, and suddenly the ground was gone. My scalp tingled, and the light peeking through the far-away tops of the trees wavered. A blanket of green folded over my vision, cocooning me in verdant shade. Numb fingers traced down my chest and spread outward.

My heart throbbed slowly.

My gut quivered.

My eyes went numb, and then I was gone.

CHAPTER TWENTY ONE

I knew without a doubt that I was in the Dark Room even before I opened my eyes. There was something different about the dream plane that was getting easier for me to identify. It felt bigger, wilder than anything I could ever experience awake. I lay flat on my back, my palms pressed against soft ground that pulsed and trembled with divine life. Roots rippled under my body, cradling me.

"Yeshua."

A shimmering pulse answered, there and then gone again.

"Yeshua?" I called weakly.

Light flared, flickered, touched every inch of the enormous labyrinth that was the sacred tree, then faded to darkness again.

I tried to sit up. Couldn't.

I dragged a dry tongue across cracked lips.

"Yeshua?" I forced my voice out a little louder.

Brilliant light ignited in the heart of her, surged down her roots, engulfed me. Then just as quickly, the light faded away again. As my eyes adjusted to the deep darkness that followed, I saw that my own flame hovered beside me.

"Hey." I murmured, grateful for its familiar company.

I'm not sure how long I lay there, watching as my flame flickered, bobbing on air currents I couldn't feel. My eyes grew heavy, a sense of peace filling me from the roots below. I could stay right where I was and fall asleep. Finally find rest. My lungs lifted on a deeper breath and I felt myself sink a little more into this place of spirits and dreams. Invisible tethers anchored me, pulling my limbs down heavily, relaxing my spine.

And yet, I couldn't shake the sense that there was something I needed to do. My brow furrowed. I worked my mouth until I remembered how to form words.

"I need—" What? What did I need to do?

There were no tasks that needed doing in this place at the foot of Yeshua. No urgency to get up, go, do, survive. The reprieve was welcome, and staying still inside the peace that seeped into me was so very tempting. I could just exist, wrapped up and becoming one with the love and light that saturated the very air of the Dark Room.

Holding onto thoughts and ideas was becoming more difficult. And yet, even with every care stripped away from me, at the very core of my existence, there was a pulse. A compulsion to complete what I'd set out to do. A need to get up and go after my purpose.

*Why am I here? Those same words had come to me days ago, one of the first times I remembered entering the Dark Room. I hadn't gotten a clear answer at the time, only a sense that there **was** a purpose for my being here. And the only way I would learn that purpose was if I chose to seek it.*

My body was too heavy to move, but I reached with my mind. Reached into my memories and tried to dig up something familiar.

"Follow the tap root," my mother's voice, almost forgotten in my memories, whispered across my ear. "Follow it all the way down, Penny-Girl."

Moisture gathered behind my eyelids, pooling and spilling down my cheeks. I wanted to stay in the Dark Room. Stay where I could hear Mother's voice, stay close to the woman whose life and death shaped so much of who I was. It had been so long since I could clearly recall what she sounded like, what she smelled like. The shape of her smile and the comforting weight of her arms around me. I breathed in, pulling the longing and the love inside of myself.

And then I breathed out again.

Mother was a part of the Dark Room. She was safe, loved, comforted and, I believed, had been since the day she died.

In my memory, I could see how young I was with a clarity I hadn't had before. How I lost both of my parents the day I gained a sister. How well-meaning friends and neighbors offered platitudes and what food they could afford to part with, but none of their offerings could fill the gaping hole in my chest.

Father had been devastated. Barely holding himself together. I had no way to comfort him in his depression. Grandfather withdrew, gone most of every day to work the land, to tend the crops and livestock. I wasn't strong enough to go with him.

But I was strong enough to wrap my arms in love around the bundle of my sister. I was able to strap her to my side where she felt safe and comforted. And, in offering her those things I lost, I managed to regain some for myself.

Taking care of Missy became a large piece of my identity from that day forward. It was up to me to protect her, up to me to be a good example for her, up to me to have the answers she needed. Even if I didn't have the answers I needed for myself. And even though she didn't need me in recent years the same ways she did as an infant, I never stopped trying to take care of her. To take care of everyone I loved. But when did that transition into not taking care of myself?

I shut my eyes tighter, giving in to the impulse to sink just a little deeper. I couldn't move, could barely think. Somewhere on the physical plane I was certain my body was dying. My connection with my body, with the world I knew and understood, seemed about as substantial as smoke. A gentle breeze and all of that would drift away.

But this place was real. This Dark Room full of mystic fire and power and endless potential surged through me and lifted my soul. I sighed, letting myself drift a little further.

The ground beneath me rolled, roots groaning as they pulled free of their entombment and curled gently around my body. Twigs tickled, combing through my short crop of hair and tracing along my skin as I moved over the ground. Closer and closer the roots pulled me, passing me from one sinewy length to another, until I slid to a stop at the very base of Yeshua.

I cracked my eyes open, peering up through her towering height at the network of her branches. There were so many paths, so many connections and bifurcations, it was impossible to map them all as they spiraled away into oblivion. My mind struggled to comprehend her magnitude, so I gave up. I didn't need to understand her to be in awe of her. Mesmerized, I watched tens of thousands of lights float gently through her branches. In the quiet beauty of that moment, I decided to let her take care of me.

"Yeshua," I eventually murmured. "Why am I here?"

The ground trembled beneath me, a torrent of whispers rising on the wind. My ears rang with the intensity, my helpless body somehow cocooned from the quaking earth. With a shudder and moan, the mighty tree twisted and bent, curling and compressing but somehow never shrinking, until a lithe column of radiant fire stood beside me. The brilliance of that light burned my eyes, though I didn't want to look away. Long tendrils of fire drifted around the form, rippling like water. What might have been a face, but had too many eyes, smiled down on me as a hand with startlingly long fingers rose up and covered my face.

My heart stuttered, my breath locking tight in my chest. Dazzling light seared my eyes and I blinked against it, wincing, but even with my eyes closed the light burned through. After-images danced in my mind; faces and places I'd never seen or imagined.

An old woman.

A rowan tree.

A desk with tools.

Executor fire.

Chains.

Flowers.

It was too much, too fast, the chaotic blur of images ripping through my mind like a storm, churning and demanding and consuming.

Four plots in a cemetery.

A Mountain Canid nursing her pups.

An old grave.

A river.

Snow.

A mountain.

A crying baby.

As suddenly as the onslaught started, it ended. The images faded from my mind and darkness remained.

My heartbeat slowed, echoed by the throbbing of my own flame in my chest. I opened my eyes again, looking up at Yeshua illuminated, sparks and flames dancing through the air around her branches. Her radiance surrounded me, consumed me, bolstered me. I gaped in amazement, not caring about the tears that continued slipping down my cheeks. She was truth. She was power. She was love. She took my breath away.

"Pen!"

* * *

"Pen!" The urgent voice tugged me awake.

Pain swamped me as awareness settled into my body. My skin felt flayed, my head pounded. My tongue was fused to the roof of my mouth. I struggled to open my eyes, only to find them sealed shut with crust.

A dismayed sound croaked out of my throat and I struggled feebly. The roots wrapped around me tightened.

No. Not roots. Arms.

"Drink." The familiar voice ordered across the shell of my ear and relief suffused every cell in my body. *He found me!* Relief, a wet whimper, sobbed out of my chest.

Something that smelled like compost touched my mouth and I gagged, turning away.

"*Drink.*" The voice was firmer. "Swallow it, Pen, or I'll Persuade you and take the consequences."

A strong hand cradled the back of my head as the liquid touched my lips again. It filled my mouth, loosening my tongue, surging to my throat. My stomach kicked, tried to expel the foul stuff, but he wouldn't let me go.

Abel.

The canteen stayed pressed to my mouth, the hand holding my head just so, until some slipped inside of me and down into my stomach.

Heat bloomed in my chest, blossoming outward as the vise I hadn't realized was clamping my lungs shut eased and I wheezed a breath. The canteen returned, forcing more of the stuff into my mouth.

"Swallow." He growled quietly.

My throat worked. The drink stayed down, though just barely. I couldn't feel my arms and I couldn't keep my head upright. But I could breathe, sucking noisy gasps into my chest.

I fluttered my eyelids again, trying to see.

"Shh," Abel placed a damp cloth across my face. "Your eyes are swollen. I'm putting a poultice on them. Let them rest."

His arms shifted beneath me, jostled. The rustle of plants being brushed aside. My head swam, lolling as I subsided against his chest. The frantic beat of his heart under my ear was soothing, like his scent. He stiffened when I pressed my face into him, breathing as much of him as my tight chest would allow. I drifted off to the cadence of his walk.

* * *

"Drink."

The command pierced into my clouded mind again. The canteen pressed against my mouth. I scowled, turning my head away.

"Dammit, Pen, work with me!" Abel's voice, though quiet, was tense with worry.

The sound of night creatures filled the air. The wind caressed my face lightly, full of the scent of green things and earth. I cataloged more sensation as awareness returned. The heavy weight of my legs draped over Abel's lap. The burn of my skin down my shoulders and back. The hunger that clawed at my belly. I squirmed, trying to move into a more comfortable position, but my body felt disconnected and unresponsive.

"Stop that," Abel hissed. I froze, trying to get my body soft and pliant again. "Drink." He repeated when I'd quieted.

I shook my head as much as I could.

"Pen, *please* drink."

"Piss." I groused, pressing my lips into a thin line.

A surprised laugh huffed out of his chest. "It's not piss, and you know it."

"Wa...ter." I suggested.

"Are you negotiating?" Relief and amusement colored his tone, his arms pressing tighter for a moment. "Tisane first, then water."

I capitulated, choking the nasty liquid down and chasing it as quickly as I could with water. My throat spasmed, small spurts of fluid trying to climb back up and out my nose.

"Ugh." I worked my tongue and swallowed, aware of myself enough to realize throwing up would mean throwing up *on Abel* and I really didn't want to do that. Again. Plus, he'd probably make me drink more of the stuff if I didn't keep it down.

"I know." I felt the heat of his arms snake around me again, burning over irritated skin that made me writhe uncomfortably. "Sorry," he grunted, readjusting me once he was standing.

"Pack?" I murmured to his collarbone.

"I've got them." He replied, taking a deep breath and relaxing the grip of his fingers where they bit into me.

I frowned, still not satisfied. "Gun?"

Another relieved laugh, more felt than heard, rolled against me. "I've got it, Pen. Don't worry."

I was too exhausted to worry, so I let my head rest against his shoulder and counted his heart beats until I was asleep.

* * *

The next time I woke up, I felt dirt, cool and damp, beneath the side of my face. Rocks pressed into my tender back. The overwhelming numbness from before had retreated down my neck and shoulders, leaving my hands and forearms ghosts to me. But the feeling that I did have was enough.

I moaned as pain swamped me, crashing in heightening waves as awareness settled back into my bones. A cloth pressed firmly over my mouth, my bleary eyes snapping open in surprise.

My vision was horrible, fuzzy and undefined, but I recognized Abel's outline above me. On top of me. Covering my body in the dirt.

I sucked a breath through my nose and blinked, trying to clear my sight as my heart kicked over inside my chest and heat charged over my skin. He pulled his hand back, wrapped in linen, and pressed it over his own mouth. I nodded, the top of my head bumping into our packs.

With one hand, Abel pulled one of the blankets from his pack, covering us both from head to foot.

The blanket and the nearness of Abel's body were stifling. Sweat trickled down my chest and between my shoulder blades, igniting discomfort across swatches of irritated skin. I clamped my teeth on my lower lip and forced my breath to keep moving through my lungs.

We were under some sort of crack in the ground. Bare, rich earth stretched out all around me, filling my nose. Behind Abel, the pale gray of dawn showed through a jagged opening that looked like jaws. Cicadas, that constant pulse of the forest, droned hypnotically. Songbirds stretched their morning voices. The rustle and scuttle of smaller animals indicated we were alone enough for the time being. Though I couldn't believe that would be true for long. Only a dire situation would have Abel going to ground in a bolt hole with me.

I stared into his incredible eyes, mere inches away from me, focusing on him instead of the discomfort that twisted into my skin. Trusting him. He breathed with me, silently matching inhale to exhale. The pain lessened as I pulled him into my lungs. I curled my tongue over the flavor of him on the air, letting myself savor his scent in my mouth.

Something had shifted between us at the pool, and shifted further when we were separated in the woods. I didn't know what it was, but the change was undeniable when we were pressed close together, exchanging air. I felt that reel in my chest start pulling again, subtle but no less profound. The attraction taking root started to bloom gently.

And this time I knew Abel felt it, too.

His lips parted, his mouth wrapping around my name soundlessly. He held himself back, the careful space small but insurmountable. I fought the urge to move, to shift, to satisfy the deep ache of pain by sinking into him. I would never take what he didn't give.

There.

The snap of a twig. The silence of the birds. Only the cicadas continued to screech, unperturbed by a new presence. Abel stiffened, his gaze sharpening as he listened carefully.

Tense moments passed as I shifted my blurry gaze over Abel's shoulder. The blanket blocked most of my view, the shadowy darkness and distance to the opening making it harder to see, but I could tell where the light filtered in. And I could tell when a set of legs eased through that light.

One. I mouthed for Abel's benefit.

The legs progressed slowly, thoroughly, melting through the foliage like magic. I held my breath, adrenaline cranking through my system. What would we do if they found our tracks? What if they decided to look deep into the hole? What if—

A second pair of legs joined the first outside of our shelter.

Two. I formed the word carefully with my lips. Despair dug into my chest and tightened my throat.

Abel held himself rigid, his vibrant eyes tracing my face like he was trying to memorize it. Desperate fear distorted his features and I felt the same terror pounding in my veins. This could be it; our last moments together. My lips twisted against a sob.

I took a slow breath, pulling the scent of Abel inside me again. Straining my eyes to see him more clearly. Wishing that I'd had more time. To return home. To make amends with my family after running away. To figure out who I was. To learn more about the incredible man *yet again* positioning himself between me and danger. We'd gotten through so many impossible situations together, our luck was bound to run out.

But maybe not quite yet?

I eased my breath out, imagining water pouring over my head, tunneling through my hair, licking at my raw skin. Urging myself to remain silent and calm, to become invisible to the scouts outside.

Oh Stars, each pulse of my heart desperately chanted, *oh Yeshua, oh Stars please.*

Somehow I followed my exhale away from my body, drifting to the side out of my pores. I felt stretched thin, stuck uncomfortably between two places. My spirit or essence or whatever and my body didn't quite occupy the same space like they should, like images on thin paper that didn't line up quite right. When I would've panicked at the thought, I kept moving air through my lungs that tasted like Abel.

I was on the verge of something, some knowledge that I could almost realize. There was something I could *do* all stretched out, I was sure of it. But I couldn't grasp the slippery idea. When I tried focusing harder, I fell heavily back into my body, stifling a gasp.

One of the pairs of legs crouched, pulling down a torso built like a tank to block more light. I froze, praying the dirty blanket would do a good enough job camouflaging us. I counted the rushing beats of my heart until the torso finally straightened and both sets of legs moved slowly and silently away.

We stayed in the dirt, pressed together, motionless, waiting for the sound of birds and rodents to return. And then we stayed longer, until the sun passed its zenith and started slanting in the other direction.

When Abel finally eased out to scent the air and look around, I tilted my head back in the dirt and thanked the roots for hiding us. Relief had my heart stuttering and a giddy wash of chills surging over my skin.

"Thank the Stars," I breathed, fear and gratefulness and adrenaline filling my chest to the point of pain. "Thank Yeshua."

My mind flooded with images of what would have happened if we'd been spotted. The scouts would have shot on sight, like we were taught to do in Arberdon. My gut clenched. Abel would have tried to protect me, but I doubted even he could dodge two guns at close range. I tested my fingers, managing to shift them slightly before searing pain cut through the numb haze of my hands. Unable to move or defend myself, I would have just been laying there, completely useless, waiting for them to collect me.

Would my arrest warrant have made it to the Executors on the other side of The Sands? If I'd been recognized, I would have been strapped to a rover and shipped to confinement faster than I could say "Mercy." Within days I'd have been returned to Ben's jurisdiction.

A shudder worked its way through me and I shut my eyes against the fear. We *weren't* spotted, and I needed to focus on what was real. Worrying about what could have happened was a luxury we didn't have. We needed to keep moving.

Abel leaned back into the hole, dragging the packs out one at a time. I shimmied around until my head was angled toward the opening, then dug my heels in. The ground scratched and tore at my back, but I gritted my teeth and started making slow progress.

"I've got you," Abel murmured before hooking his hands under my shoulders and tugging.

"*Knees!*" I wheezed sharply as pain exploded across my back. He immediately released me with a curse and an apology that I barely processed through waves of pain that radiated up my neck and stabbed into my skull. He crawled in farther, changed his grip, swaddled hands tucking behind my legs, before pulling again.

I could only be grateful for being unconscious when he managed to get us under the tree in the first place.

Out in the open air, I gingerly curled myself into a seated position and pulled my knees beneath me. I felt ready to shatter, hot and cold chills washing over my body. Fear and pain roiled together, nausea tugging at the back of my throat.

"Are you okay?"

I nodded firmly, not trusting my voice yet. After giving me a moment to catch my breath, Abel hunkered down to wrap a supportive arm behind my ribs and prop me onto my feet.

He dropped his arm as soon as I was stable, slinging both packs onto his shoulders and gripping his staff.

"Ready?"

"Yeah," I straightened a bit and looked at the fuzzy blur that was Abel, mentally preparing myself for an uncomfortable hike. *Being alive feels good,* I reminded myself.

But still he didn't move. The fingers of his left hand agitated his staff, the red tassels twitching just above the ground. His body angled toward me, and I could only imagine what he saw: my face swollen beyond recognition; my dark skin covered in angry rashes; my shoulders folding under the weight of discomfort.

"It's pretty bad, huh?"

His silence lengthened, the squeak of the leather strap being crushed in his palm the only indication he'd heard me.

"Abel," my brow crinkled, a new wave of anxiety curling through me. "What's wrong?"

"I just..." he took a step closer, clumsy, like he wasn't in control of the movement. "I—" his voice cracked.

Graceless, he dumped the packs and dropped to his knees in front of me, a broken sound squeezing out of his chest.

I looked down at him in silent shock, feeling that shift between us again. Something impossible. Something incredible. Awareness of him sparked inside me like a swarm of lightning-flies. How his powerful body crouched there, the heat of him reflecting against my thighs. Heat that echoed in my middle, stretching out and thawing parts of me that had been dormant for years. Excitement. Anticipation. A shaking breath left my lungs, my mind racing incoherently.

His shoulders rolled with his breath, rising and falling. Rising and falling. Slowly, cautiously, he leaned forward, lightly pressing his brow beneath my ribs.

The contact rocked through me, pushing me off what balance I thought I had. My mind abruptly emptied, every swirling thought dissipating like mist. My heart thundered, warmth pooling, as I instinctually clutched his head to me with my bandaged forearms. His body shuddered beneath me and I struggled to swallow.

"I thought I lost you." His words were barely audible.

I didn't know what to say, so I didn't say anything, wondering distantly if this was real or if I'd drifted off into another dream.

He exhaled sharply, the warmth of his breath melting through my clothes and shivering over my skin. *This is real,* I assured myself in bewilderment. The heat of him, the feel of his body pressed against mine, not to mention the pain that still gripped me, were all too visceral to be imagined. I rolled my forearms over the knots of his shoulders, wanting, *needing,* to touch him back.

"What's happening right now?" I whispered.

"I don't know." He pulled another breath, like he was bolstering himself. "I thought I lost you," he said again, his voice thick with some emotion.

"I'm hard to kill, apparently."

He looked up at me then, his nose tracing along my middle until his chin settled against me. My belly fluttered, tightening under the contact. Golden eyes shone out of his face, taking me in, and I wished I could see his expression more clearly.

"Good."

We passed a landmark, and I wasn't sure if we could return to the way we were before. Did I want to? Or did I want to see where this new path could take me?

Thoughts were too slippery to hold onto, but I could feel. And the sensation radiating all around me was of *rightness.* I could be safe here. I could be cherished and respected, secure in a way I'd once dreamed about. Yearning tightened around my throat. I could be free. My heart pulsed, attempting to open to that hope, that impossible reality.

"You make me forget myself." He said softly, part disgruntled confession, part growling accusation. I felt the vibration down the length of my legs.

"Forget we're different?"

He shook his head, rubbing the side of his face against me hungrily, the movement sending electric sparks all over my body.

"Forget that I shouldn't do this. I shouldn't get too close to you."

With another breath he pushed to his feet and turned away, gripping and pulling the hair at the top of his head. The hair that I'd braided. It was starting to fall out after our chase through the woods, but valiantly held its weave. That small claim I'd put on him.

After a moment he visibly collected himself and started grabbing our things.

"I'm sorry. We really need to keep moving."

I felt confused and bereft, missing the heat of him pressed against my thighs and the comfort of his touch. The finality of his words resounded in my mind like a door slamming shut. My fragile hope shattered.

But he was right. We were from different worlds. We would have to go our separate ways soon. I would find a way to survive the accusations against me and make it back home to Father and Missy, to my life inside Arberdon and my parent's farm. To Grandfather and Randall, Levita and little Randa.

And there was no place inside the walls for Abel. No place for an *Unnatural*. The term filled me with revulsion. There was nothing unnatural about Abel, but could anyone in an Executor city understand that?

"Can you walk?"

"Yeah." I cleared my throat. "But I still can't see very well so we'll have to go slow."

Chapter Twenty Two

We did move slowly as the bright light of day cooled to shades of evening. Every now and again Abel would stash me somewhere safe and do a thorough search of the area to make sure we weren't being followed or to leave a false trail. I ground my teeth against self-pity, hating that I was injured. Hating that I couldn't do more. Hating that I couldn't pull my weight.

Fatigue pulled at me. We kept a cautiously sedate pace on account of my severe allergic reaction to the Ferox-Nettle tree toxin, but we had to keep going. Those scouts were still in the forest somewhere and Abel was determined to put a greater distance between us. I was fully supportive of that plan, even though every sore inch of my body clamored for rest. I urged my limbs to take just one more step. And then another.

The shadows stretched, running together to flood the forest floor in darkness. Moon-birds replaced song birds, the cicadas continuing to throb and screech no matter the time of day. Finally, with a breeze shivering through the branches above, Abel ushered me into a natural cavern and declared we would make camp for what was left of the night.

The air smelled damp and old inside the rocky crevasse, the heavy scent tickling the back of my throat. I shuffled ahead carefully, keeping my elbow on the wall to my right so I wouldn't run into anything. Abel crowded in behind me, the heat from his bulk blanketing my back.

"It opens up a little further ahead." His low voice rumbled in my bones. I looked over my shoulder, meeting his amber eyes shining like two flames in the thick darkness. Assured I wasn't about to crash into a stalagmite, I took a few bolder steps into the unknown.

The sound of our steps expanded, echoing in a larger space, and Abel peeled away from my back to set our packs down. I ignored the disappointment that joined me with his distance.

"I'm making you a pallet."

"Thanks."

I listened to him rustle through our bags, keenly attuned to each shift and step he took, my senses amplified without my sight. The patter of unease that would usually accompany being unable to see or fend for myself never appeared; maybe because I had grown accustomed to being blind after so many trips to the Dark Room in my dreams. Maybe because I was too exhausted to worry about anything anymore. Or maybe because relying on Abel had become synonymous with safety.

"Come here." He called to me and I couldn't stop the flutter under my ribs. I pressed my teeth into my lower lip and savored my memories; Abel kneeling on the forest floor, pressing himself carefully against my belly. His piercing eyes as he looked up at me, the rasp of his jaw against my shirt. So close to actually touching my skin, but still so carefully not.

I shouldn't do this, he'd said. *I shouldn't get close to you.*

I swallowed the attraction, stomped on my yearning, and followed his voice.

"Easy," he cautioned as one of his bundled hands took my upper arm, carefully guiding me to the bed he'd made. "Are you alright?"

I cleared wayward feelings out of my throat and reminded myself that he was only asking after my physical wellness. Whatever understanding we'd come to in the forest wasn't compatible with reality. The sooner I accepted that, the better. "Yes, I'm fine."

He helped me find a seat and my muscles immediately turned into a puddle. Relief had me groaning and stretching my legs out in front of me.

The darkness of the cavern was complete. I couldn't even make out the end of my nose. Curling my hands to my chest, I gave up on trying to see anything and closed my eyes.

"Let me see your hands," Abel instructed, his voice tight. I held them out obediently, the bindings tugging against me as he carefully unwound them.

"How can you see anything in here?"

"How can you not?" I gave a tired snort and nudged what I thought was his knee with my boot. He chuckled before continuing, "There's some phosphorescent growth high on the walls, and the light from the stars filters back here. It's not much, but it's enough."

"Doesn't sound like enough," I groused with a smirk on my lips. "I can't see anything."

"You should try opening your eyes." A twist of my ankle had me tapping his knee again in a half-hearted protest. "Or don't, actually, since resting them is a good idea."

More rustling preceded a cool paste being spread across my palms, and I sighed. Abel used the flat of his blade as he steadied my arm against one of our packs, tending to me carefully while carefully not touching me.

So close, you're so close to touching me—but no, we couldn't do that.

"I found some yarrow, comfrey, and rosemary. It's not a perfect poultice, but it should help speed up your healing. The rosemary was an unexpected good find. I thought it would be too late for it at this time of year..." He narrated as he worked, filling the quiet space between us.

I nodded along as his voice rolled over me and soothed me, savoring the feel of the paste as he spread it over my shredded hands. Savoring the feathery warmth of his breath that caressed me in waves.

"You need more tisane," he proclaimed as he finished rewrapping both of my hands.

He shifted closer, a strong arm bracing behind my shoulders. His canteen, full of more of that awful swill, pressed against my lips. I held my breath and opened my mouth, determined to choke some down without complaint. A few swallows was all I could manage before it started trying to climb up the back of my nose.

"That's good. Here," he traded his canteen for mine. I rinsed the water through my teeth before swallowing.

"Stars, that stuff is terrible."

"That it is." He agreed. I heard sloshing before the stink of the tisane hit my nose again.

"I can't drink any more of that right now." My gut churned just thinking about it.

"It's for your eyes; I'm making a compact for them. It should take care of the rest of the swelling."

I curled around my middle and eased onto the ground, gingerly finding a comfortable position on my back. The pallet beneath me bunched when he braced a hand beside my head. His knee pressed against my hip as he leaned over me. Even with my eyes closed I was aware of his nearness like an electrical charge in the air, the same way I could feel a storm building. Potential. Power. Heat. His presence shivered across my skin. That tether between us coiled, tightening the muscles of my belly. My heart fluttered in my chest, making it hard to pull his exhale into my lungs.

The cloth was cool as he draped it across my eyes, the feeling immediately loosening the tense muscles of my brow. I hummed in appreciation, shifting a little deeper into the layers of cloth that smelled like Abel. My scalp tickled as he gently brushed my hair back, probably thinking I wouldn't notice the soft stroke.

Don't get used to this, I reminded myself, the ache in my chest having nothing to do with my physical discomfort. *There's nowhere for this to go.*

But I savored it all the same.

Hurting, recovering, and tangled with nameless feelings and anxieties, I sank gratefully into oblivion.

* * *

I pulled life into my lungs. Fresh, vibrant, hopeful life that surged into every cell and fiber of my body.

I picked my way through the forest, following my whim instead of any set path. The same motes of flame that always filled the Dark Room danced and lilted through the branches, alighting on my cheeks, sparking against my skin, before drifting on their way again. My own flame pulsed in my chest, content to mosey along instead of leading me anywhere in particular.

A soft smile pulled at my lips, feeling content and maybe even a little at peace. It had been so long since I felt like I actually fit into any place, either waking or dreaming. With the kind of clarity that comes inside dreams, I recognized the first drastic step away from the security of the familiar. And who I would be, who I was meant to be, was waiting for me in the thick of the wilds.

I lifted my gaze, taking in the myriad of different growth around me. Maybe that was what was so special about being in the Dark Room with Yeshua; there was a place for everything to develop in her circle. All you had to do was give her some roots to plant.

"Penny."

I paused, my flame quivering with recognition in my chest.

"Penny."

The voice whimpered through the maze of branches around me, coming from everywhere and nowhere.

"Penny."

"Where are you?" I called out as panic began to grip my throat. A shift in the air as the voice focused its attention on me.

"Penny. What have you done?"

"Where are you?" I demanded again, starting to push through the underbrush with urgency. "I can't find you!"

"Penny."

"Tell me where you are!"

My voice shook the forest, the whole plane holding its breath in a trembling silence as the final echoes of my shout drifted away. Disappointment crushed me; there were no words twisting the echo into guidance and feeding it back to me. I stepped in a circle, my eyes scouring the trees for something. I had no idea what I was looking for, but I had to believe recognition would grip me when I saw it.

I didn't think the voice would answer. Then—

"Alone. I'm alone."

Fear surged through my veins, making my tired feet run and my lungs quicken. I scanned, searched, gripped at every plant and tree and bush. I needed to keep going, I needed to find—

My foot slipped, tossing me down where I didn't fall but melted through the ground and sprouted, gasping, on my feet on the other side. Color bled into the space as I stabilized, soft greens and tans and blues of young birches collected alongside a burbling creek.

"Pen?" Abel turned to face me, jumping down from the boulder he liked to meditate on and striding over to me. "What's wrong?"

My lungs burned, desperately sucking air in beside my wildly galloping heart.

"I can't find her!"

"Can't find who? What do you need?"

The peaceful scene siphoned my adrenaline. My limbs shook, too weak to support my weight. I folded to my knees, Abel following me down with serious concern.

"I'm not sure."

He frowned, golden eyes flicking across my face.

"I heard her calling,"

"Can I help you search?" I was already shaking my head before he finished.

"I don't know...I thought—but I can't remember now." A heavy breath shivered out of my lungs.

"Fever dream." He finally said with a decisive nod. "It's no surprise. Stars, Pen, you've been through so much—I was going to say 'today,' but it's been longer than that."

The explanation fit and I huffed, settling on my backside as the dregs of my panic melted. "Right. I'm really tired. How many times have I almost died recently?"

"Don't joke about that." He held my gaze steadily, his words sinking straight into my bones. "Please."

"I won't," I promised. I reached out to pat him on the shoulder, my hand pulling back to my lap when he flinched. "This is a dream, right?" I waited until he nodded. "It's not real. Not tactile, at least. It's all in our heads."

"Actions have consequences." He recited.

"What consequences are you worried about?"

He opened and closed his mouth, struggling to find words, before giving up with a shrug and a growl of frustration.

I considered him in silence. Then, "Why are you afraid of me, Abel?"

"I'm not." He shook his head firmly, his brilliant eyes turning dark and shadowed as he looked across the water.

"I won't touch you without permission. Not ever." I swallowed old shame, shutting painful memories out of this place, out of the space I shared

with Abel. I had nothing to be ashamed of. I had to remind myself of that, believe in it, to make it true. When I had collected myself I continued. "You more than anyone know how important that is to me. I just thought...well, it doesn't really matter what I thought. I'm sorry for making you uncomfortable."

I wrapped my arms around my knees, feeling like the back end of a plow-equid for reaching for him in the first place. He'd made his position on touching perfectly clear while we trekked across the continent.

Then again, he touched me in the forest. The memory washed over me deliciously. He caressed my hair in the cavern. Did that mean I could assume his stance had changed?

"Not you," he said abruptly. "I don't want to hurt you."

I turned my head to rest on my cheek so I could watch him. He picked up a stone by his hip, pinching it between his first finger and thumb before whipping it toward the water. The quiet plip-plop-plunk *told me how many times he managed to skip it, though we should have been sitting too far away.*

"You won't."

"I have." He growled, staring at the ripples before the moving water whisked them away. "I have hurt you—"

"That was an accident!"

"Even at my most diligent, my most careful, we are constantly in danger. You most of all! I won't put you at more risk just because I want..." the muscles of his throat worked as he swallowed. "I want..."

"What do you want?" I murmured, breathless. Needing him to continue. Terrified he would.

Those eyes that always saw so much of me, all of my dark places and missing pieces, held me in thrall. Molten amber, churning like the tempest brewing between us.

The moment pulled taut, vibrating the air that I moved in and out of my lungs. It lengthened, straining, neither one of us blinking in an effort to hold time still before—

It snapped.

He turned away, staring back at the river, and I knew the time when he might have answered me had passed. The ache bloomed in my chest, only marginally comforted by the knowledge that he just wasn't ready yet.

I watched the water lap along its banks, swirling in dizzy eddies and slipping between rocks. My limbs grew heavy, my heart finally slowing.

"You should rest."

"I am resting. I'm dreaming, remember?"

"Dream Walking is hard on your mind, Pen. You need to rest. Mind and body."

I sighed. "I don't know how to leave."

"You need to remember your body. How it feels—"

"Like crap, probably."

"Do you want help or not?" He snorted, taping his shoe against mine.

"Fine," I groused, pushing back against his boot. I couldn't help the amused smile that pulled at my cheeks.

"Remember something that you associate with your physical self, not your mind. Something tangible. Something only your body can feel."

His voice layered over me like a blanket, each phrase acting like an anchor that tethered me to him. The sound of the creek faded away as I listened to his voice, as I let his words wrap around me, sink inside of me.

I remembered hot summer days, when the sun cooked me into the ground but still managed to feel good so long as I didn't have work to do. The heat of a fire as it crackled the air near my cheeks, tightening my skin. And the deeper burn of muscles straining at chores, the sacrifice the earth demanded in exchange for crops. The ache of limbs well-used. The strength that was built in that forge, the deep, pulsing power—

—the warmth of Abel pressed against my thighs. The spark of his chin against my softness. His breath, his heat, surging under my clothes and under my skin.

What if he had slid his hands up my legs? Those large palms molding to the strength of my hips, making me feel weak. What if I had pressed into him, clutching at his shoulders and drawing him to stand beside me where he belonged?

Would the ridges and valleys of his frame caress against mine as he rose, his nose tracing an unerring path toward my neck? If I pressed against his jaw, would he turn and hover his lips over mine while we shared our air? Anticipation simmering between us, the pull of that precipice taunting, tempting, teasing, until we finally succumbed, igniting the space between, leaning in to each other to taste—

* * *

I gasped a breath in surprise, my lips parting helplessly on a trembling exhale. The muscles of my belly shivered deliciously as I sank deeper into my pallet. Somewhere nearby I heard Abel breathing deeply in sleep, the sound enough to lull me back into a dreamless void.

Unnatural

CHAPTER TWENTY THREE

The next morning I felt rested despite my aching body. The cavern was still impossibly dark, but a watery gray light bled from where the cave opened to the forest. My ravaged skin felt tight, but less raw. The tisane Abel continued to make me drink must have been doing what it was supposed to, helping chase the deadly allergic reaction from my body. I tested my hands, getting a bit more dexterity before pain stopped me with a muffled curse.

"Don't push it." The shadows condensed by that weak gray light and started striding toward me.

"I need my hands to work, Abel."

"They'll work better, and sooner, if you don't push it." He countered, the air around me disturbing as he lowered himself to my pallet. "And until they do you have me. Let me see."

I held out my hands for another dressing, trying to ignore the excited flapping in my chest. I was acting like a young idiot instead of a woman who'd lived almost three decades of hard years.

It doesn't mean what it sounds like, I reminded myself again. *This can't go anywhere.*

His touch was light and steady as he carefully unwound my bandages, confident, conjuring a reminder of when I'd watched him shaving just outside The Sands, curious about what a familiar touch from him would feel like.

I hissed as the last of the bandages pulled free from my healing palms and between my fingers. Soon he had my wounds coated in that cooling poultice, relief making me press my teeth into my lips against a moan.

"*Stars*, that feels good."

The clatter of Abel's blade had my eyes flying open.

"Are you okay?"

"Yeah," he cleared the gruffness out of his throat. "Yes, I'm fine. Just lost my grip."

I hummed in understanding, feeling languid as the paste soothed the burning of my skin. "Happens all the time when I get slick."

Abel inhaled sharply, his growling exhale sending heat charging up my neck. Realization came over me like a wave, embarrassment chasing the flush on my skin and adding to it. I was supposed to be *ignoring* my attraction to Abel, not making thinly disguised innuendos! I pressed my lips together, resolving to say nothing until he was done, though my heart still kicked excitedly behind my ribs.

Wisps of my dream slid through me, my chest tightening. Had Abel been aware? When my mind wandered to fantasy and satisfaction, had I projected the same to him? I swallowed against a dry throat, unsure if the thought mortified or thrilled me.

A gravid silence settled between us while he treated my hands, making it hard to breathe. I couldn't see him in the dim, but I could feel the energy coming off of him and charging the air between us. Anticipation simmered, thick with the memory of Abel pressed against me, of his breath on my belly, of everything we said before...and everything we wouldn't. Everything we *couldn't*.

I fought the urge to lean forward. So long as neither of us said anything, I could pretend that he didn't feel what I did. That my longing wasn't real but a fantasy derived from chaos and trauma. I swallowed hard, pressing back against the desire to find him in the dark, to seek out the scent that curled around me and told me I was safe. That I wasn't alone.

"There." His voice was low and rough as he pulled his bundled hands back.

But he lingered near, the heat of him tantalizing me. My skin prickled. I held my breath, both of us hovering on a threshold we'd acknowledged we couldn't cross.

He cleared his throat and I looked away.

"Hungry?"

"Starving."

"I managed some foraging, so we've got a little to eat. Do you want it before or after the tisane?"

"After." I said firmly. I wouldn't be able to keep any of the food down if I tried to drink the tisane on a full stomach. "Definitely after."

He chuckled, the sound of a sloshing canteen already making my gut churn. "Bottom's up."

It was just as foul as I remembered, making my throat constrict and burn against its invasion. But I managed, choking the last of the tisane down. He switched canteens, holding mine gently against my lips so fresh water could rinse into my mouth. I swallowed greedily, runnels of water trickling down my chin and neck.

"Go slow." He instructed, and I could've scowled at him if it weren't for the way his voice got under my skin and made my toes curl. I opened my throat and welcomed the cool water, shivering as it traced past my heart and spread outward.

Quenched, I wiped my chin on my shoulder to collect the wayward drops. It wasn't particularly effective, but it was better than nothing.

"Here," Abel shifted, bracing a smocked hand against my shoulder. The simple touch, through layers of fabric, still had me freezing in place and holding my breath. The ambient light grew as the sun rose outside, his large frame doused in shadows that I traced with my eyes. Broad shoulders, long limbs, tentative hands. Gently he brought a cloth to my mouth, chasing the damp trail toward my neck.

This means nothing, I begged myself to believe as his golden eyes followed his hand down my throat. As I closed my eyes and tipped my chin back so he had better access. *He's not for me.*

Grief lodged between my lungs, making me suck in a sharp breath.

"Sorry," he murmured, releasing my shoulder and putting the rag down. "I know it hurts."

"It's fine." I pushed a smile onto my lips. "I'll be fine."

"Of course you will be," he replied, and I could hear the gentle smile that quirked his lips. "You're the strongest person I know."

A startled laugh jumped out of my chest and I shook my head. "I'm not strong. Look at me Abel; I'm small and weak and broken—"

"You're determined," he interrupted, shoving a bit of food in my mouth. He chuckled at my disgruntled chewing, the sound sparking delight in my belly. "You're persistent. You don't give up, no matter how much the odds are stacked against you, which is probably the most incredible thing I've ever experienced." He shook his head. "Being around you, listening to you, watching you repeatedly pick yourself up and rise to any challenge...it changes the way I see things. It changes the whole world. For me, at least."

His voice trailed off, the shape of him curling in at the shoulder as he turned away from me to get more food. I swallowed and licked my lips.

"And even though you're strong, in more ways than I could ever tell you, it's okay to let yourself be weak for a time. To let someone else take care of you." I felt the next bite against my mouth. "Just for a little while." He whispered.

"Abel." I breathed. I tasted berries on my tongue. "We shouldn't—"

Fabric rustled as he shifted closer, his voice deepening urgently. "I know I can't give you...I can't do other things. But I can do this. Let me do this."

My lungs stopped working, my heart picking up tempo in response. I wanted him to know how a fire of yearning lit up inside my chest, how I wished I could see in the dark like him so I could study his face. I wanted to assure him that I understood his boundaries and didn't begrudge him for having them. That the companionship and respect he gave me was the salve my battered soul needed. That I hoped to live up to the esteem he held me in.

"*Please,* Pen. Let me have this."

My mind was a jumble of words, too mixed up to string any together coherently. So I said nothing, just opened my mouth. I lingered over each morsel, savoring each bite, trying to forget the fact that what we shared was temporary. Forbidden. Impossible.

His eyes tracked my every expression, like he could sate his own hunger by feeding mine. Every involuntary hum, every dart of my tongue on my lip, every swallow was echoed in him. I found myself devouring his reactions just as voraciously, willing time to stand still and hold us together in the brightening dark.

But time didn't stop, and the only path forward was to keep moving. When I'd had my share of the foraging we set out again, slowly making our way to the other side of the forest. The urgency to put space between us and the scouts burned in the back of my mind. But as the sun continued to rise and warm the world around us, in spite of the threat of discovery and my healing injuries, I could almost pretend that we were traveling together for the joy of it.

Abel identified birdsong and plants for me as we passed. In return, I told him stories I remembered from the books hidden in the cellar of my parent's home. Sometimes fictions that had entertained me as a child. Sometimes facts about the earth as it was before the Great War, the tales so wild they seemed like fiction on their own.

The day passed quietly. Dutifully, he helped me with every need. Each bite of food came from his carefully bundled hands, each drink from my canteen steadied by him against my lips. We didn't talk about the longing and confusion that saturated the air, though I often wrapped my lips around his name in silence.

I managed to convince Abel that I didn't need any more of the tisane. The symptoms of my allergic reaction had abated enough that I could manage with hydration and patience. The tingling numbness continued to fade down my arms, leaving a burning ache in its place. I drank enough water to drown a plow-equid in an effort to chase the toxin from my system. Fortunately the forest was obliging enough to provide many options for streams, which had the added benefit of making our tracks harder to find though it also kept my boots permanently soggy.

By the time we made camp to rest I was exhausted. I happily sat on the pallet Abel made for me while he checked that we were secure, resting my eyes and counting my heartbeats as they slowed. My ears pricked at the sounds of the swelling night: cicadas, *always* cicadas; the hoot of moon-birds; the yip of a distant Canid. And, very softly, footsteps.

I opened my eyes and met Abel's as he returned to me, a smile on my lips.

"You're getting better at that." His sharp teeth flashed in a crooked grin.

"I am." I preened, shifting in search of relief from aching muscles and itchy skin.

"I brought some water for washing." His voice deepened, cheeks flushing above the new growth of his beard. "If you permit."

He held my gaze, and there was no embarrassment, not after everything we'd been through. Only the want that existed quietly between us. And something deeper, more resonant and sacred.

Trust.

I took another step into the unknown and nodded.

He lowered himself beside me, taking out strips of the blanket he'd cut to make covers for his hands. Staring into my eyes, he wound the fabric into place and I felt my belly tighten.

When he was done, he lowered his eyes to the buttons that marched down the center of my chest. I took a breath that shook as it left me, sitting a little straighter.

"I'm ready."

I studied his face as he meticulously unfastened my buttons. At first nerves gripped me tightly, stretching me until I felt thin and quivery. The reality of him touching me, *undressing* me, blitzed through my veins. He was only going to wipe the grime from my skin, but the intimacy of the action couldn't be ignored.

Did I want to share that intimacy with him, share my physical self with him the same way I'd bound our minds together in Arberdon? *Absolutely.* The vehemency of that certainly startled me, making me gasp as Abel loosed my second button, his breath coasting down my neck and between my breasts. My heart pounded. I was certain he could see it under my skin.

Would it be so bad to let myself enjoy what time we had together? To ignore the pragmatism that I usually prioritized and just let myself *feel*. Feel the way the backs of his hands, covered obnoxiously with too much fabric, rustled against my skin. The way his thighs pressed into mine, his body so close, so large, so real. I bit my lip when he jostled me, struggling with a fastener, the reminder of his strength driving like lightning through my middle. He could overpower me, of course, but I knew he never would. His strength was *for* me, never against me, and that knowledge was heady.

The tension broke when, after fumbling for some time, the button he was working on broke off in his hand. The startled, guilty expression on his face when he looked up at me had me snorting with laughter, that tight anticipation dissolving into effervescent joy. He chuckled, scrubbing his face against his forearm.

"I'm sorry!"

"It's fine," I gasped, my cheeks hurting. I watched as he tucked the button into a small pocket on my leather apron, fondness softening my smile.

The front of my shirt gaped when it was finally free of its fasteners, letting fresh air coast over the skin of my upper chest. I shifted my shoulders as he gently peeled the fabric away, my skin pulling in places where the blisters had burst and dried. We worked slowly to get the sleeves past my hands, which were by far the worst, until I was sitting in just the battered binding that covered my breasts.

Cool water soothed the raised patches that bubbled across my shoulders, streaked the length of my arms, and consumed my hands. Abel's movements were unhurried, washing my tender skin as though it were sacred. I curled forward around my knees, giving him better access. His breath dancing over the skin of my back, still damp, sent shivers across my skin.

"Almost done." His voice growled beside my ear. He shifted around, carefully stroking the cleaning cloth down my arms and between my damaged fingers.

"Take your time." I encouraged him, my cheeks tightening with a smile.

He gazed into my eyes, our faces closer than ever and yet not nearly close enough. And though I wanted him, wanted to taste him and breathe him and know what he felt like, there was something more under our connection. A closeness that was more profound than anything I had ever experienced. Slowly the smile faded from my lips as I savored the feeling, his expression warm and relaxed. I was battered and disheveled, helpless and dirty. But the way he looked at me...I didn't feel pretty, that would be impossible. I didn't feel attractive or anything so centered on my physical form. I felt radiant. I felt seen. I felt lo—

"Pen, you're crying." Concern sharpened his features. "Am I hurting you?"

"No! Not at all." I blinked through my watery smile. "I'm just washing out my eyes."

The realization was too big, too much. I pushed it to the back of my mind, something to work through later, and reminded myself that we had farther to go. Miles to cover. And an inevitable separation at the end of our journey.

Now was not the time for any of those problems, though. Not if I was going to allow myself to savor the moment and the way he tended me. The stroke of his hands, steady and sure, across my shoulders and down my neck. The way his breath deepened when I tilted my head out of the way. The shiver of my skin when his hand coasted down my stomach and across the top of my hip.

When my torso was as clean as it was going to get, Abel carefully navigated my arms through a new shirt and bandaged my hands again. Getting my boots and pants off took a substantial amount of wiggling and amused frustration, but the long press of his swaddled hands gliding over the backs of my legs made it worth every hassle.

The satisfied hum behind me told me that he agreed, desire blooming over my skin as my imagination latched on to that sound and made it more carnal. I pressed my teeth into my lower lip to stifle a moan, gingerly resting my chin on my bandaged arms. The pulse in my belly throbbed against the pallet.

"You're looking somewhat unraveled," he rasped.

"Hmm. I hope you're not done." I teased, feeling giddy and reckless. "I think you missed a spot."

"Ah yes," I inhaled sharply as he shifted over me, one strong arm suspending his torso while the other ghosted across my back. My pulse galloped away, my breath turning shallow. *Surely, he wouldn't,* I thought. He was still so careful about keeping our skin apart, despite the unspoken want that burned between us. And yet, I couldn't help the needy sound that eased past my lips when his large palm lazily traced the globe of my ass, because *maybe he would.*

"I see. Right *here,*" he trapped my ankles under his arm in one swift move and took his time washing over each toe, sending me into a fit of giggles that had him laughing freely.

"Enough!" I finally gasped, tugging my legs free and rolling onto my side. He smiled down at me unrepentantly, tossing me a wink before unpacking his own pallet. A soft tune rumbled out of his throat.

The night was warm enough to forego wrestling back into a pair of pants. I languished in my clean tunic, enjoying the sensation of the breeze against my skin and whatever song Abel was humming. Feeling cleaner than I had in a while, I settled down with a light heart.

"You're staring," Abel smirked.

"I'm allowed to."

"That you are."

I admired Abel openly as he busied himself with our camp, the smile staying on my face even as I drifted to sleep.

Chapter Twenty Four

"Penny."

Awareness surged through me, bringing the Dark Room into focus. I let out a slow breath, an attempt to keep calm in spite of the beginnings of panic twisting through my chest and speeding up my heart.

"Penny."

That voice! Familiar, and yet I couldn't place it. Fatigue evaporated. The voice couldn't be ignored; I had to get up.

Rolling to my side, I eased to my feet. My joints protested sluggishly, echoes of pain glancing down my arms.

"It's not real," I gritted my teeth. "That pain belongs to my body, not my mind."

Repeating the mantra helped, and after a few strides I was able to move more freely.

"Where are you?" I called. My voice was absorbed by the forest, not shifting and echoing back to me. My own flame stayed nestled inside my chest, encompassing my heart. I felt its throb of heat in every pulse, taking comfort from the quiet sensation. Looking around, I blew my cheeks out, sending the small flames that filled the air around me into dizzying spirals.

I wouldn't find whoever was calling for me by staying put. Tentatively, careful not to crush any of the smaller plants rising up around my feet, I waded farther into the heart of the forest.

"Penny."

I stopped abruptly. She—because it was a woman—had gotten quieter. Turning, I moved in the opposite direction.

Time passed. Adjusting my course based on the volume of my name, I cut across the expanse of the dream plane. Unlike hiking in the waking world, my muscles hummed along without fatigue. Whenever I needed to check my bearings, I only had to wait a few minutes.

"Penny."

The constant refrain of my name quickly became unsettling. It vibrated the air, shivered over my skin, filled my thoughts. Whoever it was didn't seem to be searching for me. She wasn't calling out, seeking an answer. Just...saying my name. Who would do that? And why?

My steps slowed. It could be a trap. Maybe another Dream Walker was trying to lure me deeper into the dream plane? A chill worked its way down my spine. Was there a limit to how far I could travel before my connection to my physical self became too thin to anchor me?

"Penny."

I could turn back. Pretend I didn't hear anything, reconnect with my body and wake up on my pallet with Abel close by. The thought was tempting; I knew next to nothing about being a Dream Walker. It would be smarter, safer, to slip away and forget all about it. And yet...

"Penny."

I firmed my shoulders, flexing my fingers into my palms.

"Who are you?" I shouted.

Silence swallowed my question, the stillness of the air making me sweat.

"Penny."

I stretched my lips over my teeth, clenching my jaw to prevent fear from rattling them.

"What do you want?"

Desperation cracked my voice, my heart beating hot in my chest.

"Penny." The voice came from everywhere at once, tugging at all sides. I spun in a circle, shaking my arms as though I could fling off the strange, mournful sound of my name.

"Stop it! Who are you?"

"Penny." Louder. It was getting louder even though I'd stopped moving toward it. Digging into my ears, tugging at my hair, pressing against my chest.

"Who's out there?"

"There!"

The echo swelled suddenly, crashing over me like a wave. A thousand thousand voices twisting and weaving into one loud shout. I felt my body ripped around, millions of tiny fire lights surging to blinding brightness in front of me. I threw my arms up, protecting my eyes from the burn. In the image seared onto my retinas I saw the outline of a maple tree.

And when I opened my eyes, the young tree stood before me.

"Penny." It throbbed.

Swallowing my trepidation, I reached out my hand—

* * *

Pain surged from my palm, searing up my arm and burning the backs of my eyes.

"Aah!" I cried, curling around my bandaged hands.

"Pen!" Abel's voice became clearer as the claxon of pain settled into the background. "Are you okay?"

"Yeah," I sucked air in through my teeth, letting it out on a groan. "I must've smacked my hand on something while I was sleeping."

"Here," Abel helped me to a seated position and offered me a drink. I closed my eyes and savored the cool sensation, letting it chase away the discomfort.

"That's better. Thanks."

"Bad dream?"

A skitter of unease tickled my neck.

"I'm not sure. It was certainly weird."

"Do you want to try to sleep some more?"

"No," I said decisively, rolling my neck on my shoulders. "We can get going now if you're ready."

It didn't take long to break camp and set out again. With fresh air in my lungs and my legs working to put more distance behind me, the unease from my dream began to unravel. Though the questions it brought still remained.

How could another person, who knew me, know how to call out to me in a Dream Walk? I had gotten the impression from Abel that Dream Walking wasn't a common trait. And yet, how else could I explain the strange encounter? I scrubbed my face in the bend of my elbow, growling in frustration.

"Do you want to talk about it?"

"I don't know." I sighed heavily, dropping my arm and turning to look at Abel. Ignoring the guilt that twinged at me whenever I watched him carry both of our packs. "I don't even know where to start."

"Can't remember the dream?"

"No, I remember it. It's like I'm getting better at recalling my Dream Walks with practice, if that makes sense. I'm not sure how I'm doing it, but it's getting easier."

He nodded, using his staff to move some branches out of our path. "You're more open to it, I think."

I didn't agree or disagree, choosing to look at that statement more closely another time. I did go into detail about my most recent Dream Walk, about how the voice seemed to act like a beacon. How the maple tree appeared to me, almost encouraging me to connect with it.

"Did you touch it?"

"No, I didn't have the chance. That was when I bumped my hand."

"Oh." The tension left his shoulders. "That's probably good."

"Really?" Memories flashed through my mind. A damaged rowan tree and a massive oak I'd connected with in the Dark Room. "Why do you say that?"

He shrugged, spinning his staff around his arm. "The spirit plane is vast and confusing. I'm not sure I would start connecting to anything found there without understanding it better."

"You mean like how I connected with you all those months ago?"

"Something like that." He flashed me a crooked grin, like I was hoping he would. "Though I have to admit that turned out well."

I laughed. "Once I stopped trying to shoot you, maybe."

"Makes for a good story."

"But who would we tell?"

We chuckled and then subsided into silence for a time, sobered by the reminder.

"How do you Persuade?"

It was clearly not a question he'd been expecting. He hummed in his throat, tilting his face up to stare unseeing at the branches above us.

"I'm not sure how to describe it. I hold a thought as well formed as I can make it. See the words, feel the intent behind them. Visualize the person hearing my words the way I mean for them to be received. And then," he shrugged, his features twisting to one side. "I *push* the thought at them."

"And they think it's their own thought?"

"Not quite." He glanced at me sheepishly, no doubt thinking about the start of our friendship. "It's like presenting a solid argument. If it aligns with what they expect, what they think already, then it's usually accepted. But if not, or if it's poorly formed, it can be dismissed."

"Then how did you wind up so deeply embedded in my brain? I'm not mad," I quickly assured him when he grimaced. "I just want to understand better."

"I'm honestly not sure. It might be because you connected us in a Dream Walk first."

"You said minds are better protected while asleep?"

He nodded. "That's what my mother taught me."

"Was she a Persuader?"

"No. But she said my grandmother was."

I digested the new information for a few minutes, ducking under branches and being mindful not to bump my arms into anything. Abel continued to lead our trek, careful not to disturb the foliage too much. While we seemed to have evaded the scouts, we had to be careful to not leave an obvious trail for them to pick up.

"Do these traits normally manifest in family lines?"

"As far as I know, but I'm no expert."

"Compared to me you are. And I don't have anyone else to ask, so you're stuck with my questions."

Abel snorted and helped me up a rocky slope, his strong arm braced behind my ribs.

"I will consider myself stuck."

"So how is it that minds are better protected when sleeping?"

"Think of it like a sol-flower," he extended his hand, palm up, between us. "During the waking hours, the petals are open so the center can absorb light. But at night," he curled his fingers into his palm. "The petals create a shield, trapping heat and light inside. Behind that protection, the sol-flower creates food to help it grow."

I nodded, my brow furrowing. "When dreaming and the spirit is off growing, the mind shuts the door so it isn't disturbed."

"Right. If I were to Persuade a wakeful mind, my suggestion only reaches the outer petals. They have to choose whether to take the suggestion into their mind or not."

"But you can make it convincing, with a well-formed thought. As a Dream Walker, though, I can get past the petals?"

He hummed in his throat again, waving his hand from side to side. "The metaphor might fall apart a bit here. You can connect to minds on the spirit plane because you aren't even trying to get past the petals. You just appear at the center of the sol-flower."

"The sol-flower thinks I'm part of the plant."

"That works."

"What if a person could Dream Walk and Persuade?"

He slid me a sidelong glance. "They would be formidable."

* * *

It took three more days to get through the forest, and my hands continued to improve. By the time we edged through the younger growth along the outer reaches of the wilderness I could manage my clothes on my own. But that relief was tempered by disappointment. For every independence I regained, I had to press away my longing for the intimacy with Abel I lost. Permanently.

I kept my longing to myself, not wanting to make the end of our temporary arrangement more painful for either one of us. Based on the hungry way his eyes tracked me when I opted to change my own clothes, though, I could guess how he felt.

We didn't see any signs of the scouts or a search party, but that didn't mean they weren't looking for us. We slept in shifts, keeping me out of his dream plane, and cut our way out of the forest as quickly as we could.

The dawning of the fourth day had us peering out of the trees to the valley beyond and the distant mountains. And nestled against that rolling landscape was a dark cut across the land with heavy smoke curling toward the sky. Terrah.

I readjusted my lightened pack on my shoulders, careful of the blisters under three layers of shirts. Abel insisted he could continue to carry both packs, but I needed to carry my own as much as I could. My gun, however, was still attached to his pack. I frowned, testing my stiff fingers as we gazed at our destination.

"I'm going to need my gun." I groused.

Abel shrugged beside me, shooting a mischievous grin my way. "At least I can use it right now."

I gave an amused scoff. "You don't know how to use my gun."

"Sure I do."

"Uh-huh."

"Just point and pull."

I rolled my eyes, a smile tugging at my mouth. I was so grateful for the connection we shared, our easy banter soothing my ache for home. It would have been unbearable to do without, to feel completely alone so far from everything I knew.

Which I would be shortly, so I needed to pull myself together.

I shifted my feet, cast-offs from the forest compressing under my boots. The ground eased away from the tree line, slowly settling into a long, shallow valley that butted against the abrupt rise of the Hacknor Mountains. Tall grasses swayed across the expanse, rippling with currents of wind that never fully cleared away the heavy heat at the end of the growing season. A smattering of indigo flowers interrupted the monotony, sturdy stalks of brown reaching for the sky. A very few trees stood stoically among the foliage, small and isolated.

There would be few places to take shelter in this last stretch of our journey. This close to Terrah there would no doubt be more patrols and guard activity, too.

"What's your plan?" I asked Abel, my mind working over the details as I came to terms with what I knew would need to happen. Braced myself against the pain.

He folded his arms across his chest, rubbing his hand over his jaw. "We've been over it."

"Right." I replied absently, calculating the distance and how fast I thought I could travel. "Have you ever gotten that close to Terrah?"

He took a deep breath, squaring his shoulders, and I knew the answer before he opened his mouth.

"Never closer than this."

I nodded, not surprised considering what we saw. Despite knowing it would need to happen, knowing that every step closer to our goal brought me closer to this point, I hated that we'd arrived. But lamenting over things I couldn't change had never been in my character. I could set my sentiments aside and be practical when needed. Like now.

"Well. I'm going on alone."

A choking sound rushed out of his throat as he spun toward me, prepared to argue.

I raised a bandaged hand and cut him off. "No really, think about it. There is *no* cover out there. We're within two days of the walls, maybe one if I can hustle. That close to a city, you know there are going to be guards and Roving Patrols. If anyone sees *you* it'll be 'sound the alarm and grab your guns!' If I'm spotted?" I shrugged, trying to convey more confidence than I felt. "I'm human. Maybe I got lost. Maybe I'm a traveler. Maybe I'm another guard. It's a big city, I'm sure all of the guards don't know each other on sight."

Abel treated me to one of his heavy scowls. "No, I don't want—" he screwed his lips up, rearranging his words. He'd been doing that a lot over our last days together, trying not to mention anything he wanted. Like he was trying to prepare for the inevitable, too. "You shouldn't go alone. It's dangerous."

"Ah, Abel." I gave him as saucy a grin as I could manage, relishing the way his name felt in my mouth. Trying to quell the sinking of my heart as I reminded him and me both of our reality. "I am alone. Especially once I get inside the city." I turned back to the thick scar on the horizon. "You know I'm right."

I listened to him growl beside me, knowing he would agree once he thought about it.

"You need that message."

"Pen, I—" he shoved his fingers through the thick hair that fed into the knot at the back of his head. My braid had long since unraveled, kind of like our time together. I closed my eyes and tried to sniff quietly. "We could just keep going? Just forget—"

"Abel, you *need* that message. It's life or death, like you said."

His jaw ticked while he stared at me, hungry and conflicted. Finally he pressed his eyes shut, his head hanging on his neck. "It could change everything. *Everything.*"

"Right," my lips twisted with the reminder that there was so much more I wanted to learn about Abel. So much I might not get the chance to learn. *He's not yours to know*, I shoved my feelings deep into my chest, clearing my throat so I could keep talking. "You need it. And you need *me* to get it. We've been following the same plan all along. I don't know why we're still talking about it."

"*Stars Above*," he dropped his arms to his sides and studied my face, looking torn. "I don't know about this."

"I promise I'll do my best to get that message to you." I said instead of addressing his concern. I didn't let myself think about how unlikely it was. How this could very well be the last time I looked into his intense, burning eyes. The last time I heard his growling voice.

The last time I did anything, really.

But I had to try. Since the beginning, Abel had been doing everything he could to keep me safe and deliver me to a brighter future than what awaited me in Arberdon. I wanted to be able to reciprocate. Help him complete a mission he had no hope of finishing on his own. And, hopefully, give him the *everything* it promised for his future. I wanted him to have the future of his dreams.

Even if that future couldn't include me.

"Pen,"

I ignored his voice, dashing my cheeks against the backs of my bandaged hands as I circled around him to take my gun from his pack. I swaddled it in another tunic, trying to conceal it, in case Terrah followed the same weapons restrictions Arberdon did. Though there was only so much disguise a shirt-wrapped gun was capable of.

"Thank you, for..." Where could I even start? For believing in me? For showing me trust, intimacy, safety? For depositing me outside of Terrah where I could start a new life and try to reclaim myself? "Just, thanks. I'll come back out as soon as I can. And I'm sure you'll find me. You always have before." I said through a suspiciously thick throat. My vision wavered.

I turned away, blinking furiously, and had started down the slope when Abel called out to me. I paused, glancing over my shoulder.

"If you get in trouble, if you need *anything*." He tapped the side of his head. "Just reach for me. I'll be listening for you."

* * *

Alone.

For the first time since I left home, I was completely on my own. Longer than that, if I accounted for the fact that Abel had been mentally with me in Arberdon for months before I'd run away. I took a deep breath, lifted my chin, and forced my feet onward. The grass hissed around my hips, tugged against my clothes, soft fronds of seeds crowning each jagged blade. I trailed my gaze over the expanse, absent-mindedly rubbing my bandages against my thighs to quiet the itching inside.

A high wind rushed down from the mountains almost constantly, buffeting into me like it was asking me to turn around. But there was no going back, no unwinding the clock. The choices I made had irrevocably changed me. Had changed the path of my life. I had no choice but to keep going, even as each step took me farther and farther from the version of me I recognized. My heart tripped painfully in my chest; would I even fit back into my life in Arberdon, if I did manage to make it home?

Don't worry about that now, I commanded myself, refusing to glance over my shoulder for another look at Abel, at the familiar. *Keep going.*

The sun's caress warmed my cheeks as I tilted my chin up, reminding me of its constancy. Whether in Arberdon or outside Terrah, or even across the stark pains of Yeven, the sun was the same. It burned, blazing on a set course, and no power in the sky or on the ground could deviate it.

Similarly, I knew what to do when there were challenges to face.

Abel needed that message. Needed an ally he could trust to bring it to him from inside a walled city. I didn't know how I'd do it, but I knew I'd give my all while trying. I'd take a deep breath, lift my chin a little higher, and keep going. It was the least I could do, really.

I would always keep going for the ones I loved.

334

Keep Reading for an exclusive excerpt from

UNTOUCHABLE

Dream Walker Book 2

Chapter One

The ground disappeared under my feet, sweat coating my body in spite of the chill in the air that whistled down from the Hacknor Mountains. Overhead, the sky was a brilliant blue tinged with the crispness that would signal the end of the growing season in Arberdon. Homesickness, like a familiar wound, throbbed in my middle. The rigorous pace I set was exhausting, making my limbs tremble and my healing blisters throb, but necessary. The exertion made the messy tangle of feelings constricting my throat easier to tolerate.

It was hard to believe how far I'd walked since leaving Arberdon, how many hard earned miles separated me from everything familiar. I had been desperate when I'd run away from home, leaving behind everyone I loved. All except Abel, the one person who'd walked across the continent *twice* to be with me. The one who taught me what freedom and trust looked like. The one who taught me that I still knew how to love.

My chest twisted painfully, making me struggle through my next inhale. I clenched my jaw as hard as I could and kept moving.

In the end, I'd left Abel behind as well. It was the only choice I could make, just as defecting from Arberdon's armed forces had been my only option. As what most humans considered an Unnatural, or *Unnat*, he would be shot on sight by any of the border guards outside the walled city I approached.

I grimaced at the derogatory term. There was nothing *unnatural* about Abel. Over the time we'd traveled together even his blue skin, sharp teeth, and incredible physical capacity had become familiar to me. He was just *Abel*. My friend. My confidant. And a future I would never be free to embrace.

I blew out a frustrated breath, rolling my shoulders and trying to let go of regret. Although Abel had been torn when we'd parted ways, the path before us was obvious. He needed a message from Terrah, a task he could only entrust to a human who could slip in and out of the walls of a human city. Entrust to me, the only human I knew of crazy enough to ally with one of the preternaturals who inhabited the deadly forests outside haven walls. Whatever the message contained, he'd said it was the difference between life and death. I didn't understand it, but I believed him. So when he suggested we forget the message instead of separating, I couldn't let him sway me. He needed that message, and I was set on getting it to him.

Besides, it was only a matter of time before we would part ways permanently. I had to live within the walls of cities, and he had to live without. Better to get used to the idea before I got even more attached.

I rested when I had to, rationed my water, and kept an eye out for guards. By noon, with the sun high above me but tempered by the wind that never seemed to stop, I could hear a rhythmic beat in the air and felt a rumble under my feet. The sound of cicadas faded as I got farther from their trees. In its place, the clanking, churning sounds rose. Step after heavy step, I plowed on toward the smoking beast that sprawled on the horizon and grew ever larger and louder.

The day passed in a blur of physical exertion and buffeting wind. If I let myself stop, I would have no overnight shelter. Slowing down would give all the thoughts and feelings I was avoiding the opportunity to accost me. I would accept neither.

As the sun settled within the embrace of the distant Western Ridges, I hunkered down in the tall grasses that reached my waist. My muscles trembled with fatigue, pulsing and twitching even though I'd stopped walking. And though I wanted to guzzle my water and devour my rations, I fought the urge. I didn't know how easy it would be to find food once I was inside Terrah. In fact, I hadn't spent any time plotting how I would merge into the city. I scowled at my carefully portioned resources. I needed to come up with a plan, and quickly.

The blackened land that was my destination squatted in front of the Hacknor Mountains, the mighty formations cutting off the horizon and striking at the sky. In the waning light I couldn't make out much detail, though I did see silhouettes running the length of the scar, crude boxes set on risers that stood at attention with equal spacing.

"Watch towers," I muttered, scratching at my bandaged hands again. The persistent itch was getting bad enough for me to consider ripping the bandages off so I could tear into my palms with my fingernails. I took a deep breath and let it out as slowly as I could stand, imagining cool water coursing across my scalp and carrying the discomfort down to the ground. The familiar exercise embalmed me with peace and I finally relaxed my jaw.

I needed to leave the boils from the Ferox-Nettle toxin alone. Abel had given me a crudely prepared poultice to apply once I had the chance to stop and change my bandages, but made it clear that another day or two of swaddling my wounds would be best. Itching was a good thing, though. It meant I was healing.

"It's part of the process, Pen." I closed my eyes and rolled my shoulders. "Being alive feels good."

There was nothing I could do to make my hands heal faster. Nothing I could do with the grief and fear that threatened to bubble over my carefully constructed calm. But I could work on the next step, follow through with saving Abel after all the times he'd saved me. If I were clever and quick enough, I could be making my way back to the forest and my surly companion before the sun rose over the Hacknor Mountains again.

Feeling slightly more settled, I opened my eyes and studied the settlement before me again.

I had to assume that each tower was staffed by Executor guards, and they probably had a way to communicate with each other. I pressed my bottom lip between my teeth, wondering how I could get close enough to enter Terrah's gates without getting caught.

Come on, Pen, I flexed my fists. *What would Abel do?*

Abel, who'd taught me how to forage, cover my tracks, and make fire without a Flame-start. My constant companion for months, without me even realizing. The man who'd made me ache for things I thought I'd given up on long ago.

I breathed through the grief of leaving him again, through the fear of being alone and unsure. I needed to focus. I had the tools to take care of myself.

I was a survivor. Always had been, as living in Arberdon required a certain mettle. When Mother died birthing Missy, I had to step up and mother us both. It didn't matter that I was only ten and felt woefully unprepared. It needed doing, and I did it. Over the seventeen years since then, I'd learned harsh lessons that could have crushed me. I grit my teeth and flexed a sore fist, using the physical anchor of pain to banish the specter of *Commander Benjamin Joshen* from my mind. Oh yes, it could have crushed me. Spending five years under the thumb of that manipulative, Stars-forsaken man...

But no, I hadn't let it crush me. I'd used the experience instead, manifesting myself into someone more powerful than I was before. A grim smile tugged at my mouth. My time with Abel had only added to that skill set, teaching me to adapt, to be patient.

I firmed my jaw and looked to the horizon. I had a job to do.

The rest of the city must have been set into the ground, as there were no other buildings visible beside the watch towers.

Odd choice, I thought. It would make the city incredibly vulnerable to attack from above. It would also make it hard for me to get past the towers and down onto the streets below. I'd thought it would have a wall, like Arberdon. I needed to get closer, take my time and observe before figuring out how I would get inside.

The light was in my favor as I shrugged back into my pack and got to my feet, shuffling forward at a slow jog. If I kept the setting sun at my back, I should be able to see the shine of oculars pointed in my direction before any guards could see me. The tall grass provided good enough cover that I could drop to my belly if needed.

If these Executors ran their city like Arberdon, the likelihood that they would shoot a human on sight was low. I swallowed against my nerves, wiggling my fingers to keep my hands loose, and pressed on. Even if I was unlikely to be shot, I still wanted to get in undetected. I didn't have my papers, and if I did they wouldn't be useful. By now, notice of my supposed assault and subsequent defection would have reached every Executor post, along with a detailed description of my appearance. I grimaced, shoving thoughts of my past aside. I would have to deal with that later. My first priority was to get inside and find a safe place to rest.

"One thing at a time." I reminded myself.

Waiting until full dark could improve my chances, considering the limitations of human eyes. Assuming they didn't have night-sight oculars.

I sighed. Terrah was a huge city compared to Arberdon; they likely had access to more resources than I was familiar with. With effort I stopped chafing at my bandages, shaking out my fingers again to hang gently at my sides. If nothing else, I could tell them I was lost and seeking asylum from the wilderness. It wasn't even that much of a stretch from reality.

The truth is always best, Penny-girl, Mother had taught me. *It's a lighter burden over time. And always easier to remember!*

A sudden concussive blast echoed through the night, shattering against the Hacknors and channeling back into the valley. Thoughts scattering, I threw myself to the ground. My palms barked in protest, my heart rate spiking as I swallowed a ragged scream. Had I already been compromised? Were the guards firing?

The loud hum of electricity swelled as brilliant white light filled the air, pressing back against the growing darkness. I blinked until my eyes adjusted, carefully looking over the sea of grass toward the guard towers.

Painfully bright spotlights shone from the wooden structures, already swarmed by gnat-stingers and other flying insects. The areas beneath the lights were perfectly illuminated, the overlapping beams leaving no corner with a shadow. And while that was not good for my plan to sneak in, another detail had my brain stuttering to a halt.

"What the—?"

The lights were angled *in*, toward the settlement, not out at the wilds.

I eased onto my haunches, absorbing this information. Why on earth would they need to shine spotlights into the city at night? Were the people not allowed to sleep?

"Unless..." I sucked in a breath as another thought occurred to me. Unless the massive crater in the ground before me, coughing up smoke and rattling incessantly, *wasn't* Terrah.

My stomach dropped, anxiety screaming through my veins with every heartbeat. If I wasn't at Terrah, where was I? And what would I find if I approached?

The story continues in

UNTOUCHABLE

Dream Walker Book 2

H M DuVal

345

AUTHOR'S NOTE

UNNATURAL is one of those projects that sank its teeth into me and refused to let go. As an undeveloped story, it camped out in the back of my brain for years; through the end of my high school experience, college, and early motherhood. I had made some false starts and valiant attempts, but they never felt *correct*. Then I set it aside entirely, not giving Pen and Abel a single thought.

But here's the thing about heart-projects: they can take on a life of their own in the dark corners of our minds where we forget to sweep. So when I did start looking in those forgotten places again, I wasn't all that surprised to find Pen, more fully realized than I'd experienced her before, waiting for me.

Ah, she seemed to say. *You're finally ready.*

While this work is no doubt imperfect, I do feel ready. Ready to deliver their story with integrity in a way that hopefully moves you, dear reader, to take brave steps away from what you accept because it's familiar and into what you pursue for your best life. And I further hope that by stepping into this intersection together, here where you hold *my* heart-project in *your* hands, you'll be inspired to take another look at those pipe dreams that you've carried for so long. They might be more attainable than you thought.